ORIGINALS

THE CITY SHALL BE HOT TONIGHT.

Feel the heat.

It's coming down.

And is this ville cranked up, or what?

Yus.

It's full of Other People.

Other People are the bit-part players in a mad, mad movie dreamed up by some sado-monetarist director, so enwrapped 'n' entrapped in this splendiferous period costume drama of Jack Dante's Rockin' Beach Party Inferno à Go-go, that he's long gone stone-broke stark-naked bare-bum crazy and then sum. The equation here is that it don't add up, so where do you fit in?

You other person, you.

No one told you?

OK, they didn't tell the others either. The extras, the urbanites, remain ignorant that all bets are off. The grand plan's been super-slammed because the shooting's stopped.

So they're living on the edge. It's the edge between reality and dream.

In its wake, every edge leaves a gap. And inside this gap is a blur where moments catch in the frieze of the social mind.

Miss Memory – who can resurrect her? The way she feels? The way her sticky moments congeal? The big slow blur of – gosh, ya remember the first time? Yeah yeah yeah you know, the way the wise-cracking blond wine-waiter watusied with the girl in the blue wig and the pink micro-skirt in Jefferson's Bar, underneath that scruffy cinema? That evening, on returning to your flat, you found, in the block's vestibule, an unsolicited colour TV – freshly factory-wrapped and vacuum-packed inside its anonymous brown box. A box with your name on it. 'But whys should anyone send me a TV? I don't get it,' you kept repeating the next day. 'I've got two already and no one owes me any money. I *definitely* didn't order it – haven't entered any competitions or anything, either. I don't understand – it couldn't have been meant for anyone else because it was clearly addressed to *me*. What gives?'

By mid-afternoon you and Eustace between you were making my head twizzle. You'd persuaded yourself that someone whose window you could watch was going to be murdered – and that the killer was setting you up for a clear run by ensuring you'd be tuned out to the tube. Eustace kept snickering evilly, the same potty cackling that continued all through that winter.

He seemed to get a particularly fiendish bang out of winding up that albino micro-man who'd parade around Brandenberg Square in his filth-smegged black and white herring-bone coat. It dragged along the pavement, his head just peeping out from above his tiny, sandwich-boarded body concealed inside the wood, safe behind the yellow sign's bright red letters that energetically exclaimed DO YOU JUJU?

The little fellah sold meretricious costume jewellery as a side, from the top of his U-push trolley stacked with three suitcases bound to its metal frame by ropy cord. He had a hell of a job pushing it, what with the sarnie-boards and all. Remember how he'd try and fiddle with the merchandise he kept in the display box on top?

Eustace'd spot him, usually after we'd wolfed a skewered

ratburger ritually flashfried over the smoky chargrills in the street. He'd catch sight of the poor guy, track him for a while – then close up and cruise him so he'd know he was being eye-balled before he moved in. Eustace, long-faced, the make-up emphasizing Fagin-eyes, full-court-dressed in his sable cloak and dayglo fake furs, looked like an El Greco polaroid of a transsexual Barbie Doll; his long, pallid spindly fingers protruding from his pink mittens, precariously balancing that dumb-show fenderful of barbed-wire, plastic dolls' limbs and broken glass coronet on his noggin as he sifted through the homunculus's carefully displayed knick-knackeries.

That little chap must have been really desperate to take that kinda crap. Maybe he really thought that one day Eustace would buy something. No chance, babe. The Vauvatier boy would sift and fiddle among the artfully arranged merchandise for as long as his anorexicly chilling digits could stand it, only to inevitably spin capriciously on his high high heel in an attitude that suggested his long, fine-boned features – sunken and drawn in the shiver wind as the nights came down – had once more allowed themselves to be duped and betrayed by the manikin's tawdry showcase. And he'd snort: 'Well, little man, I don't care what you say. At least my crown jewels are real fakes, anyway,' or some such brittle nasty.

It seemed funny the first couple of hundred times, the way the street-vendor would always go for it, the disdainful camp sneer Eustace'd lay on him, the smug simper he shot aside at us as he'd earnestly inquire the price of some terrible trinket. But that long, low conspiratorial glance of his would start to wear thin by the time the ice was melting in Da Vinci Park, and we realized that Eustace was just a sad little queen who needed someone weak to feel superior to.

Now I just feel sorry for the poor runty bastard. He's still around between the boards, but he doesn't have the jewellery box or the suitcases or even the U-pull trolley any more. He strides the streets, small and squat, muttering incandescent oaths and primeval gibberish spittle curses in a non-seq alphabet of angstsome anger and bewildered incomprehension.

You can feel him coming two blocks away – he shouts, 'Q-Q-Q-Q-Q-Q-Q-Q,' or whispers whatever languorous vowel, hissing sibilant or crispy crunchy constant takes his fancy.

But we were younger then when the snow fell thick in a suffocating blanket, preserving all still beneath.

That winter we'd track cross-town, head out to Pookie's Polka Bar and Grill or Two on One to warm ourselves, and chat and sip. And on the train our posse would vibe it up and test the litmus of our luck.

How far to go?

Once, an immaculately dressed black dude in a hand-cut, charcoal pin-stripe and clean, freshly laundered white shirt offered his seat to Eustace and Tranny Saul, erroneously taking them for gurley girls. He had a red briefcase that matched his tie handcuffed to his thick ebony wrist, and stood up as the subpath train pulled into Victory Zoomway. Eustace sat down as if he bossed the carriage and, *de jure*, all within it. The cringe of recall replayed for the bitchen iron whim of who we thought we were, yikes, the doors closed – a goshdarn *frisson* of sliding plates – and the mind's eye frames chug chug cha cha ah ha ha-shaking rattling rhythms of the train as it thunders through the tunnel, briefly out into the light, then pulls into Ultimo Station where two bona fide females pile on, all light and giggle.

'Get up,' said the man with the briefcase handcuffed to his wrist. Tranny Saul jumped, Eustace V. rose, the girl sat down and the train took off. The black man, I noticed, had an earpiece with a clear connecting chord that ran down somewhere inside his shirt.

And Eustace V. turned and stooped his skeletal bag of bones down suddenly to growl in the guy's face and, as the train pulled into our stop, he spat at him because – he later bragged in Alchemy at the Mystic City Sign – that he lusted tenaciously, and merely sought to provoke some response.

But there was none.

It was the season of the Black Rose.

He slept all day and went out when the lights went on, for as the stars were out so too were we. Remember now Vanda, the heartbreak waiting in her deep, dark, almond honey-pool eyes?

Remember that party at Belleville? The barking débutante, the crowd, the Sephardic trader in old wares who took us to that room and peeled his shirt to flaunt a barrel chest on some private shrine of self-exposure and orgiastic fantasy?

Remember Outside?

Outside: some wisecrack chollo homeboy all pompadoured and quiffed beyond his years, clad in the slick-as-silk crimson leather Bee Zee You Melrose zip-and-panniniro jacket, this dudester shouted at the passing yuppy couple deep in social intercourse: 'Hey, mister, can I fuck your wife?'

The loafered yupster turns and throws a snarling jeer; his hands are bruised, cut up and battered by overnight wreck-ravages from swill liquor spill and pyschotropic capsule crash; and the streetside interloper of their social i/course whispers at the tip-top of his lungs through the morning air: 'Does that mean yes or no?'

He gets the laugh from the gang in which he hang and his jacket, as the other gang-bangers', is emblazoned with the colour legends of the All Planet Evil Stone Overlord Dread Klan Blood Brotherhood of Dead Mau Mau Def Masters.

But the y-word couple keep moving like they're taking their faces some place out of Plaza de Soto Market four five six and sure.

And cha cha cha the movie dance, moves smooth grooves as sprockets mesh and script-romance runs the couple both to plan.

Which is one easy-peasy piece. A cinch, it's cert. Dead set, mon fils.

There is no plan.

So c'mon everybody and get that act down now. Yesa, yesa savvy up, youse urbanites. Now listen: one day to life, no holds, no falls, no ifs nor butts – your belt is something others may hit below. You may leave the metroplex at any time by throwing in the towel, but there are no retakes and positively no refunds, since all engagements are final. Make it good, keep it clean – and remember, this time it's for real. Time's started running, keep it coming, c'mon – what are we waiting for?

What happened to your omnipresent mate slash attorney? Have you defused your attitude and glamour bombs? So where's your media cool?

You know the rules. You make the moves through the city and define the shapes and surfaces that cause-effect each frame.

So keep moving.

Here's the way to go – come . . .

CARIS DAVIS'

STEALTH

THE WHITE EDITION

PENGUIN BOOKS

PENGUIN BOOKS

Published by the Penguin Group
27 Wrights Lane, London W8 5TZ, England
Viking Penguin Inc., 40 West 23rd Street, New York, New York 10010, USA
Penguin Books Australia Ltd, Ringwood, Victoria, Australia
Penguin Books Canada Ltd, 2801 John Street, Markham, Ontario, Canada L3R 1B4
Penguin Books (NZ) Ltd, 182–190 Wairau Road, Auckland 10, New Zealand

Penguin Books Ltd, Registered Offices: Harmondsworth, Middlesex, England

First published 1989
10 9 8 7 6 5 4 3 2 1

Made and printed in Great Britain by
Richard Clay Ltd, Bungay, Suffolk
Typeset in 10/12 pt Lasercomp Bembo

To the memory of my grandfather Ahron David Halevi and to the futurity of that Poodle Person

Each reader reads only what is inside himself. A book is only a sort of optical instrument which the writer offers to let the reader discover in himself what he would not have found without the aid of the book.

– *Marvin Minsky*

It is not the houses. It is the spaces between the houses.

– *James Fenton*

. . . out of nowhere.

It breaks the earth of the up-country flatlands beyond the city, bursts through the very ground – a monstrous tarmac artery, an affront to nature, a man-made shock that socks all senses real to really reelin'; knocks your breath away by its sheer scale, the magnitudinal pungence of its busy cells' gasoline vapours, their collective decibel surge like an oceanic roar that never ebbs, but on-rush crashes crests ever more mightily upon your aural dip of shore.

It's –

It's –

It's –

It's the 56-lane Shakespeare FlyDrive SuperZoom.

Savage no-mercy asphalt slashes dark black path in a straight straight line clean through 17 Don't Stop kilometres of adulterously homogenized western suburbs.

(The citizenry refer to these stupendously unnatural phenomena as 'Shakey Zoom' and 'The Slurbs' resspectif.)

On on it powers, till, at the hydra hub that's the Von Alvensleben Interchange, the superhighway soars skywards; it rises violently like some mythic reptile that elevates itself on high, brutal pillars of massively reinforced, titanium-riven concrete to swooooop through the vertiginous, crystalline glass obelisks;

sweeps swiftly past this New Jerusalem's towering slabs of icy steel, and thunders through its glass and molten stone and on and on a Keep Moving arc suspended among, along, and around; darting and diving between the metroplex's iridescent shimmer cylinders of cost-effective people-stack to heart-stoppingly drop, straight down through Victory River, low below into four submerged klicks more of parabolic banking trauma-stretch; an eerily hygienic robo-monitored floodlit tunnel that quite quite unexpectedly veers back sharply onto level road, sears further forward on relentlessly on on on for seven bonus bitumen-burnt, relentless dashboard dial-rotations, only to hit Point Supernova at Machinegunreefer East – where the tiny details of complex intra-state bureaucracy with their Right Cash Now t-tollbooths and bureaucratic shadows fragment it into a tangled web of seamless, tiny tarmacadam tributaries.

No doubt about it, Shakey Zoom is There.

And its movement is but one vector of the velocity which raises the temperature round here –

There. Everywhere. But not just anywhere does this one singular dot among the masses move off Shakey Zoom.

The emetic point progresses on its flat trajectory through the metropolis in the heat.

Heat.

Bitch you right out – like breathing in a stoker's furnace.

Something, a foot depressing on a pedal, actually, causes the point-dot to slow and stop.

Check the drop-dead leg which steps, all elegancy, from within the industrially power-polished diamond hard gloss of the black Electro Powerglide De Luxe custom s-t-r-e-t-c-h limo out onto the streetwalk straight into a corrosive pool. This toxic puddle comprises red and yellow bile slime gut-gungin' yueuch, coagulates in a brown trail of blood and urine that's trickled down from some old bum – another anon derro-drift wood-be myth-hit manimal – kitted out in vet's green 'n' black combat fatigues and rotten, stink-blue T-shirt rank in its decay (THE PERSON WHO DIES WITH THE MOST TOYS WINS, its white-letter-write-on proudly proclaims). Around BumBum's neck is a string of pearls, funky little costume paste; and up top crow-nesty resty on his bonce once natty locks, now matty dirt and scuzzy beneath the frayed gold-flecked beret that's absolutely apex. Four tears are tattooed above his chin, below his eye, the right eye, left as a sign. Right now this cat's left the out-field, spun off. Off the whirling centrifuge that drives the people and the objects in this ville round and round and he's crash landed here. Down on the ground back back back from some idiosyncratic personal peripatetic metro-manic urban frenzy mission: he's dizzy, so dizzy in the giddiness of the hell-weeping city-world. So he snatch forty and naps snoozefully on the flagstones which rest around, all brown scrubbed clean, leanin' 'gainst the aircon vents that're inset inna the shiny white marbly wall of this utterly civilized hostelry. Hotel Swankomodo's courtesy anti-depressant harlequin chocolate truffles (that appear on cue with your steaming, frothy cappuccino) will cost more dosh than the sleeper is likely to see in a year.

The puddle flashes a section of expression back at the girl who's got out of the car. If she'd been looking.

But no. Just for once she isn't narcissistically examining her face. No.

The young, tall photogenic woman's sleek, well-bred features register something between backboiler irritation and peripheral self-disgust. She shakes the lizard-skin-shod leg. Her nostrils flare, her chill blue eyes resume their customary mask of repulsive languor. She reposes her lips in their hooded pounce of ever-ready routine cruelty and, preoccupied, strides past our image-

O D'd refugee up up the marble stairs towards the lobby where a gold-braided livery-form flunkey-Joe pushes the revolving door into orbit. Round and round. She comes out here as she walks through and –

Discovers her dress caught in the door?

Goes to room 1962 to shiatsu massage her mother's last-but-two toyboy?

Clocks on for the night-shift with all the other barstaff?

Makes her way to the conference room where she will, with scary equipose, sit down with her papa, one Eddie Eisler, and listen most politely as the associates of Eddie all-hail the chief, while beneath the mannered veneer she savours the thrill of her very first board meeting?

Incident? Assignment? Role-play? Encounter?

Or something fresh again?

Anything can happen to anyone at any time in this city. It is designed by humans who live within the architecture of appearances. They build on the foundations of frustration and burnish the interiors' backdrop with dreams.

Every day, new buildings go up – and others blow away, collapsed in rust rubble dust or abandoned to decay. The Fear has cleared some city streets where once the people bustled. Deserted, dead, dangerous.

Elsewhere, 'cross some invisible line machines define and vandalize, develop and construct, erect-a-section; reclassified, rezoned, hi-hi glass towers glitzed with luxury one millimetre thick and bid bye bye to ethnic smells and funked brownstones.

YOU'RE EXPERIENCING ANOTHER EXCITING ENVIRONMENT BY 21st-CENTURY PROPERTIES – PROUD TO BE A SUBSIDIARY OF EISLER REALTY INC.

The sign of corporate manners.

But even at the centre of the chaos and the debris the city's emotional temperature remains constant in its mercurial flux.

It is hot.

It is cool.

But never lukewarm.

And how is it right now?

How is it with you?

No mind.

You know the rules.

Keep moving.

Now you're here, you don't want to waste any time, do you? OK, so you've arrived: thus far, you've made it. And perhaps it's begun to dawn on you that there's already been a rule-change, a whole new set of rules going down.

Rule One: *YOU'RE WORKING FOR US.*

Rule Two: rule two is –

– a rule of ink around a picture.

The picture blows down the street, pushed away from the hotel wall by the air from the vent next to the absurdly garbed man who snores near by.

A photo in a newspaper.

A message in the city.

Pick it up.

It shows a group of people's bodies: five men, two or three women. They lie down together on an apartment floor.

'Study the picture more closely.'

Zone in.

One woman has her back to the camera, her face buried in the patterned carpet as she slumps in drowse. In the background a singular man in a short, grey beard and *crime de fashion* nylon shirt sits up. He is middle aged, he is thin – his short neat grey tousled hair sticks up in slightly odd tufty angles off his long bony face, his small blue crow-wrinkled eyes are tired, habitually wary. He looks as if he's just been wakened suddenly. Perhaps some sixth sense alerted him to the picture being taken?

Media Cool.

Got it like that.

Back off.

Underneath the photograph is this drawing, this sketch-wash of the group, an artist's impression of the face of the woman with her back to the camera. It's a paradoxical picture. The woman's dressed like a teenage groove-thang; but the young female face is savaged with ravaged, craggy, deeply etched time-lines.

Acidic burns on a movie-face: the clock has run its race and caustic liquid hisses as it eats into the metal plate.

To expose –

– the newspaper headline: THE CULT THAT SLEEPS WITH AIDS VICTIMS.

The photo has been taken . . .

You guessed, didn't you? You were hip to it all along, right?

. . . through the apartment window by a paparazzo with a long lens. A colour by-line runs vertically up from the picture's lower-right corner.

It identifies the photographer.

The Ministry of Happiness.

They're putting them in camps now, aren't they?

Routine MO.

'It's the Agency Jack.'

Whip-pan.

Over in the Barrio, the old part of the city, trams still run through the rocky rolling cobbled streets. Some vehicles are now painted with the hard-graphic laser-edged posture posters with check-it-out rapid-recall slogos of the omnipresent multinational electronics giants. They're in your eyes, your face, your hair, baby they're stupid everywhere. Their garish pop canonizations (PLANT A TREE FOR MARC B – CATCH TEEN-TIME

ON 0/62 FOR DETAILS) have gradually begun to displace the more traditional names and motifs that once denoted the munificence of some local sweatshop manufacturer or fortune-lucky clairvoyant street seer.

Mid-day: hot sun, high overhead.

Inside the Barrio, the banks are closed and the stores have pulled down their grey metal shutters.

Nowhere else within the central zone would sleep through lunch. Out there in the metro-mess, the temperature's rising as Other People target-niche battlegrounds, massage each others' messages, sell sounds, tango figures and bounce deals round and round and round in the 24-hour romance of gimme gimme numbers that count baroque in the courts of high-style, aspirant aristocracies collectively curious, increasingly predatory in their wargasmic check-the-brand raids, furious flurries which gradually erode the spaces between the buildings – and exorcize their power to soften and dilute memory,

to crush the ghosts that beetle with lightning scuttles dimly rekindling the shadows of our fantasies,

to dilute the pain of phantoms that tramp the streets of an older simpler city, now buried beneath the on-stomp of their feet in unmarked graves covered by drifting snow.

These streets have seen some tyrants come and go.

But now the sun shines out. And in the square behind the intricately carved, grey stone gargoyles and grotesques guarding from their high top vantage point, between each pillar that supports the stupendous symmetrical portico of the Museum of Discoveries, two men stroll along the circular path that coils around the small, semi-tropical gardens of St Francis the Discreet.

The blessèd white statue of the saint features the index finger of the right hand placed to the lips of his face. The blissful eyes stare directly up. From within the painstakingly crafted folds of his meticulously sculpted robes, St Francis the Discreet's left hand perpetually beatifies a menagerie of dubious heaven-gazing beasties.

Already there are moves afoot, set in train (no doubt!) by said corporate creeps, to replace him with a portrayal of the newly canonized St Buddy. Oh the shame! When, as sometimes happens, curiousio touristos ask about Francis's right hand, the guides point out the utterly fascinating architectural aspect of the Military Hospital visible immediately behind you, built fourteen years ago when 18,000 tons of liquid were poured into 3,211 cement mixers to . . . excuse me, I must've dropped off for a couple of years back there.

The city is filled with such monuments to explorers and divines. Leave the gardens and find y'self on a narrow Barrio street; it rolls down a hill and back up again. The Barrio is the only part of the city where the topography has not been flattened, thumped, pile-driven and brutally repressed into the service of genus-cruel human-kind. Somehow in the Barrio, nature holds still vestiges of turf.

Memories linger.

On both sides of this particular Barrio street run rows of diminutive pink, brown and white houses. All are set back at individual distances from the road – yet all are melded together in one continuous cramped zigzag along the worn cobbles to define the street.

Some have washing hung on lines outside. Some emit the noizak of domesticity. Some have open windows to let the sun shine through. Old relations sit ravelled deep in reverie on odd porches, intermittently to doze and drift and watch the world and its life pass by.

Other houses – Other People – have pulled down the shutters.

Move closer.

The shapes of the architecture are remarkable, the detailing, peculiar. Look at that house, with its tiny dust-bowl of a front yard. The roof's layered with crooked red tiles. Upstairs, the wooden shutters are drawn in. But in the front yard there's an envelope, a pink envelope in the dirt. A black cat pads lazily along the ground. It stops. Its paw investigates the paper.

Stop frame.

Enhance

– the cat.

The animal's upper-left ear has a bite-size contusion. Mr Tabbatha Whiskerypuss sports a wire around its neck that (horrors!) turns out of its scrawny fur towards its stomach wherefrom hangs this ridiculous multicoloured cable.

We'd like to show more but –

Keep moving.

Enhance

– the envelope.

There's a mark on the back of the pink paper. A monogram in blue. Writing. Initials. Initials say NCKG.

Turn over.

The handwritten name ran in yesterday's rain.

Cress . . . D. Cr . . . ne. Personal.

They walk, meanwhile, a few paces up the hill onto the Rua da Infante Sanctites, these two men.

Other People.

They wait in the queue and Fatso Urbanite buys two tickets. The duo enter the wood-panelled lift. Also in the lift: a bearded man in shorts with a backpack strapped on, his four-year-old boy in tow, glancing round this pantechnicon that moves.

He sees: a primly coiffured mid-twenties girl with her brown hair in a neat bob. He notices the ancient artificial latex-covered arm she partially conceals within the crumpled linen of her lightly faded apricot jacket.

The small's boy's blue eyes widen and stare, fascinated.

The lift attendant, rumple-haired and crumple-faced in his shabby grey uniform, slides the door. It bangs shut woodenly. Mechanically, he pushes the old but buffed, why-just-last-week, brass lever down and the lift climbs smoothly upwards. 350 feet above the boulevard below, it stops. Another man, whose lights-out dimness of eye, weak droopy lips and drearily submissive expression suggest all feeling had been interred long ago in some carnivorous catacomb that closed in around his fading light and soul, puts their tickets in the pouch attached to his Bee Z. municipal uniform. Its new purple cotton and shiny red receptacle built on the belt afford him no pleasure. He weighs his life in fluttering batches of lift tickets, cheap paper litter, each more orderly and habitually boxed than the last within the piles that will by clocking-off time nearly – but never quite – overspill from the officially marked bin-line bag beside his clumsy scuffed brown leather shoes.

It's the Barrio.

These two men leave, the plumping pink-suited Urbanite and the Other. Stroll along the small bridge which affords them a panoramic view of the city built on hills. The Japanese diplomat observes the freshly painted political graffiti. It's in lingua Barrio, urban hipspanic: LA TRANCHA DI CENTURY 21! VIVA HOMBRE DE 44 VISAGO! VIVA REVOLUTION!

Outside at the table of the café, mercifully an undesignered mass for real people who fancy imbibition, a career-waiter in a clean white apron appears smartly to take their order.

'Two Bicas,' says the Urbanite and begins to fiddle with the chain that hangs around his neck with his fat fingers. Attached to the chain is a shiny medal that depicts St Ignatius the Ignominious; one solid gold foot; a tiny silver hand; a pendant which contains a wispy lock of hair. A blue and red double decker bus passes among the traffic in the road. Over somewhere to their right the Shakey Zoom's mid-town heavy traffic non-stops. But they've adjusted, natch, and filtered out and yet . . .

. . . both men simultaneously become aware of a high-pitched hum. It is a noise and also a smell. These disagreeable stimuli become increasingly difficult to ignore.

A cross-eyed beggar, shabby-shod and dead-thread in one torn trainer and an old grey cold-weather suit, propels himself lop-sidedly towards them. His hand's outstretched. The other side of his misshapen bod leans on a metal crutch. He drags a club foot. He glares at them piteously as he emits his shrill whine.

'Tch tch,' says the Urbanite and waves him away.

The diplojap produces a coin – the smallest denomination among the two sets currently in circulation – and drops it into the beggar's hand.

'You were saying?' the fat man resumes. But now a boy appears at the table. The urchin rustles something inside a piece of harsh, rumpled white pseudo-tissue paper.

'Gold?'

A ring glints.

'No, no – go away,' the businessman snaps irritably.

Later, the Japanese stops outside a shop façade, identified like so many others in the old city, with the owner's name picked out in mirrored letters against a plain painted-glass background. The small bay-window displays (on either side of the stairs that lead up to the premises above) contain old black and white photographs. Their subjects' poses and attitudes, their clothes, their hair styles seem stunted, curiously dated, distant. The pictures seem as if they were taken at least forty years ago.

'It cannot be,' he mutters to himself, rubbing one knobbly finger against the dust on the glass as the other searches within his pocket for his notebook. The attaché carefully annotates the name and address of this photo-studio before carefully returning the saddle-soaped, bound brown leather organizer back to the right pocket of his black jacket, which sags somewhat from its accumulated weight of downpull.

This double-agent for the Ministry of Happiness stares sadly once more through his small, round metal-framed spectacles.

HAPPINESS IS KEEPING YOUR EYES OPEN says the slogan on the poster on the wall facing the small table in his cramped, locked-room at the embassy. He'd leered intently; opening his eyes as wide as they would go, trying to move closer and then back off, to elucidate the mystery. But it's no good.

One particular picture, a full-length portrait of a man in his mid-30s about six feet three inches tall. Yes, this is the focus of the agent's attention. The subject's hair-line recedes from the front of his forehead. He wears a leather flying jacket, twill trousers and high, tightly-laced early-issue air corps knee boots. Underneath his right arm he clasps an aviator's flying helmet.

Zone in.

Check the features.

Nothing. No features. No landscape in the face at all. No nose, no mouth, no cheeks, no moles, neither teeth nor brows. And no eyes.

The closer you go, the harder you try to specify, the bigger the grain in the blur becomes. It is as if the molecules of the skin are do wop wop boppin' in some bug-dance.

Back over on the main drag, the black man in the ersatz pearls sleeps and dreams.

He dreams he flies. A human missile.

It twists and turns as it hunts down its prey. He feels frightened. Subconsciously an unfamiliar notion strikes him:

Possession.

A babble of voices in his face, a Japanese man, yammering

incomprehensibly. In his consciousness, he is still flying. The mind, accelerated beyond its normal limits, lands more slowly. Gradually, in fragments of lucidity, he recognizes a doctor in a white coat, a nurse with a hat like folded paper, a jet-black cat that sometimes strays in his room and lies underneath his bed. He never sees it leave. But occasionally at night, he imagines he can hear its claws scratch the wooden floor.

One day, as usual, his luncheon arrives on the metal tray. He looks at the newspaper underneath the white china bowl from whence steam soothingly nutritious vapours of tongue and vegetable broth. There is a date at the top right-hand corner of the newspaper. He strains for detail. (His eyes are accustomed to a bigger perspective – orange flare, kill kill kill.) It says 15 December 1942.

He knows he is well enough to leave the house. He is surprised more than somewhat to find his skin has bleached. His hair has disappeared from much of his forehead. What's left is straight, brown. His tattoos have vanished. A bubble car drives past him. He sweats. The bubble car is made from wood. The wood sweats. He feels for the talismanic coral beads he has worn around his neck since childhood beneath his clothes – but there are no beads. He looks at the palms of his hand. They are black. He sees a white cat. The cat has a multicoloured collar that trails away – he wants to follow the trail. The nimble feline pads past him on four paws.

It keeps moving.

Now so does he.

He tracks.

Until eventually he finds himself in a small trailer caravan, parked behind the red terracotta arch set up on the dry yellow scrub and dust of the flatlands.

'But I want to join your circus.'

'Don't be no my voice,' he notices as he pleads with the woman who stands at the cooker with the brass pot on the hob, by the window that looks on out into the vastness of the land and empty, bending sky.

The woman is in her mid-forties, and wears a threadbare, checked Chanel suit. Once she had blonde hair: now her features are sharply honed to a wasp's as it stings, a vixen as it whelps.

He notices the large diamond ring. It signifies, he knows ('But how?' some inner impulse prompts. 'This not be my seein' or my scene') that her husband is dead. He hears her say he must clean out animal cages, must work to erect the giant red pagoda.

'But first m'sieur . . .' The woman scarcely looks at him. It's as if she's daydreaming and her mouth forms frames of words autonomously. Her diction and her Francophone vocabulary suggest she must be connected somehow, sometime to the coast.

But first, she says, looking over his shoulder at the light green, tinny metal trailer's door, she 'finds herself obliged' to give him a test to ascertain his suitability as a Probationer.

Which is how he comes to spend that evening in a shiny pseudo-silver metal garbage bin with 55 daubed on its lid in yellow paint. He totes a pro-camera with its long, heavy telescopic casing that protects the ground glass telephoto lens around his neck.

'I seen this camera one time when we and Simple Alice is foragin' up Mattimoe Town.'

And he watches. He watches the small apartment in the residential Barrio street. Periodically, he takes a picture through a crack in the opaque bedroom window. He looks inside the red briefcase that's chained to his left wrist, jammed down open and hurtin' like a motherfucker rubbin' on his knee down thar. Inside the gap, he can, when he concentrates for long enough, see the rolls of film (exposed already through this night) lie glistening dully there.

He does not understand the necessity for this surveillance. Only that she told him that it must be done, and he must do it tonight.

Now.

She knows – that woman with her sharp features distended in mid-vision, that diamond-toting widow-woman with the coastal patois – how desperately he now needs to must clamber oh please once more again into that now familiar cockpit and fly away over the city into powder-blue sky, leaving behind him only a vapour trail, so that others might make good their escape from the zoo.

'She promised that.'

Yes, she did.

'Zoo, zoo, call the zoo.'

The old black guy shakes his head. His face is twitching. Blackjack pokes him in the ribs.

'Oh wake up, man, wake up.'

She looks at her companion, a lank youth in a red baseball cap. He's Boosterfish. Boosterfish has narrow eyes surrounded by a face fulla acne that's the pits.

'Barney,' she says. 'He won't wake up. Give him a shake, eh?'

'No, no. I'm awake, I'm awake. I just been havin' the most fabulous dream. Fabulous.'

'Come on, Jean Jean,' says Boosterfish. 'Come with us. We've got a little job for you. Mr Eisler wants to see ya. He's gonna give ya some money. Come on.'

'I had a dream, I had a dream,' Jean Jean begins, looking excitedly from one face to the other.

Blackjack offers him her arm.

'You can tell us about it on the way cross-town,' she says. She has big brown eyes. Her voice is kind. Her eyes – they suggest this is not always so.

As they walk down Second Avenue, the old tramp senselessly

repeating phrases to himself, Blackjack's eyes shift, they scan, search-mode. They are the eyes of an urbanite. Busily directional. They keep moving.

And she flits that focus through the frame of street, catches your eye or hits on your feet, checks your shape in the blur among many fleet, ephemeral forms. You check her back: one third of the trio who prowl along, pushing their features out of the crowd that throngs through Television City, and the trio look about as happening as a centipede with broken legs. A jet-engine roars hot in the sky. You look up momentarily. A face in the crowd.

'We're gonna make' – you hear them talk as bodies brush – 'gonna make you rich and famous, Mr LePichon,' says Blackjack, still supporting him on her arm. 'Rich and famous.'

Wasn't this what you came to the city to hear?

You notice something.

It flutters out behind from one of the three who already merge into the kinetic tide of body blur and heat.

You turn around and pick it up.

It's the square white back to a tiny photo-print.

You turn it over to view the picture on the other side.

The positive, the monochrome image blurs in sepia hues and washes black bleaches white.

Totally dazzling.

It keeps moving.

And as the traffic runs along the Shakey Zoom just twelve blocks away, the movie runs on as planned.

Last Night Wah Wah

'HIYA THRU TO BITCH INC. and the back-track to this tape is Tsing Loa Ranting's upcoming release "Perpetual Revolution in a Totalitarian State". Leave a message and see how you rate: if you make the cut you get called back, otherwise don't waste our time and drop dead on the no-tone.'

Knocker chucks Lucky, the stray black kitten that he'd found scratching at the door last week, under the chin; turned on the answer-mach, fine-tuned the adjustments to his tie in the long mirror in the corporate bathroom. He sees a fair-haired boy scraping six feet with widely set blue eyes, a nose that began below them skinnily but broadened out into ruddy red cheek-bones. He sees a deep scar, a mark that resonates with a now familiar ambiguity. He views, with pleasure, the razor-revered, blue leather double-breasted suit in which he is clad. He measures that pleasure, the *bon ton* in adjusting the bespoke skin's detachable cuff buttons.

He passes his hand across the particle-beam console-stat to squelch the lights, carefully triple-locks the joint, heads down the narrow flights of wooden-then-metal stairs from the converted studio apartment – which serves as the operations base for his nascent infotainment empire – and trips on out the door into the Rua de San Phocas, popularly known – among the pretty, shiny young things Knocker hangs out with – as the Emulsion Belt.

Out-time.

In the past Knocker – as he was universally dubbed among the multitude of tireless young media-aspirant metropolitan funsters who constantly re-grouped in fortuitously fresh combinations to synthesize The Scene – had been the universally acknowledged Prince of Hip. Record company big-jobs called him Mr Goodtimes, and chicks constantly mythered and manoeuvred for dates on his mobile go-go Al Capone. For Knocker had been suss incarnate.

This dude has run many hundreds of one-nighter party palaces, in locations as diverse as a Mantran intercity express train and the isolation wing of a recently abandoned psychiatric hospital. On or off the rails, he knows how to keep after-dark happenings in line and on the right track. Apart from his facial scar, Knocker has the mien of a boy who'd nearly been a pop star. He keeps the numbers of the 5,000 people who really matter about his person on an electronic organizer. Knocker'd had the smarts, at the time when it really mattered, to hire the savviest young party-planners to deal with the relentless morass of detail club-running entailed. He'd had the bottle to deal with drunks, aspiring hunks, rough-cut gang-bangers and their limpet hangers who tried to hustle their muscle onto his turf; cops who'd think they could close him down because he'd neglected to apply for a dance licence. And he'd had the wit to hit on the hottest young art-stars to take care of décor and youthquake breakthroughs such as the planet's first telepathic nightclub invitation. Knocker'd organized the indulgence of peccadilloes for global stars of stage and screen: with one-time partner 2Can-Bone (now smacked out in erratic-stylee for some shit-hot-shot animatic movieco) he'd ferried minor members of royal families from three continents to an island paradise where the resultant week-long total wipe-out binge had been the subject of an emergency debate at the United

Nations on post-colonial moral pollution of the Third World. Knocker had employed inchoate and sometimes incoherent legends like the Toy, Tranny Saul and Fat Tuesday as hat-checks, barkeeps, bouncers – door staff even. He knew what to say when the fire marshall arrived. Ask him a question – Knocker has an answer.

'What's happening?'

'Come wiv me and I'll tell you abaht it.'

Go out.

Out blurs the edges between aspiration and achievement. For this K O person, Out is In. Being In the infotainment industry is all about going Out. And getting into going out by getting out of it with the In people – the Out crowd. See be seen, right time right place, fills the void he feels during the unguarded moments that have begun creeping up on him recently. Introspective episodes when he'd cross the line and become so into going Out he couldn't functionally get into it.

It starts with the sensation that someone else might be having more fun. And that he's not having enough.

It's The Fear.

It's a bit of a worry.

The Fear was blank gap undesignerable, raw black emotion perpetrated by the person he'd once been on the persona he suspected he was about to become. It was a floating lotta loathing that unpredictably appeared within his interior landscape suddenly, without rational explanation or prior warning, cutting loose in cannibalistic, fangsome feedy frenzies of metropolitan angst, social confusion and (at its acme) blind, catatonic panic. He tries not to think about it, to block it out as 'negative'. But it lurks somewhere deep inside him, dark and low – a shape; a whispering predator: he'd feel its ripples, undermining the slickly smiling exterior façade he presented to the world with the nipping, nagging tease of its small serrated teeth.

Knocker walks towards the station past an old photographic studio. It registers somewhere that the bow-fronted display windows have been cleared out.

Long memory: Knocker'd been born 24 years before on the projects down in Stewartstown. Even today, the day before his 46th birthday, his dad, Denny Carlton retained the trim, wiry physique that had brought him some modest success as a prizefighter and semi-pro scrapper down and around the city's mid-east side. He was a man whose nose was wide, whose steady eyes were set far-spread on his round, broad-boned face, a man whose lips were thin. All of which physiognomy, bar the round face, his only loinfruit had inherited. But Moira – his mother's side of the family – had tempered this with a lighter, Nordic angle on his complexion – and the finer bone structure of a distant, but distinctly different blood-line.

Despite his youthful two-fisted flirtation with pro-pugilism, Knocker's old man retained a bright and enterprising eye, and a mind granted the gritty gift for playing to win in the Casino Society of the then newly autonomous city-state. But thanks – or not – to the associates from his boxing days, he dealt off a crook deck: Knocker, as an over-educated adolescent growing up absurd, craved exit and escape from the craven stupidity of his home-base concrete-trap. Here, though he knew it not – for he was a guy who'd rather feel the smallest thrill than think about anything in the abstract – lurked the load-spring of his Knocker's worry-clutch: pressure-cooked recollections churning over, in his dreams, like a game show conveyor-belt's cavalcade of prizes, with a bluff and tumbling hustle house forever, in his memory, filled with

obselete porta-phones;
knocked-off coffee-makers;
dodgy immunizationatrons;
counterfeit boomboxes;

hot smart-card blanks;
plainly defective mind-mirrors
and similar such in brown boxes, with a bias towards the electric small-scale, the easily carried pub-floggable.

He'd cowered in the tiny boiler-cupboard built into the kitchen when his mad-at-heart old man'd return home from the Veterans' Club, slurring and staggering after blowing the moulah from a successful selling sortie of the same on poteen and beer, a coupla lines and some draw. Knocker – and his mother, while she'd been alive – knew from painful experience that then it was time to make themselves scarce.

Perhaps the warmth within the dark, the fantasies that he devised huddled in the fearful sarcrosanctuary of the boiler-cupboard, nurtured young Carlton's metabolic lurch towards the nightlife.

Motive?

Which, incidentally, is the masthead on the fold-out funky-format mag he reads just now on the rapid-transit train that slides along on rail-wheel-roll beneath the city and next, at his stop, above it.

Motive is Getouttahere! Knocker took his old man's words to heart. They're the trigger on the block, Knock's motive for Out. He had a rationale, oh yes, that only Off-Scene provvy trogs assume clubs were all about bullshit dipsomaniac hebropheniacs shouting 'What?' at each other to ward off the grim real of the drunken dawn. They wouldn't get in, so they had no way of knowing. And if they didn't know, how would they ever understand club life? And in the metroplex, according to Knocker and his mates, to suss The Scene is to close the gap on people who ya rate. Otherwise – well, to be unsussed – you wouldn't wanna be like that, would ya? Where's the data, where's the fun, where's the Action gotta run . . .

That's infotainment.

A man comes through the connecting door and circulates deftly around the carriage, shaking down donations for a card that illustrates the finger patterns of the deaf and dumb. Knocker had at least half a dozen already – they made excellent roaches – and knows that their wording claims the vendor was thus afflicted. The man looks at him – he's short and sports a shaggy beard and momentarily eager brown eyes.

Knocker gives him a buck, slipped the ultra-deep-red cardboard into his inside pocket and continued to peruse *Motive* magazine.

More Long Memory:

Goofin' off and cuttin' up meant bunking school. But the arcade games, junk-food, new clothes, sounds, flick-tickets to the back row so you could feel up girls, booze and tabs which filled the afternoons of those halcyon afternoons all had to be paid for somehow. To pacify his da, after the school's social worker dropped by to probe about the reason for his absences, the 14-year-old rebel-without-a-car made bread as an apprentice friar in the fish-shop, where his mama had once worked among the straw-hatted batter-beating white-coat boys. His job? Load four-and-demi heaped half-piles of just-peeled chips from white plastic buckets, measure 'em on and shovel 'em off a black and white chipped china plate into the bubbling brown sea of ground-nut oil that's kept at a constant 362 degrees Celsius. Four, five minutes later (Knocker knows – 'Chips are down when soft inside and hard and crispy out' – Mama told him so) he'd take the aluminium trowel and dump 'em inna likewise metal chip box. From whence the packers match chips to fish, and plonk the polystyrene packages of crisped and scaly calorific eat-out dishes on the plastic counter for the hordes of hungry punters.

Jacqui, a pubescent cherry-bomb apprentice packer, one payday night at closing time suggested out and about go Knock and Jac round the central zone where the Big Time was. The consequences of which were manifold and multiplex, but germanely, up-shot in Knocker's first visit to a nightclub. It was called Panda's. The block where it stood was razed to the ground three years ago to make way for a high-rise of condos and duplexes called Xanadu Towers.

Drunk on Mickey Moose beer, high on illegally imported grass (they didn't market drugs in brands back then), Knocker gazed aghast at the chucker-outers' enormous muscled bodies straining inside their terribly tight posh penguin suits. Jacqui, who'd snared free tickets from somewhere, instantly met up inside with a gaggle of her gangin' girl-mates who promptly migrated to the lavatories for 20 minutes before regrouping fleetingly, only to instantly disperse en masse amongst the mob in search of the dancefloor, boys to fill it with and drinks the boys would buy them to roll over those good good times. Music played and the room moved. It was like being back in the boiler-cupboard in the kitchen. Plus some aspects of the fantasies but minus the threat. As he slowly marinated in dark, familiar warmth, Knocker drunk in the scene (already firmly up-cased as The Scene within the giddy dropbreath excitement of his young mind-time), osmosis-itized it all, frame by soft frame, setting pictures in future memory, cut to beat and soundtrackin' some savage diva beauty of the positive mod-ule girls' make-no-mistake moves, that show-cased out their coming-on then backing-off and winding-up to chill hot-gun wise guys, fly fashion spies and real warm-bodies of celebrities who up till here had just flickered distant fame on transient TV screens round Knocker's room, but now were buzzing on the Action.

Knocker too, only more so – his being there, the smell of making it making it all magi-mixed round and round here hot in the slow rush from the popocratic cocktails he drank that suddenly it pumps upside his skull, soaks his clothes with damp hot dancin' sweat as on pounds the sounds that split his head open and do it do it do it in his skull brain-fuck noise waves of free-verse rap and total

Yeah, Knocker remembered the first time.

At the beginning of that summer, he'd answered an advertisement and started work as a busboy at Magique. He never looked back. While he toiled at clearing tables, tip-hustling and copping and licking the tricks of the trade at the lavender mafia eat-to-beat risco-disco dining club, he had to wear white short shorts. This at the insistence of the proprietors, a curiously self-contained couple called Schpicshpupv. He was an ex-Odeon booker known as 'Never', ferret-eyed, totally bald with gold-caps that glimmered wickedly on his bared black teeth whenever he laughed; the woman, Jantz, preferred sardonic smiles and the wry grimace, a long-repeated – for, like Never, she was in the positively last edition of her thirties – series of which had caused her down-turned lips to curl into a thin, crabby sneer. The pierced space in her left ear was closing up, her make-up was too white and her hennaed crop offensively severe. K O noticed that Never's disco boots had been converted all wrong and that he always smelt of Armagnac and too much overreaching aftershave. He'd stuck it almost a year.

His dad was happy.

'At least the boy's earning a livin',' he'd tell his muckers at the Veterans' Club.

But one night there was another row because the till was short again – Knocker suspected Jimmy, a lank Spanish guy with shifty eyes, but said nothing. It was inculcated from birth that no one in Stewartstown would ever grass. As he was leaving, one of the regulars, Raoul, a soldier for Carlos 'Mattress' Jacquenelli's family, mentioned that there was a nine-to-five available next week at one of his boss's sex shops.

Knocker went back inside to tell Never he was quitting then and there.

On the night he'd scrammed Magique, he ran into the crew at Candybox, the hole-in-the-wall where club staff and an uncertain selection of night people drank after hours. On the Scene: White Jaqui (for it was she), Boosterfish, Eustace 'Queeny' V., Ziggy Shondelle, Muscles McKhan, Blackjack, Faceframes, Snaps, 2Can-Bone, the Toy and Tranny Saul. That night all the fly young things had got shiny and The Scene capped up for real.

Things had never been the same since and now they'd brought him here, disembarking the train with *Motive* magazine under his arm. As he steps into the arched, concrete station corridor that leads to the escalators, he reaches for the micro discman beatbox. A gust of wind blows as he steps onto the moving stair. Coming towards him on the down-bound escalator, he sees two chicks. Knocker checks 'em out. One, the prettier of the two, with a pink polka-dot bow tied in her frizzy hair, looks back at him. The gap between them closes. He holds her gaze and explores the look. She's fly! She checks him with a correspondingly sexual scrutiny. The escalator keeps moving. She breaks the eye-lock. Knock hears them giggle and pretends to view the posters passing by on the wall for a moment. Then he glances back down at her – to discover she is already gazing back at him. She smiles and he grins right back at her.

'Ooooohh' he moans. He hears her laughing with her best friend.

The silver stairs flatten on their grooves and Knocker jumps the turnstiles. He feels good – yeah, sure he could've turned around and chased her – but random lust is one of many multiplying possibilities within the metroplex for this Knocker person. He intends to explore them – selectively.

He turns right outta the station and struts his displaced teensome angst in pants swank, heading on towards more Out among the crowd of urban bio-massing Other People with whom he's spilled shoulder to shoulder, pace to pace, away from the subpath station down Fortino Boulevard, moving through the Crowd, wondering if Tonight will yield that ultimate one-time good good feeling.

The escalator flirtation has banished any trace of black undesignered mode or terroristic sleepwalk coma creep. The Fear's on hold.

Pulse on, Knocker.

Well.

Cred moves. Like the citizenry it is volatile. Like Out, it has a market and inherent momentum. Both of which travel at a pace that blurs.

Get an edge in the blur.

Yus.

As Knocker throws a left to head for Tilt, where he'll meet the boys for drinks, the light changes and he's nearly run over by a black-factor limousine.

'Bastard!' he yells, banging on the bonnet. Pedestrians have rights, he thinks – unless, of course, it's Knocker at the wheel.

'Hi, Knocker,' smiles Polliana, the greeter at the oft-chronicled yo-life retro milkfood bar.

'Hi, Polly,' he says and smiles. It's genuine – normally he'd stop and chat and wheel and deal – but after a hard p.m. of creative telephonic frenzy he wants to kick-back and unwind – talk pussy and trade turf tips with his posse.

Leaning on the wooden bar is Richard Rayban, style-czar, detail-Meister, gossip guru and arbiter of in and out.

'No, no, no,' he's saying. 'You've missed the point – it wasn't a black boy; she was lying on the bed with a black goddamn poodle.'

His audience is attentive for a group whose median attention span averages 20 seconds. Nicolai Josh Rambuen, the rising-starred talk-turk crew-cut talent-scout, laughs phonily as his eyes reflexively shift over Rayban's shoulder to check the flicker of the TV and ensure he isn't missing anyone or anything among the busy throng who brush by along the crowded walkway that runs from one end to the other of the long and narrow bar.

'Two Becks by the neck,' Dick says to the bar boy. Knocker thinks he looks fucked up. As usual – good old Dick, supremo of the Naff Café.

'Yo, scenester!' exclaims Tallboy (what that off-beige hustler did no one would say) and plays along with Knocker's honky handshake ritual before floridly outlining the scope of the evening's potential to the newcomer, whom, he felt reasonably sure, would imminently be paying for his next drink.

40 minutes later they roll on up to the opening of O^2, the happening new oxygen bar, where aerobic advisors in cling-film dress would politely but firmly (according to the data-pack distributed on the door) transform your filthy lucre into metered units of pure fresh air, delivered through individually industrially sterilized face-masks bolted in a row to the narrow, ragged-round-edged limpid transparency of the huge glass bar. Almost immediately, *inter alia*, Knocker meets the world's self-proclaimed second greatest bottle-player and an anorexic blonde in a seriously aggressive Anonymous business suit who burns a hole in her stocking with her Now cigarette as she shows him her garter belt.

'Lingerie is so much sexier when it's worn discreetly, don't you think?' she says, recovering. 'I'm a lawyer and it really turns me on to dress like this for some old drone at a client meet. I know exactly what he's thinking, and it gives me a real angle on his fantasy connection that makes the meeting easier to manipulate. It's like a double life.'

Rayban had just stood-off from a set-to with Tony Burgoyne

about the latter's new straw boater, when Knocker slides up and asks after his mucker's younger kidult brother.

'He's having an operation, actually,' Rayban, relieved at an excuse to avoid the artist's evil eye, says. 'He's convinced one of his testicles' – occasionally the ambi-sexual social sultan developed a fastidiousness re details anatomical – 'is smaller than the other.'

'Bu' I fort everyone 'ad one ball smaller dan der uver,' Knocker replied, his accent glottal-stopping automaxin' cred override.

'He's convinced it's atrophying every day. He wants to catch it before it disappears completely.'

Rayban pauses to contemplate his Kamikaze Slammer (the brain-threatening supplementary house speciality consisted of four parts brandy, three of tequilla and liberal measures of champagne and peach juice. It also seemed to be available in a life-threatening double dose, but apparently the night was still only middle aged).

'And then he's going to have a nose job.'

'Like Michael Jackson's?' asks Russell, an up-scale, under-employed film editor with glinty eyes beneath thick brows, of swarthy skin, of short black hair long at the back and a mean-streaked mien. He'd never had a paying gig in his chosen field of endeavour but liked to keep busy. Currently, Rustle One Muscle Daktari Snake Bite (as he was known around the Scene) eked out pin-up money as a semi-pro game show contestant.

'No, no, it's not cosmetic,' Rayban taps his nose. 'Inside. His sinuses are blocked up or something.'

Knocker, Tallboy and Russell exchange a knowing glance.

'Yeah?' says Nicolai cynically. 'And I'm James Dean selling fax machines.' He enjoys publicly chastising his quondam mentor; until he'd acquired, quite recently, economic autonomy as a freelance talent-spotter, the black-clad hover-booted boy had been a protégé of Rayban's, for the ageing Binge King enjoyed patronizing the intelligent twinkies with which he surrounded himself. Perhaps he too harboured nascent Fear in his interior.

The style-führer chooses to ignore the interruption and blithely continues his narrative, hinting at familial resentment about paying for his sibling's indulgence. Their wheelchair-bound father is a self-made man who'd devised Soul Kitchen, the city-wide fast-food chicken 'n' fakefat giblet crashmunch, which offered opportunities to religious junk-noshers in a rush – eat 'n' worship to the pre-taped non-denominational hippydip New Age TV evangeligush that pours forth from every franchise's fifteen viddy screens. The cadet Raybans live on a wing and a prayer to inherit as heirs.

'I mean, you can see him at a party where someone asks him "Whatdaya do?" and he'll say, "I'm contemplating a career in surgery." And they'll say, "Oh, you're at med school?" And Chris'll reply, "No, between operations."'

'Isn't this just totally drabulous?' says Rayban, as Splinter, the young maître d' of Pasta Primadonna, waves them on inside the newly opened, tiled restaurant which had once been a bath-house but more recently – until last week – the basement of one of the innumerable videoporn shops along the Strip.

'Drabulous?' queries Nina, the city's only titled insomniac oral hygienist.

'Oh, it's so chic and bleak and underbudget,' asserts the publisher, gesturing vaguely around him in the general direction of a young freelance stylist who tries to attract the style-leader's attention as the group pass her table, where her outrageously clad companions clatter noisily along into the restaurant's resonantly ambient soundtrack as they drop their cutlery on their crockery upon sighting the maverick magazine maven's approach.

The trio have just ordered the aperitifs when Rep, Knocker's itinerant girlfriend, flounces in. Rep has red hair and green eyes.

She wears a black dress accessorized with discreetly placed pieces of cod-jewellery that foil her lizard-skin boots.

'I'm sorry,' she says, bending to lip-brush KO on the cheek as she takes her seat. 'I've just been to a board meeting with daddy and it went into injury time.'

Knocker and Rep have a glass of beef apiece. The hygienist plumps for hand-knitted tofu Spageroons and Rayban the Ravioli à la Urban which the waiter, only 40 minutes later, serves directly from the can he opens before their very eyes, right at the table. The motormouthing group share two bottles of mediocre Château Parvenu, four Cognacs (the dudes do doubles) and the bill comes to 284 notes plus service.

Motive magazine's publisher charges it on his Status card.

They detour via Mystic City Sign. This was demi-duty, since Rep's papa Eddie Eisler owns the joint, although he doesn't go there overmuch.

Inside, next to the bank of total-protocol interactive self-maintaining user-empathic seventh-generation databases, they run into that incidentally Irish, absolutely atavistic celebutante role-model Fat Tuesday.

'He's lost so much weight. So fast. Where's it all gone? The visual crime bank?' Rayban whispers loudly.

'That isn't it,' Rep hisses. She desperately needs to write for *Motive* – that wondrously exposed window of young talent that chronicles the interplay amongst the millennial generation – if she is to stay on schedule and front her own chat show by the end of the year after next.

'That boy is really sick,' she whispers into the balding groover's hairy ear. 'He's got these kinda barnacle things growing underneath his arms. His glands are up and he's lost tons of weight. He's really worried that . . . you know?'

Rayban nods sagely.

'For Chrissakes don't tell him about it,' she says. 'Don't let on you know.' She's talking in that breathless way of hers. 'He'll kill me if he finds out I've told you. I mean, God, can you imagine – how embarrassing.'

It isn't a question, so there isn't an answer. Only the inevitable grind of Boosterfish's swagger-brag wheels of steel from the DJ box above the nighterie within.

'Oh you,' says Fats, diverting his attention from introducing Knocker (who always pressed the flesh with his itinerant star-employee) to the leatherboy with whom he'd hung with as the quartet first blew in. Tuesday's slickered hair is short, his jacket black to match his baggy trousers, his tight polo-neck and square-toed shoes. But, Rep notices, the black rings that line the hollows beneath his eyes serve only to make his features seem still more gaunt.

Tuesday's sussed – he notices her noticing.

'Well, you can wipe that look off your face for a start, you hideous old cow. I know what you've been doing.'

'No you don't,' says Rep.

'Yeessss I do,' Tuesday lisps, and eye glistens. 'You've been making some career moves. Rep's always making career moves,' he explains for the benefit of the sideburned acolyte beside him, who clutches his ticket-hero's Desert Orchid cocktail within easy reach. 'You know it's like "I'm sorry mummy, I'm going to be late home tonight – in fact, I might not be home at all." And so mummy says, "Well as long as it's a good career move that's fine, darling, wonderful, we'll see you at nine o'clock tomorrow morning then, in time for school."'

Tuesday does the accents brilliantly too.

Inside Rep positively shrieks at Tuesday's shriving – familiarity with his *modus operandi* has bred respect – but her exterior remains unflustered, equipoised, calm, cold as diamonds, marble-tough and granite-hard. The sideburned leatherboy is bafflegabbed, bezonked by too much, much too soon – he's looking from one to the other for some sort of clue as to what's going on. But Tuesday just laughs at him, and then at her, but it happens simultaneously – now he's taking the piss outta the botha them.

Thus chastened and suitably up-wound on the sanguine nerve, the foursome pop along to Discodrome (frat slobs, empty suits, dumb doxies and dodgy bodgie-birds who couldn't make a buck on a battleship) before ploughing on to Rififi, the club set within a converted ancient grace-and-favour warehouse leased from the local hysterical society. On stage, a Japanese Beatle-clone group mime parodies ('Suchi in the Sky with Diamonds', 'Hey Judo' and a *hari-kari* cover of 'Twist 'n' Shout'), while Knocker and his gang burrow through the building's labyrinthine maze, up up into the darkened topadashop VIP room's standard cast of social succubae, gangster groupies, washed out popsters on the drinks-tix shake and brunch babies up way way beyond bed-time.

Rep wants to book.

'Some of us have to work in the mornings, you know,' she snaps tartly, pointedly fixing her squeeze with the fish-eye. When she sees this is not producing the desired effect, she stands up to leave, her green eyes blazing, her red hair tossed, her skin a furious white that'd darken milk. 'Don't worry about me,' she fumes. 'I can make my own way home, thank you.'

He laughs off her petulant exit as Rayban flirts with a soulless black boy, and the anorexic sex-Sloane producer of *Eating for Quids* inquires if he knows the whereabouts of Rustle One Muscle Daktari Snakebite.

'Wha' time zit? One firty? Well 'e could be anywhere, cun'ne? The G, Alchemy, Power Exchange, Em Cee Squared. Tried 'em?'

Indeed the producer has not. Actually.

'Well, eel be rhand Jefferson's later. Rus always goes dahn Jefferson's. Wanna cume and have a squiz later, eh? Fancy that?'

She does.

Jefferson's is sited beneath a porno-store and mini-cinema that lurks halfway down a dark alley. The basement afterhours instantly confers the sensation of instant criminalization on all who pass through its dingy portals.

Furnished with old armchairs, lit by bare red bulbs, Jefferson's subterranean walls stink rank. They reek of cheap perfume, hard liquor, stale smoke and distant barf. The dank rooms emit a unique engrained, entropic gloom suggesting imminent forbidding forebodings that presage horrid doom.

Jefferson's is the most cred.

So now Knocker and Rayban and Rentboy and the tall, dark titless researcher chick ('Well, I'm not actually officially a prodicer yet, but I shell be rilly rilly soon. My uncie's Jimmy Hennessey and he like owns the network, word yah?') head for the Green Line, the popular pre-op transsexual hangout down-town and east. Knocker talks them through the door, and fast – the night has turned cold and breath vaporizes in the icy air. Since leaving the restaurant, they've given money only to the taxi-drivers. They never pay to get in anywhere, not cash: it's a principle of face, especially for Knocker when he's with some girl. Face is all when out. Rayban, not to be outdone here, eases his squeeze to flatter the leather-studded clone-'tached bouncer inside into handing over a wadgy fist of comp-drink ducats.

Jammed inside the matt-black oblong chicane that runs betwixt the stage and around its two crowded bars, Knocker sees the action's already well in hand. An oblong pit, roped off like a boxing ring, has been erected on the raised dais. The late-night launch of the washable version of *Eat Trash and Die Y-Plan Diet Book*, penned by a 31-stone former landscape gardener who in some previous half-life answered to Reginald but now has re-tuned its tag to Daphne, is well under way.

'Are you sure you don't want to meet the author?' pleads the flack.

'More positive than life itself,' Rayban asserts.

'But you will stay for the match, won't you?' Stinkabelle doesn't pause for answer. 'We're having transvestite mud-wrestling and the girls will be so upset if you don't stay.'

Now she pauses.

'Richard?' she says.

But Rayban is looking at a celebutante who has just been illuminated by the burning battery of portable lights toted by one of the three pro-TV crews covering the event. Knocker, returning with two organically made Margaritas, recognizes instantly from his posture that he is furious that no one has interviewed him yet.

'Hey, mister . . .' says Stinkabelle, waving her Aqua bottle at him. 'Knocker!'

Carlton manoeuvres to try and distance himself from Rachel, which is the name of *Eating for Quids* anorexic representative who's hanging on his body and planting lipstick on his face.

Stinkabelle is Rep's best buddy: they'd been the youngest-ever editors of a metro gossip column when, during the school holidays, they'd worked for free for *Pink News* the year they'd hit their teens.

'Yo, Stinker,' he greets her, struggling to ward off a baffled Rachel's ferocious grip.

He relaxes the ambitious teenager, nodding smiles as Stinkabelle chatters about her paranoid flatmate's suspicion that he's about to be hit by the KGB – mysterious late-night calls from Wanda, long-distance wondering about a home address.

'And he's weird, Knocker, really weird. He hasn't been out of the house since Christmas, not for anything.' On the Scene that was sure-fire and damnation a rad bad red mark in the copybook o' cred. The blot of that other f – word, a confession of soul-dead; of unhappingness, no cashflow, zilch social skill and wearing inappropriate clothes. In is safe: so to stay home was – a floppertunity. Out was to be alive – to dance not work, to yay the risk of life, to be yourself, double up the stakes and gambol on the frolicsome play of Personality, perchance to survive and thrive. The entire cluster culture of clubs and Out and Scene is based on the cold cash and hot animality of people that do not do – yet plainly are.

Knocker suddenly feels a hand around his waist.

Spinaround.

'Hey, I've just remembered there's this super party at the Wah Wah Bar, let's go.'

He looks in horror as Rachel brushes her face and the 'I Spit on Your Filofax' T-shirt up against him salaciously.

'He just writes these vicious chain letters all day long,' continues Stinkabelle, apparently unfazed. But he knows that she can't have failed to notice. She'll report back and dis him to Rep.

So on the way over to Wah Wah in a purple bus (all the city's licensed taxis are painted thus) trauma thrashes and whumps about him. So much so that when the putative producer leaves 20 minutes later – she pleads overwind and PMT – he scarcely notices.

Looking out of the lavatory window as he ingests yet another slug of drugs, Knocker sees the icicles and freezy grunge that coats the pavement. Some time during the their nocturnal haji, snow has fallen, lightly dusting the sidewalk with a pure sprinkle coat of white. But already, like a once-pretty woman run out of her mind by too many kids because she married too young for all the wrong reasons, busy urban feet have trampled the white crystalline carpet's flimsy picturesque fall into a sludgy mass of grey gunk. Emerging past the snakelike line waiting for the cubicles, Knocker notices that water drips from a pipe on the wall at the end of the bar. He looks around amongst the tightly packed mass of milling bodies snouting down to drink, chat, snort and smoke. The Wah Wah Bar's packed out. He surveys the crowd. Anxiously, he realizes he can see no one he knows or recognizes. No one who matters. No one who can help him.

Immobile, he feels The Fear rush in.

Desperately he forces himself to move and mingle amongst the surging sea of bodies. A dark-haired girl turns round, reads him and turns back.

'So who are all the big fish in Futures at the moment?' she asks the dark, diminutive monkey man with big eyes.

'Fish?' he replies as Knocker wedges his way past them. 'They're not fish – they're sharks.'

To his right, a gangling bean-pole woman with enormous glasses and loud shoulder-length red hair berates one of the barmen.

'Look at it!' she urges him. 'I used to work in a pub, and I'm telling you that is a dirty glass.'

The barman looks at her, takes the empty wine-glass, holds it up in his outstretched hand and cursorily, but theatrically, examines it.

'And what I'm telling you,' he says, replacing it between two ashtrays on the bar, 'is that they're all like that.'

In front of him, Knocker finally recognizes a familiar face. It's Tannia, the model. She talks to another girl who's been naturally endowed with great beauty.

'I used to be the same age as her,' Tannia says. 'It's a shame the way she looks now.'

They're both wearing jeans and loose, plain shirts whose deceptive simplicity can be borne only by great expense at point of purchase. Knocker is about to talk to them when he's seized with a terrible doubt – is that her name? Or is it Tallia? Or Talai? Or Titania? Or . . .

Oh shit, he thinks. The Fear.

He lunges for the chrome shaft that curves along just below the bar as it moves in. He makes it just in time. But en route he's bumped some up-tight tyke in a blue suit, who turns and glares at him aggressively.

'I'm sorry,' Knocker mutters, grasping the rail for dear life. Now he knows he's got it bad – he had apologized. The man, a dude in his mid-late twenties is still staring, and Knocker realizes that he's still staring back.

'Look . . .' the guy begins belligerently. But then Kirk, the head-barkeep (who doubles up as booze-savant for the yewf niche on Channel 001) taps the geezer on his exposed elbow.

'Would you like me to open, or would you rather?' Kirk asks pointedly. The Wah Wah Bar, as always on a Friday night, is going cra-z-ee.

'No, no, that's OK,' says the gook, peeling off the wrapping round the top of the bottle of Krug.

'Oh, darling,' swoons Katy, a débutante hipster Knocker knows somewhat.

'Champagne? Oh – not champagne,' she says. He tries to catch her eye – but she's staring, glassy-eyed, at her date. 'I'm soooooo bored with champagne,' she says peevishly.

'Stevie! Stevie!' somebody shouts.

Knocker looks around. Rayban has disappeared somewhere amongst the crowd of Other People.

Fear. He feels it zoning in, tightening. Desperately, he forces himself to listen to the noizak swirling around him like a blanket.

'. . . drinking with Destiny – every time one of the characters on the screen has a drink, everybody watching has one of what they're having . . .'

'. . . then these swans came at me, all vicious-looking . . .'

'. . . what I want to know is why they always seem to commit suicide during the rush-hour . . .'

'. . . well it's a known fact that the only reason he got it was because she gave the creative director a blow-job . . .'

'Yeah, I do still fancy him, really, but he's been a bit mental since I stabbed him.'

'. . . and Rayban told me he found her on the bed with two black boys, a Brazilian pre-operative and this black standard poodle . . .'

Disconsolately, Knocker looks into the middle distance. His eye alights on the pipe. The leak has become a fracture from which water has begun to run more vigorously.

'Must be the cold weather,' Knocker thinks.

Someone slithers past him. Fillet.

'You're so lucky being small,' she's telling the model whose name had triggered Knocker's current crisis. 'You can get away with wearing cheap clothes.' He reaches out to snag her, but she's already bolted beyond his reach.

'Look, Jasmine, you must realize that life is not a video,' he hears an intense, short-haired type tell a pretty girl in a suede snood.

'I want to tell you something,' Katy confides to the man standing next to him at the bar.

'Yes?' he says expectantly. 'Feel free.'

'You're a real drag,' she says and ups sticks.

'Anyway, she's well past the fuck-by date,' says the confusingly named mannikin to her friend.

Knocker looks weakly at the patterned carpet.

'Well I can foresee problems with your brother,' asserts one of the waitresses bustling up beside him. He looks up at her, frantically seeking eye-contact or some other form of ack. But none's forthcoming.

'Why?' asks the rockabilly boy with the flat-top and two-stone denim jacket standing next to her. 'He's not drunk.'

Knocker's body sags as he reaches for the fag burning in the ashtray. His fingers fumble, he bungles, and the cigarette end burns his hand as it falls to the floor.

'Exactly,' ripostes the waitress triumphantly.

He stoops to retrieve it. Picking it up, he notices that the carpet is damp.

The pain from the burn encourages his reflexes to reassert themselves. To flee The Fear, he forces himself into active mode and starts moving. But, as he jemmies his way through the crowd's vicelike coherence, he comes across no one he knows, no one to talk to. Something has gone wrong (The Fear rises within him again). Two groups away, he notices Blackjack. But such is the dead touch within him that he can't summon the bottle to interrupt her conversation.

'Prince?' Daz, an unemployable session musician who plays part-time with a no-hope thrash-metal band, is saying. 'Yeah, I dueted with him once.'

'Shut up,' Blackjack says disdainfully, pinching one of his cigs.

'No, I did,' Daz insists. 'He was on the radio while I was in the bath.'

Shyte, muses Knocker. It's bad when I can't even talk to Blackjack.

He's meditating depressively on this thought as he checks the change in his trouser pocket to buy another drink when, at last, he hears a familiar voice.

'Knocker!' cries Katy, moving round to greet him.

They power-kiss.

'Ooze 'ee?' inquires Knocker of her erstwhile companion, who's now seeking solace with a long-legged, liposuctioned bimb in a rubber micro and patterned tights.

'Some geek I met at a dinner party last week,' Katy says. 'I was told he was a sexual athlete – but actually he's just a physical jerk. Do you realize – that man keeps Jelly-tots in his hip-flask? Darling, listen,' she says, running her fingers down the line of his lapel. 'Knocker, will you talk to PJ for a moment 'cos Cindy's coming over for Fillet to see what Emma's done for Nick while Cressie isn't here.'

'Sure,' replies Knocker. Katy is making it slightly better. He feels the carpet squelch beneath the tread of his two-tone Mohicans as he trots along behind her. He looks down.

'PJ's just come back from the east,' Katy's saying.

Knocker is standing in a puddle.

'. . . these amazing statues of Nemrut Dagi in eastern Turkey – there are five of them. They're colossal. They were built by Xeroxes I, the photocopy king . . .' PJ, a dishevelled, loose-limbed spaced-out hippy brat, rants. Knocker looks around. One or two of the others have noticed it too: it's a bloody big puddle. He glances at the wall. Water's cascading from the broken pipe.

'. . . must be a bloody bisexual necrophiliac, 'cos he'll screw anything that doesn't move.'

'Where are they?' Kirk is frantically asking the white-shirted minion who Knocker'd watched inspecting the wine glass earlier.

'They'll be here any second,' he replies petulantly. 'That was what they said – *any second.*'

'The waiters refused point blank to serve Bulgarian wine at breakfast . . .' brabbles a fat-man with glasses in an up-country accent.

'You know we're going to join hands around the base and turn all their stupid missiles into fish fingers . . .'

He recognizes that speaker as Suzie Splash. Ultra-cred. She'd squatted with the Toy just before he'd made it; worked for St Andy just before his death; been an IV drug addict and, lately, run a conceptualist boutique in the Barrio called Slag on premises she'd rented from a feminist prostitutes' collective. Sometimes Suzie would sell designer clothes cheaply from her flat. Others, she could be found hanging out with a toyboy *manqué* Italian count. Reputedly, she's Bee Z.'s silent partner in the snoot Melrose fashion store. Knocker finds this hard to credit, since it is so rare for Suzie either to stop talking or to have one penny to her name. As always with the Outcrowd (the ones who were really in) nothing is certain, since every time she's asked about her invisible means of support Mz Splash'd throw back her head and laugh a husky cackle hotter than an eskimo on an equatorial beach.

'Angabaht,' he tells PJ, staunching the seasoned traveller in mid-flow. Suzie's eyes twinkle mischievously as Knocker routinely air-kisses her sallow skin.

Soright again, he tells himself as she talks at him. Sgone away.

'You call me, darlin',' she advises. 'I have these trousers you will love. They are by Gino Jacometti, made from grey velvet and when you walk into the room every one will say, "Rrrrrr-some. Quella Hombre?" You will love them, I promise you – come over tomorrow, try them on, see.'

'Si,' he replies, feeling marginally better now.

'It's angry type,' he earwigs Rayban lecture a tall, short-haired Scandinavian-looking chick whose long, tanned neck protrudes from a preppy suit.

He sees a bimb tear her tight micro-dress as she climbs up onto a table, clutching her shoes.

'Hey, are we on fire, or what?' Daz asks the overweight, overtanned bottle-blonde harridan in the unflattering fringed orange micro-skirt, who's been pushed in the crush next to Black-jack.

'Fire?' she says, alarmed.

Indeed, the Wah Wah Bar is being overrun by fire-fighters in blue jackets and liveried yellow hard-hats, none of whom seem to have the slightest trouble moving through the formerly impenetrable crowd, as, with a quietly effective and practised drill, they rapidly start operating the two pumps that have appeared in place at either end of the venue.

'It's a like theme party, right?' Daz guesses out loud at his female companions.

Blackjack screams. A burly fireman turns and smacks her swiftly round the chops.

'It's OK everybody,' Kirk shouts above the taped mega-mix of the George Gershwin rap. 'Everything is totally under control.'

Scarcely has he spoken when he disappears from view as one of two fire-fighters clambering onto the bar, to reach the broken pipe, puts his weight on his head, and leaps across towards the central row of optics.

'What are you doing?' screeches the bar manager from the floor.

'Watch yourself,' shouts the other fire-fighter, a middle-aged woman with a fat face.

Kirk flinches as he is covered with a shower of flying glass splinters.

'My boyfriend's a fireman,' exclaims the scrutineer of wine glasses as his boss looks up. 'Isn't it great to have friends in high places?'

'Jeus H. Christ,' whimpers Kirk as the fat-faced firewoman stuffs a table-cloth, purloined by one of her brigade, across the aperture.

'It's a fire-fighter party!' exclaims a bald, elfin individual in a long black Japanese coat with whom Knocker is currently not on speaks. 'Get it? It's a fire-fighter party without a fire. That's quite neat . . .' he continues for the benefit of anyone who might be listening as he too searches for a vacant spot at one of the increasingly crowded tables.

'. . . a strong, silent type: Futura Clear Inverse.' Rayban blathers on obliviously at his embarrassed, giraffe-necked girlpal who's nervously trying to draw his attention to the events unfolding around them. 'The architecture's pillars of strength eye-snatch the down-page distractor through all that clear, white, yet paradoxically aggressive space to reverberate and activate the read-me triggers . . .'

Back at the bar, a lone fireman continues the destruction of the bottles on the shelves with merciless hacking downstrokes of his two-handed axe.

'OK, OK,' says the fat-faced firewoman. 'It's all over. Let's get out of here.'

The fireman standing amidst the debris at the back of the bar pauses in mid-swing and turns to her.

'Caspar and Tharg have shut down the valve at the mains,' she says. 'They've cut off all the water for nine square miles.'

He looks incredulously along the wall. Knocker follows his eye-line. The cascading torrent has abruptly become a tremulous trickle.

'It's like – intense,' Daz says, gazing in awestruck stupor at the mêlée around him. 'Totally intense. We're on fire!'

'Is someone videoing this?' asks the woman in the fringed orange micro skirt and bulging pink latex boots.

'Over?' cries the fireman crouched on the bar in horror. 'But it can't be over. We've only just started.'

'Now now, come on, chief. Get down from there and we'll get back to the station,' the firewoman tells him soothingly. 'You can do the invoices and the boys can have a brew.'

'Oh God,' says the fire-chief, reluctantly climbing back down again. 'That's so unfair.'

'Listen,' says the firewoman. 'There's a geyser on exit 84 of Shakey Zoom. You can go and see to that if you want to.'

'Are you sure it's fixed?' the fire-chief asks her, glancing suspiciously back at the dripping pipe as she leads him away.

Kirk is almost immediately surrounded by a bellicose bunch of angry scenesters.

''Ere, look at these shoes,' Blackjack shouts, thrusting them in Kirk's face.

'Ruined! Ruined! I want instant compensation. And if you don't hand it over – I'll sue!'

Knocker is on his fifth double Bloody Mary since Kirk declared an open bar, and morosely wonders why Rachel had high-tailed it, when he suddenly feels a jerk on his jacket.

Someone is pulling him up onto the stage.

Knocker is only slightly surprised when Lady 'Tiger' Lily Curzon – much to the delighted squeals of the fun-drunk night-birds and bawdy catcalls from a few loitering firemen – strips off her clothing and flings it untidily on the floor, capriciously allowing her G-string to fall within the resonant depths of the white Steinway piano. But when the toast of Cappuccino Society slowly repeats the process, beginning with the unravelling of the Windsor-knot he'd tied so laboriously in his favourite M. Rocas neckwear that he'd taken all that trouble to put on after getting up especially early for the two o'clock lunch with Stinky Eddie, Knocker is utterly got-whacked. It isn't that he minds Tigs's lilac eyes, or indeed any other aspect of her lithe anatomy, go-going walkabout all over the dubious mystique of his physique. Hell, no – normally he would've pushed a peanut with his nose across a zillion miles of jaggered bottles just to sniff her tight tops.

It's the other 70 people who happen to be in the bar at the time that make him feel a bit shifty.

He can't understand why they're laughing at him. Goddamnit, he's done them favours – this place is like his local.

Knocker gazes bemusedly as the nubile society beauty writhes her perfectly proportioned limbs in a grindy melt of wet frot mere inches from his nude frame on the Wah Wah Bar's venerable boards. Now people are standing on tables to get a better view. Of, he hopes, the metropolis's most depraved débutante.

As she wraps the hips that launched a thousand quips around the microphone stand like a snake, Barney Boosterfish, his small dark eyes wickedly incandescent in their deep-set slits, seems to be dangling a giant plastic spider around the suddenly hermetic form of Knock's cock.

'Am I too old or sumfink?' Knocker blurbles ingenuously into the stage microphone. ''Ave I lost der plot? Aghhhhh – waassa point?'

Gales of hilarity greet his manifesto: wind-chill factor 23. But he can't see the joke.

There is, it occurs to him dimly, something utterly shameless and too indecent about all this.

As Boosterfish, Tallboy and Fat Tuesday noisily hoist three and four more crates of champagne from behind the bar, KO finds himself pushed along, half-naked, in lemminglike egress through a crowd that greets him with cheers and jeers, towards various vehicles parked around and about in the chill night outside.
He shivers involuntarily in the cold.

Then he's in a car. It starts. Someone has turned the hot-blast aircon on. His stomach churns like memory, glut-sated. He feels sullied, spurned, bloaty and distended. Tiger Lily pushes something in his mouth.

'I got it from my cousin Arturo – he's f-faaaaaaabulous. You know, the hairdresser out on the coast? He knits these amazing sweaters out of dental floss and designs studded seatbelts for lavatories. You'd adore him.'

Then some guy says he's going to make smile magnifiers for kidshrinks who practise psychology on myopic tots.

Outside, the city of night rushes by. A sign on Shakey Zoom says DIRECTIONS BELLEVILLE AND ST CLOUD.

'. . . really humuongous statues,' yatters Katy. She's bobbing up her blonde hair and pouting her lips as she adjusts her big black Spanish hat in the driver's mirror. This forces Lily to contort herself to see through the frost that covers the rear window as she negotiates the car through a stream of traffic to make a turn.

'There's Apollo, Fortuna, Zeus, Antiochus and Heracles. He says Zeus has had his toe-nail clipped and the heads have all fallen off.'

At Tiger Lily's place, the party is in full swing.

'No, no thanks, I won't actually,' Fillet, clad in her little Chanel suit, demurs, when Knocker offers to get her some food. 'I don't like eating in public.'

'So,' he replies, miffed at her brusque rejection of his chivalrous self-exposure, 'oo yew gahn out wiv eeese daze ay?'

She bridles – then throws back her head and squwarks delightedly from the bottom of her lungs, 'Bee Z.!' and deserts Knocker for the omnipresent boutique owner of age uncertain, leaving the image of her indignation imprinted on his brain like an object viewed intensely just before the lights go out.

'Well, we're supposed to do a deal with the city council. But they're being represented by Mann, Rogers & Greaves and the guy there, he's pushy, he wants a pay off. So at the moment, it's cratered. Want a piece?'

The blonde Marilyn Monroe clone who'd been at the O^2 party earlier chatters to the paunchy beret-wearing beardie who lounges next to her on the low-slung Italian sofa. He is Bobby Hot-Rock, the music merchandiser who fences stolen high-ticket stones on the side.

'I don't think so,' he says. There are flecks of foam on his dark facial fuzz. His expression looks worried, like his girlfriend has just told him her period is a year overdue. 'If Kinsella's doing the deal, it means it's mob money. I don't want to get involved with wiseguys like Casales and Culver – too many people they do business with seem to end up modelling subaquatic overcoats.'

Aimlessly, Knocker wanders through the crowd that spills out of the drawing-room of Tiger's apartment – autonomously self-contained beneath the smart parental Belleville demesne – into the kitchen, where huddles of black-clad Barrio dwellers have gathered to discuss who was hot and what was not in little knotted studies of immense intensity. The TV raves and rabbles in the background, hooked above the sink on a matching metallic robot arm.

'Well, what we're seeking here is a non-specific misanthrope, about five six and 130 pounds with bad teeth who may recently have done a bulk-buy deal with a cosmetic surgeon,' the bull-necked metropolice commissioner barks. Somewhere in the back of Knocker's brain it registers that the cop is talking about the Man with 44 Faces, the latest berserker to terrify the city. Gino Jacometti has apparently been found dangling from the ceiling of his riverside apartment in a French dog collar, amidst a mass of kid-porn snaps and rentboy paraphernalia. The Man with 44 Faces had called a phone-in on the wireless to claim the kill.

Wow, Knocker thinks, recollecting a fragment of conversation earlier. Better see Suzie about those troos. They could be valuable.

The datastream on the right-hand side of the screen pours forth a mass of spurious electronique infotell: ante-post prices on whether the cops or privatized vigilante posses employed by the Ministry for Harmonious Cohesion would nail him first.

As he stares at the flat screen, the black, undesignered sleepwalk creep-mode rumbles somewhere inside him, its lust unslaked.

It's the bleedin' droogs, Knocker tries to tell himself. After all, if he really had The Fear he would've cracked back on stage, no? Dead set. Bloody well right – that Spectre. Very rumpy-pumpy. Oioi, wazzisen?

But as he tries to re-focus his pressing attentions anew onto the screen, all he can grasp from the amorphous statistical splurge of even odds and temperatures and soft-commodity price-boom breakdowns is that it has, somehow, turned into Monday. A week after carnival. Carne Vale – farewell to the flesh: traditionally the end of the summer. The start of the fall. He'd lost a day somewhere last night. Grappling amongst the cutlery, crockery and dirty dishes that spill over from the giant sink, Knocker finds the remote-control unit nose-down in a paper cup of wine.

Zap it.

Click: old movie. Click: 24-hour weather. Click: dumb sitcom. Click, click: a sports game show and another lame repeat. Click: an Indian western with hispanic subtitles. Click: an ident for *The Teddy Bigbucks Show*, breaking for commercials –

'Hi, babes, Fat Tuesday here to tell you about my incredible new album, *U Can be Fat and Voguedance . . .*'

Kill it.

Electro-death.

Walk, sometimes a walk helps.

He staggers through into Tiger's office. It's minimally furnished. Tiger needs an office like the pope needs a bikini. Everybody who'd been on the receiving end of one of her bills at the Wah Wah Bar, or who'd had to break a note for change to buy one of the iridescent lottery cards at Alchemy, knew that the dotty blueblood thought 2 + 2 = a career crisis and that she found all the news she needed in *Hotspur's Daily Updated Turf & Track Report*. Tiger Lily was quintessential Deb Labour. She did it all with amusing inconsistency and – until she'd hit the Scene – for laughable amounts of money. When not otherwise stylishly exploited on catwalks, or charity ball committees, grease grease slime slime, she walked on the wild side the rest of the time, lay on her back listening to Miss Nazi, the situationalized artist, read to her from Chastity Van Assad's *Selected Speeches and Essential Essays* as she sipped champagne and sniffed cocaine. At night she slinked around. Her overactive imagination was capricious, playful and yet persistent in its pursuit of some never explained ulterior agenda. Some she told she was a thesp, others – the green marks, the outtatowners with wind-me-up signs visible to any who could use their loaf to make some dough – that she ran a shebeen. It was unlikely that she needed the money. For Tiger, it was a game, a cred exam.

Inside her ersatz office two lawyers – Knocker'd once had them thrown out of Le Hot Club de Now for being underexcitable, and but rarely did he forget a face he'd stepped on – lean against the black wooden desk. It had been designed by Fun-C-tion. He'd had one similar before the fire in the disused factory that was his home-base three years ago when things were really hot. Their supporter reminds him of something.

'Hav'ta gerra a new desk.'

They ignore him. Blank him out.

'No no no,' insists the bony legal with fat freckles and red hair as he reaches into his bespoke pin-stripe suit pocket for a Camelot lux-length Mentholate. 'What's really wrong with our generation is that they've never had to fight a war.'

'Well . . .'

'Our parents had the childhood experience of rationing, Simon, and their parents were bashing the boche in the trenches.'

'What about that little South American island venture?' posits his companion. This one is simian, sleek-skinned, well-manicured. He looks like a hard-faced adman who's done well out of arranging sponsorship for televised executions.

'You're missing the point, Simon,' retorts the voluble, fair-complexioned youth. He is, Knocker recalls dimly, a something slash attorney. 'That was a small-scale engagement, not a proper war. It doesn't count.' Fastidiously, Slash Attorney wipes straggly pieces of the lobster thermidor Tiger's parents had so thoughtfully instructed the staff to prepare from his mouth with a soiled white linen kerchief monogrammed NCKG. 'A proper war unites people, it really binds them,' he says. 'Gives them some sense of community spirit. And heaven knows, just looking around here should suggest to opinion-formers such as our good selves that there are significant sections of the population who could benefit, Simon, benefit substantially from a decent dose of that. She should've introduced national service and had a real war, a bloody good one. Lordy,' he adds dreamily, neatly replacing his pocket handkerchief in its habitual position in his breast pocket, 'think of the stimulus to the manufacturing sector.'

He begins to scan the room like Colonel Clot seeking Private Johnny Mudpile AWOL, and notices Knocker's ravaged figure lurking in the threshold of the doorway.

'Oh, hello,' he says warmly. 'Don't I know you from the Anti-Japanese Food Society?'

KO was about to reply when two girls dressed like rejects from the *Sloane Strangers Preppy Handbook* push past him.

'Oh, we're not intruding?' asks a diminutive blonde. She wears a startling diamond fox brooch pinned to her Joe Naggamoto red cashmere dress.

'Far from it,' says the simian pin-stripe, appraising them smoothly. 'I say, don't I know you from Bobbington's?' pipes up the oleaginous other. 'I bought a picture there recently. A Rob Shepherd – quite *risqué* – in your erotica sale.'

Simper whitter twitter. If their talk gets any smaller, it might disappear entirely.

'Would you mind terribly getting us a drink?' the blonde asks NCKG's dark-haired counterpart with a bitty pretty grin.

There's an uneasy silence. They aren't the kind of chaps who like women telling them what to do. Certainly not in public, anyway.

'I've something rather delicate to discuss with Zarah,' explains the blonde, who was indeed Bobbington's auction house rock icons expert, and turns her smile back on them with a formidably steely assurance.

Her name is Annie. She is used to her Ramplingesque looks and femme flirtality getting her what she wants. She certainly isn't about to be denied now.

'It'll take only a minute,' she tells them firmly, flashing a twinkling smile. The boys look at each other ignominiously, and then creep away in complicit silence.

Knocker hovers like a grey band on a black and white test card. Why hadn't he been cruised? Where had all the good times gone? He wonders how long the elliptical pink pill that Tiger had stuffed in his mouth during the car-trip will take to enter his bloodstream and blow away his undesignered coma and the yuppification of everything.

'I only called him, darling,' Annie is saying.

'He's a bastard, Annie, I don't know why you waste yourself on trying to make him happy.'

'Do you think he's having an affair?'

'Probably. He's a complete bastard – I wouldn't trust him an . . .'

'We haven't had sex for three months. He keeps on shouting at me, getting in these irrational bates for no reason at all.'

'I think he's having an affair,' says the other girl censoriously. What does she know? Secretly, she fantasizes that she's the sort of femme Other People's significant others have dreams of dalliance and conquest about. But Zarah's expensive clothes serve only to emphasize her dowdiness. The big-boned, horse-faced gel doesn't see it that way though. Out of fantasy mode she prides herself on her practicality – and if she'd known what pragmatic meant would've ticked that box too.

I'd rather rim a rhino than let you into any club of mine, thinks Knocker, looking at her. If she'd been a scenester – he ruminates – rather than be so self-conscious about her height, she would've made the smart move and played it up instead of stooping her body and wearing sensibly flat shoes. None of her friends, he imagines, are real enough to tell her that her look is one-way to dullsville. An admission that this side of quite radical plastic surgery the quickening of her heart, if indeed she had one, would probably remain a mirage.

'He's a loser,' Zarah says. 'He may be frightfully flash appearing on telly the whole time, but you know he really isn't PLU.'

Annie winces.

'Oh come on! You know he's never been one of us. Socially he's a total lame duck.'

'But he's a very nice lame duck, Zarah,' Annie cries and wrings her small hands. Tears well in her eyes.

He tunes out.

The two city-hitters are concluding their conversation in the hall. 'Anyway,' says the Slash Attorney to his friend with the eyebrows that meet in the middle of his forehead, 'I told Christopher to tell Nigel they should slap V A T on food . . .'

They begin to make their way more determinedly towards the mainstream of the milling throng.

'. . . poor people eat much too much as it is.'

'You're humiliating yourself by getting this worked up by a man. Do you want everybody to think you're a fool? He's nothing, a real nobody. Look,' Zarah volunteers, 'why don't you come and stay for the weekend at my place? It'd give you a breather, a bit of an opportunity to think things through. Nige's going rowing next Sunday and we could have a super pub lunch by the river. James and Simon'll be there too.'

'But he's my husband,' the blonde girl snuffles lachrymosely. 'I feel so disloyal.'

'I think you should have a good look through those mysterious exercise books of his and see how disloyal you feel then.'

Hit.

The Spectre crashes Knocker's nervous system. Colours run. Shapes of surrounding objects assume primeval meanings; people animate, and he senses himself warming to the waves of ontological energy they constantly transmit – but that his nervous system routinely filters out. It's as if a lightbulb has been switched back on somewhere deep within him, and imbues with significance the world that he watches unfold around him.

The old, dented deco silver-plated cigarette box on the low table seems riveting for what feels like days. He rotates the object slowly in his hand.

He hears a noise, a slow rumble, thunder in the distance.

He looks and sees that objects are falling from the square planet that is itself now tumbling from his grasp. Knocker watches it free-fall in slow motion – the rumbling is nearer now.

He's become aware that he's moving as if pulled by some arcanely potent *Deus ex machina*. Successively it occurs to him during an immeasurably malleable unit of time that:

The Fear that swims within his soul is a tactile, furry-celled intelligence from the collective unconscious of the gene pool;

that everything around him is vividly colour-saturated and that he can smell the ultra-violet, stringy lines of phosphorescent light that travel across the room, intersecting each other.

Then the light envelops him, transforming everything into a warm white womb that brightens to suffuse him with a great tranquillity. The warmth becomes heat and the heat is light and a charge fizzes and crackles up from the nape of his neck through his skull and explodes into a totally dazzling burst of pure energy.

At this moment, technically, Knocker is brain-dead.

Previously, all that Other People could see was that Knocker had been staring at the cigarette box when he turned it over and all the tabs tumbled out. Someone had alerted him as to what he was doing, but he'd begun to sway and bumped into a girl called Poodle – her bearded companion had supported Knocker, dragged him over to one side so that he was less likely to hurt himself (or anybody else) and set him against a wall before allowing him to slump down on the floor, where, unless the observer was himself a devotee of Spectre X7 (a controlled substance originally developed by a Chinese pharmaceutical co-operative to control bed-wetting), they'd almost certainly assume that he'd passed out momentarily.

Knocker comes to and finds his eyes staring at a headline, BABY AGED ONE GIVES BIRTH the *News* inky banner says. It'll never make the *City Tribune Times*, but who's ahead? Who's counting? What's it all mean? (It all means something, it's all true. In the metroplex even the side on which kids wear their hats and hair communicates a message to the savant: in which gang they hang. Even the lies are true in the sense that within their infinite desert of duplicity and deception lies a grain of truth revealed re the fabricator who perpetrates the falsity. Who knows?)

Don't tell.

Talk that way and nod and smile.

Some of the finest brains in the city state mooch around here, tonight at Salon Tiger Lily. But, right now, they don't want to know about philosophy, history or anybody's politics – they just want to see your underwear. They talk of yachts, tanning butter, skimobiles, Portuguese cableknit sweaters, the Dangerous Sports Club, stud farm futures, how many klicks is that from Tulsa, South American soft commodities, Black Russians, big sisters and Chinese rugs. They chat about the Man with 44 Faces, society murders, houses on empty nude beaches, Lhasa apso puppies, getting the last non-smoking seat on Concorde, room service in Haiti, Agrovational domophobia, Brazilian cuisine, robotoid dinosaurs, hot Cognac, stud flamingoes, thrashin', Kosher Italians, windsurfing and Daumier.

Able to move now, although still steaming more than somewhat, Knocker wanders up a red-carpeted flight of stairs. Then another. He pauses in the passage, takes three steps and, instinctively, suddenly opens one of the glossy white doors to his right.

Inside a tall, thin middle-aged man lies dozing on an old-fashioned queen-sized waterbed. He is bald. He is also naked. On his head is chocolate ice-cream. On his cock another dollop rests. Framed in the floor-length window is the suspendered arse of a girl with long, dank, dark greasy hair. A distinctive cobra and chain tattoo on her upper forearm. She's draped in a too-short designer elk boob tube. Something – she's watching something. Out there. Outside. Through the window-pane.

The man's eyes are closed. On the bed, above his head, is a dark mirror, supported by chains. This man is Tiger's stepfather, Jerome, known to his many intimate aquaintances as Zero-Zero. He publishes sex magazines. *Raunch*, *Bod*, *Deep Snatch*, *Journal of Third World Sexual Deviation* – they're all his. It's said that his sexual indulgences and her own chemical romance drove Tiger's aristo mama – a woman who'd never cut her own fingernails in her life – to an early deep-six.

Now the girl turns round.

She is Zero-Zero's newest bimbette, Knock assumes. The face registers somewhere.

'I'm uh, terribly sore-ry, wazum lookin' for toilets ahuh barf-room . . .' mumbles Knock, the paraposh words tumbling uncontrollably through the Spectre-triggered rush that crowds his frontal lobes.

'Cut the bootlicking, kid, I can see straight through it,' the game bird snaps back. Turns to face him full on. She is about his age, 24, 25, maybe a couple of years older – he sees the scars underneath the boobs. Reduction job. He knows this girl and she seems to know him. Who is she?

'Knocker, I'm not really inna guys. You wanna do me? I'll play. But to be honest, if you gotta girlfriend that's better. Much better.'

'I want,' KO begins but then his mouth opens and shuts as futilely as a goldfish trying to sing Jinglebells in time for Xmas.

'We all want,' the girls says. 'What d'ya need?'

Knocker nods hopelessly. (He is under the impression his mouth is filled with clouds.)

She comes over, and runs her hands through his short, fair hair-cut in the tippest top of fashion heights.

'Don't worry about Zero,' she says. 'He's had it.'

The chocolate has begun to run . . . everywhere. Jerome snores gently.

Her almond eyes and honeyed skin, her dark bangled hair and long, slim fingers seem familiar. But although Knocker flashes on the order of her 8,000 big questions of life and death, details like her origins and name elude.

'I-I-I-I-I-I,' he stutters.

'Take it somewhere else, Knocker,' she says tartly.

'Honestly . . .' she mutters as she withdraws, walking away to pull back the drapes concealing within from without. 'Stupid Spectre spackies.'

She watches the action through the gap outside on Peter Pan Park Drive. A crowd gathers around an armoured white Money-movers security truck.

He staggers over, solid gone.

'It swerved to miss another car,' she explains in a clipped high-drone monotone. Her tone has changed – she's suddenly decided to become a commentator. 'And it hit that guy in the CZeckra.'

As they look on, a paramedic crew arrive from some shonky scavenger medico posse in a shrieking red-crossed ambulimo.

'I don't think anyone can get in because the only guy with the keys is in the back of the van.'

Downstairs, Knocker hears the chewn-machine blast out an old Margot Random disque: 'I walked/You talked/Nowhere to go and nothing new to do/You fought/I thought/There's gotta be a clear path through . . . on Second Avenue (Erowwww)' Power axe-riffs rive the floor.

'He won't open up.' Her attitudinal turnaround is quite remarkable, Knocker notices. Suddenly she's become inexplicably objective. Her voice is as dispassionate as a reluctant conservative watching the election results. Outside, a welder in cop gear turns his torchin' unit off and steps back. He shrugs. Three other flics almost immediately begin to batter the van's reinforced back door with heavy hammers.

'Second Avenue (erererowww) Second Avenyew-oo-ooo (er-rowrowrow) Second Avenue.'

One of the flics now has a crowbar, attached to a power-feed inside the cop-car, wedged inside the door. Extra leverage? All three fuzz lean against the bar and start to walk away from the truck, pushing the bar very slowly like they're mimes wheeling a shopping trolley in a hurricane. The door begins to buckle.

It opens like a can.

Knocker can just see the security guard, prone on the floor inside. There's blood. His feet dangle uselessly: he's buried underneath a collapsed pile of crates, some of which have spilled their cargo of small change that's burst out of its boxes.

Someone produces a fluorescent orange bodybag.

'The dead weight of money,' says mystery girl.

The other crashes seems to be in difficulty with his vehicle. His head's stuffed inside the off-beige bonnet. His left knee's fused. Fused to the front bumper, right next to the off-side headlamp, which is totally shattered. He strains to support the chrome strip end.

Old chrome, very old chrome: badly treated and broken down.

''Scuse me,' says Knocker. ''ve gotta find my, find my desk.'

'Please yourself, faggot.' She doesn't even look at him.

He's back downstairs – in Tiger's bedroom.

Knocker stares at the wall: wall-time. He counts thirty hats suspended there.

Vieux chapeau.

Wide brimmed.

Straw.

Plain toque.

A tricorn with small silk flowers pinned at back.

A shore hat, extremely flat.

Layered and patterned, black velvet.

Brimless felt.

Silly wide and whacky flop-hat.

Appliquéd astrakhan trimmed with broderie anglaise.

Small green with pointy ear covers (made for an elf or Tiger's mother?).

Back bow.

Feathers: brown, green, black, red.

White with dark veil and antique silk.

Garland of flowers: purple, white and red, suspended on plain green loop to crown the verdant spring-time head.

Swirly. One piece of blue brimlessness.

Cossack wool in spotty purple and pink knit.

Dark blue, square brim, round crown, silk trim.

Light blue pill-box.

A green velvet Dr Seuss cat-sat-on-the-mat hat.

White-lined silk that turns in on itself.

Matching spots.

See-through criss-cross lattice white.

Trilby in brown felt with sexagonal crown.

Glitzy blue with turn-up brim that folds to where red paper rose's pinned.

Curious blue cotton and black helmet intertwined around itself.

Black and white with long black Chinesey tassel attached and dangling down.

Half helmet in dark velvet, replete with 26 small black studs.

Black decaled glitz flapper hat. And an eau de nil metal hat decorated with vents that, with a start, Knocker suddenly realizes is the air-conditioning unit built into the wall. Oh, he thinks, his brain racing.

No one owns these hats. They own whoever wears them: it's said that people with hats have character but really that's on loan. From the hat. It absorbs its wearer's traits and adds them to its own incremental persona.

'Hey, baby.' Knocker feels the voice's hands around his waist. 'Come and help me run my bath.'

He follows Tiger dazedly through to the bathroom.

For the second time in twelve hours he is totally naked with one of the 10 most fanciable females inside city limits. Daintily she clambers into the water in the tub. Suddenly she looks at him, alarmed.

'Ugh,' she exclaims. 'You're getting a hard-on.'

Tiger grabs the shower attachment and unleashes on him a furiously ice-cold jet. The bathwater leaves the tub with a clockwise schlurp. The white enamel is horribly cold.

'Put this on, come on.'

She helps him out of the bath. He tries to kiss her. Firmly, she pushes him away.

'Don't be silly, Knock-Knock,' she says briskly. 'Dry yourself down, there's a good boy.' She hands him a white towelling robe labelled REGENCY INTERCONTINENTAL TORQUEMADA. As she does so, her fine-boned face suddenly focuses in on his. She brushes the lower half of his jaw with her long index finger and traces the line up over his lip to its conclusion halfway up his right cheek.

'What is that really?'

'I just fell over, you know.' He knows she doesn't know and he doesn't want her to.

'You always say that.'

'It's true.'

'Why don't you tell?' she cajoles. 'Suzie told me how Johnny Throat got his scar. She said he got in a scrap with some guy who in exchange "diden getta retain da usea his face".'

Knocker grins, to stroke Tiger's take-the-Mickey talent. Her accent is OK. But not as good as Tuesday's. But she's abandoned the inquisition as peremptorily as it'd been instigated, slides into the purple leotard that hugs her curves and swerves out of the bathroom, dragging him in her wake.

He notices the party's thinned. He sees Jake Morrison, the Channel 95 reporter, leaving with Poodle, a girl who always dressed in black and white and had been on The Scene more than somewhat of late.

'Hold on,' that pom-pommed femme says now to Jake, who produces a phone and complains to someone he is being besieged by calls for a psychiatrist who used to live in his flat.

She, meanwhile, thrusts a card into Knocker's hand. He examines it bemusedly. On it is a retro sketch of three poodles and a telephone number handwritten underneath in black ink.

'. . . had to take the phone out of the Porsche because when you hit 90 you can't hear it ringing,' Cressida Crane, the blonde El Grecoed MM clone with the discreet lingerie says.

'Well, when people call me in the car, I always tell them I'm on the other line . . .' Bobby Hot-Rock ripostes.

'Was haben Sie am Derby Day gemacht?'

'Es ist nicht *der* Bidet sondern *das* Bidet.'

'But, darlink, that's vhy Anglos are zo depressink. Zey only care about zaire stoopid animals and zeyre ridiculous gardens. Vat's zer point in payink zer servanz eff you do all zee work yourzelf?

'Oh Lauaradonna, you're so hopelessly out of touch,' Fillet says and knocks back the remains of her Bloody Mary, which Knocker has discovered earlier cleans contact lenses from the inside out.

Fillet is, in fact, the daughter of a suit that was somewhere up-country beyond the Shockwood but south of the Mistral. He's a management consultant she now calls papa – at 17 she'd rejected wrinkled bats' first names during parental conversations as 'too too gauche'. Her mother is politically active. An only child, Fillet had grown up in the flatlands town where she'd been born and they still lived. She rarely ate anything other than a salad in Other People's presence. It was a Fillet position: an ultra-ethical condemnation of conspicuous consumption in any form. It was a rationalization: she had to keep the weight off to hold on to her pacy fast-bowler boyfriend. Her Interior Scariness (yes – everyone's got The Fear) disapproved of public mastication: self-nutrition gave away too much personal information. Someone might be watching. Someone . . . mercenary. Someone . . . hostile. Someone who was . . . getting something of her precious inner sanctity for nothing. Someone who . . . might perceive some flaw in such self-exposure, and realize that she was vulnerable.

So now Fillet eats only in her bathroom, late at night.

Yet despite her patina of puritanical Waspishness and what both her friends euphemistically refer to as 'eccentricity' (They are mad. He is crazy. You are eccentric. What am I? The barcode on an Egyptian anglepoise light. That's right.) Fillet has a loud track record on the Scene. For she is beautiful. Her wild mystery of dark fly locks, the bespoken breeding in her tough-but-fragile dark brown eyes, her fine-lined mouth, her altitudinal cheek bones, her long, louche limbs with a subtle, elegantly packaged hint of raciness around her curves – all this, and of course, a personality enigmatically both formidable and funny – pulled boys like plasma to the heart.

She spurned potential suitors by the plane-load.

Yes, she has secrets.

For a start, she prefers Led Zeppelin to sex.

Her scared Interior. Contagious Fear.

And well, there's more – but why linger long on Fillet-up-face when she'll spill blood herself? Now she's dissing the dirt to Cress's sister's art school consort.

'Don't we rather think there's something just too cravenly *hallitotal* about Kinkaid's hidden assumption in presuming that attitudes today always form the basis of tomorrow's social trends?' Fil opines.

Then kicks in bitch-mode some horrid, feisty quip.

Knocker makes his way through this brabble o' bilious babble and assumes attitudes diffusing from various bods who, one time or another, he'd said 'hello' or 'goodbye' to at and in one of his numerous night-time enterprises.

Inside Tiger's room with all that hat, Terry Kinkaid (the aforesaid infamous pulp writer of such lit sensations as *The Interactive Book of Designer Death*, *501s Go Ape on Mars*, *Plato is a Junkie*, *Excuse Me While I Self-Construct*, *Impertinence*, *How to Make Men You Secretly Despise Discover Your Shopping's G-Spot* and – pseudononymously, it must be said – *A Penis Speaks: Memoirs of My Tropical Underpants*) admires his reflection in Tiger's art nouveau wall mirror.

'It's great,' his host enthuses.

'All ties are bourgeois bondage,' Kinkaid snarls and begins to remove the fluorescent kipper neckwear.

'Here, Knocker – choose.'

He looks at the drawer full of semiotic neckwrap that lies on the patchwork quilt covering Tiger's Safe Glamour metal-framed bed. 'Haz oo seen ma ah uvver tie?' he asks as he slips on a thin sick-yellow strip of knitted wool.

'Oh very nice, Knockski,' says Vanda Jacquenelli, the sallow-skinned frizzle-tressed heiress. She straightens the tie and pecks him on the cheek. He recognizes her now . . . hadn't she been? Wasn't she . . .? (His brain contorts, trying to reconcile the image of the girl upstairs with the mental portraiture of the Vanda whom he knows so well.) She has a Tommy Goldswinger striped cravat knotted loosely around her head, but otherwise the dodgy doxy's too short elk boob tube outfit matches up. Her voice, her voice? Was that upstairs scene an act or an illusion? He wants to ask – but The Fear clamps his mouth shut.

Lost mind, musta left inna desk, Knocker thinks dementedly. Gotta getta noo desk. Find Rep. Rep find desk. Meybe iding innsigh. Rilly.

'Gonna gather up a posse to battle Big Daddy – UGH!' chants the massed electrowarped vocalnaught of Stark Naked Car Stripper from the other room. As Tiger continues to dress one and all in her selection of neckties, Knocker notices it's getting light outside.

'Let's go and have breakfast,' someone suggests.

They all pile back into Tiger's metallic mauve Isola Berlinetta Tarantula Turbo 2 + 2.

'You never took me to the Ritz, Knocker,' Vanda whispers in his ear. 'You always promised you were going to take me to the Ritz.' She puts her hand on his thigh and, despite his confusion, he feels the stirring of a baby-hard.

'We're ghan dahn Pookie's,' he says wearily. 'We're gahn Pookie's for fry-upz. I dunno, we'll see afta, OK – I've got this desk to deal wiv, ya know?'

What would Rep say when she found out about this? Stinkabelle would by now, somewhere during his lost day, almost certainly have filled her in on the prelude. Knocker couldn't bear to think about thinking about it. Guiltily, he realizes he hasn't called her. He shivers – ugh, The Fear.

Not to worry, though, he tells himself. 'Sonly a tactile furry-celled intelligence from the collective subconscious of the gene-pool, right?

'Stop, stop,' shouts Cressida the blonde lawyer (for it was she, perfect except that Marilyn Monroe would never have had a hole in her stocking). 'I'm gonna be sick.'

Monday morning commuters stare as he and Vanda tumble out of the front seat and Cress chucks up lobster in the gutter.

Vanda starts laughing.

'You can't go out dressed like that,' she jeers, pointing at Knocker. He wears nothing but the bathrobe and the yellow knit tie.

Cressida is standing head down, legs akimbo in the gutter. It occurs to him that he'd never ever seen Cressida laugh. In the back seat, Hot-Rock is buttoning his flies.

'Aw, she just couldn't take me, I'm too big,' he brags confidentially at the top of his lungs.

'U suss that sheez suckin' 'im?'

'You could call her a lot of things,' Vanda replies, looking at the girl dry-heaving in the gutter, as she considers the best way to avoid the question. 'A liar, a bitch, a junkie and a whore. But you could never say she wasn't game.'

'Na, ya could thagh . . .,' Knocker begins.

'. . . You'd be lying,' Vanda interrupts him.

'Y u av yer tattoo done, eh?' he asks her as they leave Pookies later.

The girl, the daughter of one of the city's top porn mavens and slum-lords, glances at the intertwined snakes on her upper right shoulder. The legend underneath says ANACONDAS ANONYMOUS.

'I don't know,' she replies. 'Combination of things, really.'

They stroll through the Plaza de Soto, the crossroads of downtown. It's 10.30 and the market is already in full swing.

The Pd market is most interesting, its merchandise being so diverse, the velocity of its transactions (so) erratic, and many of its vendors prone to sudden zap-zap concealment of their wares prior to rapidly disappearing themselves from the scene at precisely that moment when a familiar collection of characters in blue coats with shiny buttons and funny hats arrive.

'It's like everything changes, you know,' she says, pausing to scan and subsequently scrutinize a collection of old *X*, *Belladonna* and *Motive* magazines laid out on a checked blue and black blanket by a thin blond faggot poseur, who, despite the sunshine, shivers in his beat-up biker jacket as he rubs his hands together.

'You're involved with someone and you think, "Wow, this is it," but it's not. You know, your friends stab you in the back and you can't make the weight on your mortgage or something, or your record collection gets stolen. How much is this?'

'Five.'

'I'll take it,' Vanda hits the boy with a blue spot and slips the back number of *History of the Great Composers* into her rubber duffelbag.

These mercantile types vamoose snap-snappety sharply-fly on aforesaid occasions, because it may just be these officious-minded legal enforcers could, hypothetically, wish to discuss topics which may prove most fraught-making to the usually ruggedly robust-ing entrepreneurial temperament already so frizzle-frazzled from the cut and thrust of the day's dealings on Plaza de Soto. Topics like the whole ghastly desk-jock question of what permits, licences and the like have or maybe have not been applied for in the proper form. And, squirmier, just exactly how legitimately second hand some of the merchandise offered actually is, even suggesting that the second pair of hands, in some cases, was a tad snatch-and-grabby in dealing with the property in question.

In Plaza de Soto market lies a wealth of sadness. The items laid out are the syntenostic strands of vendors' lives, the web of metro ident.

'But you know, a tattoo is permanent, it's with you forever and ever until you die. It's like your pierced ear, right? The gap in your ear always reminds you, deep down somewhere, of that moment of pain, that moment when you're playing for keeps.'

They saunter on through the mess of items, some of which are being dodgy-hustled at superfast 'hey hey you won't believe this buddy' prices. Much of the stuff is not just second hand but more usually 3rd to 17th hand. See Jimmy James Washington, the doyen of the Ultimo Vets Club (EX-SERVICEMEN ONLY. NO NON-MEMBERS ADMITTED) going through the motions to round up the scratch.

It's pathetic such a brave man should have to take this crap, Knocker thinks. She's right. Everything changes, rearranges.

Jimmy James stands on the street amidst the cacophonic detritus of urban sleaze:

empty vials on sale extra cheap and

'hey we're virtually giving these away' pre-shrunk post-fade abstract floral print cheesecloth shirts and dresses with at least two obligatory buttons missing or mismatched, brown bereavement-forces-quick-cash-sale leather flared trousers,

two-tone brown plastic boxes that look like books but, on closer scrutiny, prove to be change containers given away by World Bank,

dog-eared back issues of *Catholic Housewife* and *Vendetta* magazines,

jumpy tapes and

chipped ceramics in questionable taste. Much of all this and similar Kipple,

obsolete foodmix components,

malfunctioning belt buckles,

entire car tape units still recalcitrantly bolted on dashboards,

four-dollar handbags,

funky old bits of crystal and dead purple neon six-point stars,

ceiling-sealing wax, and

whacky warpo hi-tack solutions to the question, 'Where the hell did you find that outfit?'

wanes and spills, maxes and swills into the cardboard boxes, abandoned shoes, old newspapers and blankets, gum wrappers and other homeless trash. Yeah, there are times when the merchandise and garbo blur into indistinguishability – and this looks like being one of them.

'No one can take it away from you,' Vanda says. She stops and puts her arm around him. 'C'mon, what about the Ritz, huh?'

She throws girlie-girlie bimbo too hot take-me pout number three. Full eyelash flutter/glossy lip pucker.

'I can't,' Knocker hears himself say. 'Rep, you know?'

'Hey, mister,' calls out some gang-banger. 'Can I fuck your wife?'

'Oooohh,' moans K O. 'Let's outta here.'

He throws a fou-off look at the kid, who can't be more than 14, in the crimson red leather jacket. Checks the laces: he and his cronies are foot soldiers with the Total Planet Dead Dread Mau-Mau Blood Brotherhood Klan of Evil Stone Overlords gang.

'Well does that mean yes or no?' the kid sneers right back at him and the others laugh.

'But I am having an INSTANT SALE,' pleads some poor old black guy at the top of his voice. 'Here, you wanna make me an offer?'

'I don't wear ostrich feathers,' the female cop says. She rolls her eyes in a glance of routine revulsion at her colleague, a blond policeman whose badge says HUTTON. They move in on the geezer with the strong-armed suggestion that he's eligible for an instant free-ride down-town, courtesy of the Metropol.

'I used to be a game show host, really, man. You remember *Pro-celebrity Shopping*? Hey, bitch, don't touch me there, get yowsar stinkin' hands offa me, woman, I demand the right to a phone call. Call my agent, I gotta right to call – don't do that – you know? You know who I am?'

No. They don't: nothing sadder than glamour on the rocks.

Knocker and Jimmy James see it simultaneously.

But he beats the oldster to the punch and pockets the 20-buck bill some sucker's left on the streetwalk.

Knocker looks at Jimmy.

'An omen?' Vanda asks him quietly, with a provocatively quizzical look in her eyes.

'Rock 'n' roll!' he cries and, animated, leaps to hail the passing purple taxi cab.

'The Ritz,' he tells the bull-whippin' freightdyke that's its jockey.

Jimmy James Washington turns to the blond faggot poseur and shrugs.

'The rich get richer.'

'Word,' says the blond boy.

Sirens wail in the distance.

Oh Where We Goin' to Go Tonight?

ON THE OTHER SIDE OF THE BARRIO, beyond Shakey Zoom – the 56-lane superhighway that bisects the city like an artery – the black CZeckra Zaftig saloon pulls up to a dead stop. Behind it lie the two lions, their ferocious expressions frozen in stone at the gates of the monolithic granite Lodge.

Behind them are thick oak entrance doors, pushed open so air might circulate to mitigate the swelter. Inside three men are visible. All three wear plain black three-quarter-length frock-coats. They stand together in a tight circle these three dark figures, tiny in their blackness against the ornate opulence of the porticos, arches and high-domed ceiling of the building's vast inner entrance hall. They discourse in whispers. As they converse, one taps his shiny black brogues on the polished harlequin mosaic floor tiles. Occasionally the second runs his hand through short, brown greased tonsorial strands, purses his small piggy lips and listens intently. The third man is more animated than his companions. Like them, he is fighting 40. But Eisler dominates the conversation – when he talks, they listen. His eyes dart and sparkle behind the rectangular golden frames of his spectacles as he speaks.

But the driver of the black CZ saloon does not see them.

He looks in the other direction, through the car's tinted windows onto the street. He is not the sort of person who sees the street as theatre: somewhere to see and be seen, a place to sell what one has to sell, a backdrop for action. No. Not just now. He notices shapes, colours, movement. But not, not yet anyway, exactly what he wishes to see: anxiously he checks the time on his stainless steel wristwatch.

Just over four minutes. He hears himself breathing heavily. Throws a switch on the dash – it's imperative to remain absolutely calm.

'The minister for state security is expected to face council questioning,' announces a voice that sounds like plums surprised in varnish, 'within the hour from the opposition parties about an incident at the Alien Detention Centre near Stockbridge. Jake Morrison has the story.

'Military police are manning seven roadblocks, set up here just over an hour ago, to seal off the Tannertown Alien Detention Centre four and a half miles outside the wealthy commuter-belt suburb of Stockbridge,' Morrison says. His voice is homogeneously classless, professionally modulated.

'As I speak I can see about a quarter of a mile away an armed convoy of some 32 vehicles – including what looks very much like a Khalichinov ground-to-ground subnuclear missile launcher – making its way along a slip road towards the fortified complex of 14 or so buildings, normally used for housing transient illegal immigrants.

'Nobody seems to know exactly what's going on. But informed local sources I've spoken to in the last 15 minutes in this normally placid community have relayed reports – and I must stress that at this time they are only reports – of an escape by what one eyewitness described as two large reptilian bipeds. The military, armed with state-of-the-art Artema search-and-kill bio-blasters, have imposed a total media black-out. Q Division Intelligence Sector Director Colonel James Montcrieffe was unavailable for comment on a story circulating locally, which claims the escapees are carrying HDV-IX, the airborne AIDS-related virus. Police and civil defence workers are going from door to door among Stockbridge's 14,000 inhabitants and telling them to stay inside because of what they refer to as "an isolated break-out by dangerous detainees". The local 700-pupil high school has been commandeered by troops as an ad hoc base, and children are apparently being sent home on town buses. The specifics of the escape remain a mystery – but one thing is certain: this conservative country town is awash with fear. But the authorities have launched a swift and massive response to contain the situation, and pre-empt the possibility of any civic unrest. Jake Morrison, outside Tannertown Alien Detention Centre, for 95 Network News International.'

They're out there.

But, he reflects, so what? He has an agenda, a strategy and a plan. He is a man on a mission. It's too late to back out now.

He re-tunes to a music station, but it's playing an irritating subliminal jingle-hit, so he flicks the unit off.

He fiddles with the popper on the glove and, just for a single moment, narrows his eyes to look back in languor at the door of the shop over the road. Neat little shop. Chic. Only the flagstones cried out for a foot-and-mouth pavement artiste to turn them into a state-of-the-heart paving stone zone.

On one side of the shop stands Pookie's Polka Bar and Grill. Pookie makes a mean saltbeef. Maria, his overweight and overwrought meaning-of-wife, works with him most days. She fries breakfasts six to six, yet somehow retains her composure and remains sanguine in the face of food that constantly spit-fires back at her off the hot slab-metal grill. She cuts the sandwiches for the office workers at lunch with swift assured thunks, smiling all the while and sometimes humming a little tune from the golden days of radio to herself, as her tanned and hirsute forearms manoeuvre with familiar grace among the re-sealable tubs of fillings, the condiments in their lurid plastic fortresses,

the chrome egg-slicer whose chop was like harp muzak to her ears,

the anonymous white paperbags – each an embryonic envelope of postage-due food as love.

Her sacklike dresses with their faded floral prints move from one chore to the next, accompanied by a constant stream of noisy-bustle and quick-fire banter as pastrami-on-rye succeeds fegato di pollo and sunnyside eggs to go in gravity-defying swoops that fly off her arm with the fluency of a bored blackjack dealer. She has no apron – Maria, like the housepainter who wears new shoes to work, is so adept within her domain that she never spills anything. But her feet are shod in funny black leather peasant boots and usually, unless like today it is exceptionally hot, she wears a gaudy headscarf. Her coarse-boned features would show a flash of searing temper – temper one minute and the next, a smile that could light up the Palladium.

In the window sits a kit.

He sees that cat.

It is a black stray called Moussaka. Inscrutably, Moussaka observes the world go by on the other side of the vitrine. Three of the youngest of the couple's children (who, like their fourteen siblings in times past, had worked around the place to earn pocket-money during the school holidays) had adopted it four years ago.

Now he and the cat watch the traffic pass from behind the protection of cold, hard glass.

Sometimes the people'd go into Baptista's, lured by the bookseller's eccentric displays of antiquarian volumes and papers provocatively pleated and plicated. But one module of the urban biomass had rolled its ass and walked on by to enter the adjacent building.

This is a black-tiled deco pile with windows covered by tropical wood shutters. They half conceal a chiaroscuro, hint at another world within. A world of the interior. Of fiercely esoteric plant life gasp-grasp for air and goddamn photosynthesis amongst the smoky cologned bohemian cliques, who'd colonize each other under the large propeller fans which swirl lazily from the pale ceiling above.

All this lies behind closed doors set under the canopy with its definitively discreet red lettering that identifies the faded beat-bohemianism of the Wah Wah Bar. At this time of afternoon they serve old-fashioned cocktails to patrons who earnestly converse about things that had mattered 20 years ago – only now they take them seriously. Finally, about an hour and half ago, she'd re-emerged, looked around unsteadily, put her sunglasses on and tottered back up to Baptista's bookshop. She'd been inside ever since.

He checks his black leather driving-gloves. They're fastened. He checks the time. It runs.

Pop.

120 little seconds, 119, 118, 117 . . .

He looks at Mickey Moose, dumb as a dodo on the front seat. Everything's ready. All set.

Inside the shop the CZ driver slyly zones in on, the delicate strains of Bizet waft through tastefully concealed pine speakers as an attractive, young, dark-haired woman approaches the cash desk. Phil Baptista looks up over his thick, elliptical, metallic, silver-framed spectacles.

The girl smiles at him.

She has buck teeth and luxuriant black tresses that fall onto pale bare shoulders. She wears a frilly black petticoat skirt and a front-loader black satin empire-line corset. Her skin seems as fair as tiny piles of powdered white marble. He can see what she wants at a glance.

'Excuse me a moment,' Phil says. Her high heels sink deep into the thick lilac carpet as he pads across to the office in his sandals and socks. The girl gazes out of the window. She sees: a young couple looking at Mr Baptista's come-hither display of wares,

a black CZ saloon on the other side of the road,

three businessmen in frock-coats walking down the steps of the Masonic lodge.

Baptista knocks on the door of the office at the back of the shop. 'Cookie' he mouths, and taps again on the glass to attract her attention. The fat woman who sits poring over two sets of ledgers at the desk looks up irascibly over her black diamante butterfly spectacles. As she rises, and waddles over to unlock the door, Baptista thinks how hideously unflattering the expensive green leather dress is to her mightily matronly figure.

With a deft, familiar touch she disengages the brass chain.

'What is it?' she snaps, opening the door just a fraction of an inch.

'Frederick's of Hollywood . . .' he starts to say.

'29.99,' she snarls and slams it in his face.

Wearily, Phil wipes the perspiration from between the tufts of grey hair on his crown. He can feel the damp patches under the arms of his grey-white shirt. 'Too bloody hot,' he mutters, trudging back counterwards.

'29.95.'

'I'll take it.'

'It's such a nuisance when the tags fall off.'

With his usual, meticulous, neo-obsessive care, he slips one of the shop's distinctive bags over the classic catalogue.

'I've been looking for this for ages,' she says. Her tone of voice, he notices, seems curiously wistful. 'No one'd ever buy it for me.'

'I designed them myself, but people will keep pulling them off.' (He's still thinking about the tags.)

She searches in her old black velvet bag with the frilly trim and gilded clasp and, finally, produces an Excess charge card. Baptista hits the button on the console and the board autodials the card co. and validates with a demi-melodic bleepy sound. Phil picks up the tricolour plastic flim-flam and mechanically runs it through the antediluvian template.

She leans forward to sign. He stares at her bosom – oh the curve and texture of it. He begins to feel very warm indeed. She tears off her copy of the receipt and flashes teeth and smile like an encore. Baptista grins back wanly and returns the card.

'Yes, yes, thank you,' he hears himself say as he watches her walk away. Suddenly he feels a twinge of pain in his chest.

'Baptista!'

Cookie's voice brings him back with a bump. 'What are you doing? Here's some money – go and get some milk from Pookie. I'll watch the till. Go on now.'

The girl dons her black and white speckle-framed shades as she steps outside, about to her feet to the Disposable TV vend-o-vend beyond the Masonic Lodge on the Sony side of the street. But she doesn't because she briefly considers backtracking into the breeze to see if Mrs Martyn has finished the repairs on her shoes in her workshop in John Stuart Mill Street. But she quickly dismisses that idea too. It's such a bright, sunny day.

Instead, she turns left to stroll up the road towards the stationer's. Her high heels ensure she takes precariously dainty steps.

The pretext for visiting the stationer's was that perhaps she should acquire some new coloured pages for her personal organizer. The context? She likes stationery shops. Stop to shop slot: she leurved that bold no-holds feeling of embryonic organization, the potential business of the neatly stacked reams of paper;

the tightly shrink-wrapped yellow legal pads;

the primary-coloured ergonomic soft-tech pencil sharpeners;

the splash-plastic and gun-metal clips of differing sizes and functions

and the argon-coated Japanese laser-writers, carefully arranged in the clean steel display stand according to their variable senso-torque precision brush-strokes.

For a moment she wonders, from behind the cool shades that hide her eyes from probing looks and lonely guys, if it was the fantasy of efficiency or the sensation of the inchoate that stimulated her more.

Yes, she thinks to herself. Some marbled grey Fidofax paper. That would be very nice. She

KERRACK! It all turns black. She gasps. Her whole body's pulled by a violent typhoon. It drags her off the pavement. It bounces her off her feet. It blocks her mouth. She gasps for air. It lets her breathe. But she can't. Her lungs have frozen solid.

The engine kicks and the black CZeckra swerves through the traffic and jumps a red light. A purple Crusader convertible pulls up in a dead squeal of rubber. In the middle of the road, some guy with a pot belly and a long white beard has got The Fear and chucks his groceries all over the tarmac – he shouts and waves his hands around like Rumpelstiltskin trying to unravel his knitting.

The motor revs as the man guns the gas and slings the car right to avoid a kamikaze biker moving left like a rat from Harley hell. She looks at him, rigid in oh-oh the horror of the frightmare.

He wears no-name blue jeans and a black silk bomber jacket. The T-shirt says NUKE THE BASTARDS AND LET GOD SORT 'EM OUT. Those black leather gloves move capably around the gear stick. He has short fair hair, but it's impossible to distinguish much else because his face is hidden behind a latex Mickey Moose mask.

'My sunglasses!' she screams suddenly. In front of them, pedestrians scatter in all directions. A horn blares. The CZ makes a sharp, unexpected and totally illegal left turn off Roxburgh Boulevard onto a feeder-road that leads to the Von Alvensleben Interchange. Lanes of traffic surge, all around. Lines. Always moving, always gaining. Where were they going? They settle into routine city bumper-to-bumper pugnacity. The man behind the wheel doesn't look back. He says nothing.

Then the mask turns towards her. Slowly.

'AAAHUMP,' breathes the predator's voice, wetly sloshing around somewhere inside.

She feels herself shiver. She wants to light up. But then she remembers she hasn't carried any cigarettes for two and half a years.

ULTIMO AND DIRECTIONS STEWARTSTOWN says the neon sign. STAY IN LANE urge the bright kinetic letters.

They move faster now. She sees the sharp brutal towers of the municipal housing projects racing towards them like fingers pointing into the sky. The car pulls up behind some funky-coloured old transit van. You could see the steps leading up to a corridor and a pair of metal lifts through the car's smoked windows. If you'd been looking that way . . .

'UNGHHHH,' says the man in the mask. He hits a switch and the door button beside her flies up.

'You seem pretty confident that I'm not going to run away.'

He locks the driver's door and slips the metal keys back into his pocket.

'GRUNNNH,' he growls. She can see his eyes staring at her across the grimy black neutron-Teuton blackness of the sunroof.

He pushes her. Sullenly, she drags herself up the steps and stares through the crazy quasi-shatterproof coloured glass of the massfacked Mondrian-look window. Some anaemic ratbag, in a dirty-grey overcoat with a tobacco-stained thatch that sits above his lip like a dead caterpillar, is talking to a small boy, who, understandably, is preoccupied in playing with his intricate 4-D space-station game,

Her heels briskly click click click across the concrete.

The lift door shuts and the glittering metal box starts its climb to the 43rd floor.

She turns away from the view to meet the lascivious glare of appraisal emanating from the eye-slits in the mask.

I can't believe this is happening, she thinks.

The man in the mask, shifting slightly in his Nike Vandals, just stares and stares and stares.

The lift stops. The door opens.

She waits to see if he'll move first. He doesn't.

'UNNNGHH,' he grunts. He prods her in the scrimshaw whalebones of her corsetry, where he might've expected to hit her ribs. 'GURRLIE.'

He pulls her roughly by the bare flesh of her arm out onto a balcony.

'Owwwwww,' she squeals, pulling away from him. 'That hurt.'

He jostles her in front of him, out to the left. They begin to walk down a corridor. She counts three apartments. Out to the right the view is breath-snatching: the city is spread out like a concrete and chrome go-go dancer transparently pleading 'take me' to anyone who'll listen.

She feels like a condemned murderer walking to the chair. Involuntarily, she goosebumps again. It's as if she didn't own her body any more. An alien firm of body repossessors has moved in and taken control.

He opens the door.

'MUUVEIT.'

She moves.

She looks around at the room. Some autistic kid, who's escaped from a paint factory with his vendetta against interior decorators intact, had hit the peeling wallpaper with a psycho-manic spray-gun.

'STRIP you freakin' bitch.'

'DO IT!' he screams suddenly.

He begins to peel off the mask. She removes her shoes carefully so they point towards the naked horsehair mattress in the middle of the room. Even as she bends down, she watches him.

Now his face is only half covered. Bloboid strands of plastic hang off his skin. Hangover stubble. His blue eyes are shot through with red. The gooey distorted remnants of Mickey Moose cover most of the lower half of his face, but a cruel, upturned lip pokes an evilly smile out of its right-hand corner. As he pulls at the mask, a scar becomes visible. It runs right down the lower half of his face.

She stares at him standing there, one foot on the lino, one foot on the highly incongruous red Chinese rug.

Is he tooled up? There's no way of telling. She unzips her long black and white dress as slowly as she can.

The zip snags on the material. She stops. His lip bit twitches. She pulls harder, but the zip resolutely refuses to budge.

'ARRRWWW.'

He snatches at her like a fighting dog. The dress falls away. He's on her. She tries to stick her fingers in his eyes, but he's too fast for that. She cries out from the pain of his grip on her finger. His hands are large, neat, tanned, manicured. He holds her in a Vulcan death-grip and pulls at the remnants of the mask. As the scar that runs across his chin and lower mouth closes on her, she screams. He forces his mouth on hers. His lips are sandpaper rubbing against her cupid-bow mouth, his face fierce acid on her alabaster skin. His hands tear at her back, ripping a hole in the black patterned tights. He rams his finger into the crack in her arse and pushes it up inside.

She screams. And instinctively, she brings her left knee up. A short sharp snap, full on into his groin. He doubles up, his face pinched in excruciated surprise. As his body drops, she smartly side-kicks him in the face the way Hutton had taught her in the attitude classes at the mid-town gym.

Then she runs.

She pulls the front door open and runs out into the sunlight. Noise rushes in from below. She bangs on the next door along, then she runs. She looks behind her and yells something. Then she runs. She stands on the balcony and punches the button to call the lift. A red light, flashing. Her teeth rattle round her face and her head flickers from side to side like a clunky robot gone bizwaz in electro seizure. Then she runs. She bangs on the door of the apartment nearest the balcony. Inside a dog barks. She looks down the corridor – empty. She stabs frantically at the lift button – but the red light just keeps winking back at her. Her arse hurts like hell. She feels violated, hateful, hurtful, desperate.

She turns on her heel and runs down a stairwell off to the left. A sign says EMERGENCY EXIT. She almost falls down the stairs, unused to clunkering and careening without her restrictive heels. Then she runs. Along the passage between each flight of stairs, she sees nothing, feels nothing, hears nothing, except the next flight of stairs in front of her. Each floor she clears is like a kind of mantra screeching at her, 'Get out of here, out of here.' She feels her lungs on fire, her legs tense and gnarl into twisty knots that burst pure pain.

Don't stop, don't stop, she hears the voice inside cry. It isn't her voice. The pain in her bum is like heat. She fights for breath. I'm not gonna make it, she thinks. She is about to collapse.

Her ankles fold – she leans on the stairwell rail, astonished that she's made it to the 29th floor. Her body fights for strength, her mind races nowhere. Pant, gasp, merde, she can't move, can no longer command her limbs to obey. She feels like she's going to crash and let all the lights go out.

No, no, no, NO! she hisses to herself, staggers over to the balcony and hits the lift button.

It stops and this time the doors open immediately.

He grabs her by the hair and it makes that whizzy sound as it flies upwards. Her heart is concrete and it cracks.

Now he peels off the remaining garments. She's immobile, desensitized, a Barbie Doll with a bloody back-end. The torn black patterned tights. The black satin corset. The small leopard-skin-print knickers. Off they come. Now she's naked and they stare at each other.

Calmly, and without any trace of frenzy, he gently forces her onto all fours on the lift floor. She hears the sound of keys and coins falling on the floor as his no-sign jeans hit the cubicle's metal floor.

She moans, makes that peculiar noise of pleasured violation.

She grinds her teeth. Her nipples are hard.

She writhes and he pushes back.

She tightens her grip on him there. He thrusts harder and she feels the last breath being pushed out of her. Her arms collapse. Her face is sunk into the stud grid on the floor. He leans right forward, pulls her face up by the back of her hair and sloshes his tongue around in her mouth.

Her fists clench and grab at the hard steel, oblivious, she wiggles, her tiny mouth opening wider, wider, her eyes shut, now the noise inside building to a cry that makes her throw her head back, that racks her body with a spasm, that pulls her together with him. He pumps furiously at her again, she bucks back. And she feels herself cum, come, coming, KERRACK.

She is spent. The lift is still.

For almost a minute they lie there together and she feels the triste, sweeping melancholy surging in their post-coital soul. She crawls over his sinewy frame, her soft pale flesh tinged with pink brushing against the harder, darker span, of his tanned torso.

She plants tiny baby kisses over his hard shoulder, on his face, and they sound like water dropping on water. And some lines run through her mind from the back pages of the time she'd spent at drama school.

> *The wrinkled sea beneath them crawls;*
> *He watches from his mountain walls,*
> *And like a thunderbolt he falls . . .*

She whispers softly as she begins working her way down his body with her tongue. But the lift suddenly lurches downwards and she feels him start to enlarge tentatively in her mouth. Should she risk it? Stop and press the manual override button?

No. The metal cabin halts as suddenly as it had started. The door begins to open. He leans forward on the button and it shudders for a second as its primitive nervous system tries to make sense of the contradictory signals. Then, much too slowly, the door starts to shut and the man with the dead caterpillar on his face shouts, 'Oi.'

She feels a frisson shoot through her body. She eyes him, ambivalent, unsure.

'Hey,' she says. 'Where do I tell my husband to pick me up?'

Ye Complete Book of Role Martyrs

'In the Valley of the Dolls lie the brightest and the best. Sleep – sleep, sleep, sleep, sleep, sleep, sleep.'

The line from the has-been band ricochets round his mind and he smiles – Flash Colorado and the Stetsons – Jack had liked them once. They were part of the soundtrack of his youth and neither of them would ever lose that. So sad that when you turned on the light, the nursery of beat-fancy should be like this, he thinks as his eyes adjust to the drab shapes in the cold darkness of the little room.

He looks at the pillow. Two things about that pillow – it isn't clean. Not really crisp and even, the way fresh linen ought to be in a hotel. Second thing: it has a face on it. The face is attached to long strands of bird-nest-mess dark hair, beneath which nestle features pertly rounded in sweet dreams of canine couture.

'What happens to dreams when you wake up?' he recalls asking her, last night on the way back in the coach. 'Where do they all go?'

His own sleep had been deep and, it seemed, dreamless. But he knows that there is no such thing as dreamless sleep – only dreams you choose not to remember.

'If you carefully removed the cobwebby gunk, that stuff that gathers around the points of your eyes nearest your nose,' she'd said, 'and dropped it each morning into a jam jar, you'd soon' –

seven minutes, seven months, seven lifetimes? – 'have something you could label as "sleep". Or, of course, you could label it "dreams".'

'But,' he'd countered, 'you'd be lying and dreams never lie.'

She'd been quiet for a long time. Then she'd told him, in a slurry voice, that she'd written a biography of Lenny Bruce because she wanted to publish a book that started with the word 'fuck'. He was going to wisecrack back, but suddenly she'd turned her head and begun to force her upper body over the seat and – splurge 'n' purge, scarf 'n' barf – thrown up on the tartan covers of the seats behind them, all over some dozy rock crity who'd nodded out from all the excitement.

Whip-lash flashback: they'd been out at a pub somewhere mid-country along with a dozen other desperate acolytes of faded hip. The smell of bad beer lingered in his nostrils. And in his mind's eye was a gap left by the bloaty old photographer with grey hair and square specs, who'd suddenly appeared to snap the hype pics set up to quench the tabloids' thirst for total truth, pics posed by busty minettes and leggy bimbettes wearing cop hats as they sold tongue sandwiches to four has-been rockers, who looked a tad uncomfortable now the time had come finally to shave their sideburns. Too late! It didn't matter any more. The only reason he, Network 95's self-styled go-anywhere-foot-in-the-door-cut-the-crap-fuck-the-style-gimme-the-facts hard man hack, had tagged along on this third-rate publicity trip for the no-rent old-timey band was because it dovetailed neatly with some unfinished business 90 miles away.

He creeps out of the bed and, watching all the while to ensure he doesn't wake his companion, eases into the crumpled jeans which had spent the night in a pile on the floor.

The grimy off-white corridor outside is frozen; bare save for its red and white fire exit notices, and the chipped paint peeling off the pipes that run everywhere.

He pads down the stairs and snatches a cup of coffee in the grungorama restaurant. The cup has a hair-line crack inside. Two paunchy businessmen earnestly try to discuss the economics of holidays and sliding aluminium door frames over the racket of the industrial vacuum cleaner motoring throatily in the adjacent bar.

'Which way is the station?' he asks the receptionist in the bright-brown polyester suit.

Taxis? Forget it.

The landscape seems so morose that to hear a suicide note on his personal stereo would've brought him into an ecstasy rush. But – and wouldn't you know it? – the trickbox won't play. Not today. Still, at least he doesn't have to drag his over-the-shoulder suitcase too far along the grimly drear of terraced streets to reach his destination.

'One way to Cair.'

The platform's packed with commuters. Contrary to media reports (many of them, he recognized guiltily, his own), life has not dropped dead outside the city. Some of his fellow-travellers carry cases and bags, read newspapers or magazines, chew things and talk to companions. Others merely double-gaze into far-away and close at hand. Commuter dreams? he speculates.

It's windy. So he waits in the station buffet. He leers at the bored anaemic girl behind the counter making piping hot mugs of tea in quasi-ergonomic green cups. At least the cup isn't cracked.

Big fun, he muses. One dead boogiepack. Suddenly he feels sadness trickle around him like paddle waves at low tide. Why are you always alone on the beach?

'On the beach' was an expression his family used to indicate things were bad. Suddenly all that familial vocab has begun to impinge on his mind-set, edging out the rock-lyric-think that had kept painful and embarrassing emotional interludes – those judged uncool by fear-group pressure – firmly on the periphery. Yes, real life cannot always be explained by a monster buck meltdown megarap or computer-animated effects linking thematically diverse album-cover concepts. Shame, really.

He watches a seccy-chick (was this the way she passed the business day?) snouting down on a flaky pastry sausage roll.

'Sometimes denial of background serves only to assert it,' he scribbles in the black and white notebook he'd bought earlier that summer. The awful drearydrab of his immediate surroundings encourages him to anticipate the worst. It wasn't even as if he was making the annual plane-trip back to visit the parentals. Their idiosyncrasies had boundaries now. Anyway, the experience of being met by aunties in exotic airports had stroked his adolescent fantasies with fierce fuel for a long, long while.

Train-time! The yellow and blue Mantran express pulls up to the platform on grit-breaking wheels of steel. Jack loses out on the mind game where you fight for positioning on the door and finds himself, as the last on board, forced to tug at the metal bar to close the heavy steel panel behind him.

Four fun-filled action-packed coaches further up, he finally finds an aisle seat and opens the inky, broadsheet newspaper. '40 terrorists killed in a revenge raid by a Syrian snatch squad . . .' '. . . he inflicted multiple contusions on his victims before repeatedly raping them . . .' '. . . dismissed reports of alien bipeds terrorizing remote locales as "perfidious scaremongering" . . .' '. . . claimed there was a political conspiracy to destabilize opposition figures by using public money and government agents to smear and repress . . .'

From the window of the train he watches the grey buildings, green pastures and grey sky roll by. He notices the trees: those clumped together in a copse on top of a hill with a white chalk mark on its side; a group of seven poplars standing sideways-on in a line like soldiers in a children's picture-book – and, when they stop at the small town station, trees in the adjacent streets that have been pruned, but whose stumps are now shooting young leaves.

And suddenly he feels very adult and responsible. And then saddened that being grown up should have to be learnt like this.

There's no one at the station to meet him. He hadn't expected it – they didn't know what time he would arrive. But somehow it seems wrong – another rip in the dignity charade: that any of this really matters, that it has any meaning or significance to anyone to whom he attaches any meaning or significance. An immense wave of despair washes over him. Show no emotion, he tells himself and pretends to be someone else. Someone hard. Someone who knows – someone like a mafia contract killer.

It doesn't work. The only thing he has to kill is time. He trundles down the road, away from the station, along a narrow path through a splash of park. Sparrows sing. Bare larches with wet, raw, pointed branches. Drizzle. He mingles with crowds of moping mothers and stumbling tots and snivel-faced brat kids in anoraks and push chairs crying out for Masters of the Universe Gobot Transformers, giant jumbo bags of tooth-rot sweeties and a lot lot more attention. As he drifts on through the shopping centre, it starts raining properly again. Signs on store fronts run across his sight-lines. They strike odd associations: Corfam, Oxfam, picking up shoe-trees, don't die. Was that real thought? Or a second-hand sentiment from some crappy indie-pop band twitchily muscling in on his emotional domain?

He shivers. 11.45 a.m. and already he's starting to feel weird. Worse than a rip-off drug rash, worse than the bit in the horror movie you're watching latenight on your lonesome ownsome where you know the hero's gonna catch it in the neck, worse than the moment where you have to meet some lover and you know it's the last time. Worse than the last time.

'He's my man and he's so strong, he kicks my butt all day long,' raps a disco diva from inside a record shop. He goes inside and, for a few minutes, loses the pain among the piles of albums and rock-victim paraphernalia. It seems like sanity, a link with city life: fast cars and smart bars and people who could put all this into some sort of amusing context, pretext, don't fret. But then he sees the jacket of the group he'd been ligging with last night. Flash Colorado and the Stetsons – 'Remember Those Fabulous 70s?'

Seen it, been there, done that, heard it all before.

Outside he finds himself following the signs to the cathedral. Was this preordained? Preprogrammed? Destiny, like an anthropologist finding a footprint in the sand? F-f-f-fate?

One hot summer day, years ago in Florianville, he'd been walking along to collect the laundry and had seen a card lying in the street. It had an ornate red back. He'd stopped, and wondered whether to turn it over or not and eventually he did because he was curious and it was curious, so he flipped it with his foot. It was an old Italian tarot card. He stared at the image lying there on the pavement, grinning at him as if it'd just escaped from somebody else's dream, to say, 'Yes – it's me. You can say what you like about me. But you can't pretend any more that I'm no longer part of you.'

Perhaps, he thinks, I can find some kind of guidance here. Or at least, some peace or serenity.

The shell of the old building had been bombed out bare to the sky in the International People's Scare. He checks the remaining brickwork. It is brown. It is ochre. It is red. It is blue.

Curious artefacts, like nails used in the construction of the roof by local craftsmen of your yore, were on display in glass cases. Tourists shuffled round in small groups, occasionally flashing minicams from Japan and Germany.

Naked sweating cameras ploughshared into the dream-time.

Oh flash those nails, photo opportunity this misery that is between me and what-it-is-out-there, he hears himself think as he pulls up the high fur-lined collar of his new black leather jacket.

He blocks it, pushes away the pain.

For now.

He walks thoughtfully across the milling pack of peoploids who throng the narrow street and continues up the stairs into the adjacent building. This is the new cathedral. Its white spire points skywards. Against the grey misty cloudscape it seems inquisitive, accusatory.

Why now? Why me?

These are the questions everyone always asks. Big questions. And the answers?

He walks along the aisles with their pennys set into the floor, worn smooth by the passage of endless trails of feet. Saints, sinners, pilgrims and perplexed populations of nuns and school kids, crazies and curiosity-seekers with half an hour to kill.

He remembers the time he'd been here as a small child: many of the coins had been nearly new then.

Then, he'd come up with his family to visit Beela. All they'd done was walk around, talk and eat because she refused to take anyone back to the sports shop above which she lived with her husband, an eccentric and unemployable opera-singer, whose baritone was no match for his splendid petulance. Beela had infuriated everyone because she ate so slowly, lining up peas on the plate like a general marshalling her forces. Now, alone, he'd come back.

I never really minded the way she ate, he thinks. But of course it is too late. Too late.

He finds himself facing the altar. An enormous tapestry of Jesus hangs above it, stretching right up to the alcove's pointy top.

What did he build in carpentry classes? Was John the Baptist really his press agent? Would Jesus have like'd to have been married? Would he have proposed on one knee? How would he have told his children about the facts of life? Did Jesus dream? Was he telling anyone about it?

'Oh tell me about it,' he implores, lost within the surrounding melancholia.

But there's no response, no answer outside of the mechanical shuffle of curious Teutonic feet.

Jack makes his way back to the station and hails a grey saloon off the rank. It has only two doors.

Hick town, he thinks and tells the man where to go.

The journey takes them through the suburbs. The driver's dark, swarthy, thick-set. He says nothing until, unexpectedly, he stops.

'This is it.'

He overtips, gets out and slams the door.

Repulsion. Revulsion. And, he recognizes, for all the worst reasons. He looks around at the hideously modern church, the surrounding housing estate. Snobbery – he hates himself for despising this place. He remembers what Grace Jones once said: 'It ain't how high you jump, it's how you land.' As the day progresses, he knows he's losing touch with the present as the past seeps from every passing minute to ensnare him. And he can't cut it off and block it out forever.

He rings the bell at the front door of the small house annexed to the church. Bing bong.

A young guy in a grey suit and grey mule shoes, opens it. He seems stooped and has a salt and pepper complexion: red hair, pale freckly skin and a dull-featured face that cries of a thousand days of clerking.

'You must be Jack,' he says, his flat voice pumped as full as he knows how of phoney-cry and synthetic, lush sincerity. 'I'm very sorry.'

His face falls. Jack notes his eyes, small and frightened, watching him.

An uneasy silence. Jack crosses the threshold of the house. It has a fussy smell: tea cosies and silver polish. 'I'm Graham,' the boy says, proffering his hand.

'Uhmmm,' Jack grunts. As they walk into the sitting-room, he feels the response is somewhat inappropriate – he can see Graham looking at the others, flashing messages saying, 'Tricksy, wrong, wrong.' A riot. But what else was he supposed to say? So you're the leech that encouraged my aunt to behave like this town's answer to Mother Teresa? Thank you for changing her bed pans while we all tactfully ignored the old basket-case?

'This is Jack,' says Graham.

'I'm so sorry,' says the vicar. He is a feeble-looking man in his late fifties with cheap specs, this vicar. There is thinning grey hair and fine bones which frame his face in a look of pained acquiescence to the perplexing enigmas of the material world, like buying a bus ticket. The bastard had made it his business to exploit Beela's guilty evangelism to the full. Bloody man is already cassocked. He twitters noises that suggest tea, perhaps?

'Very sorry,' says a thick-set chap in tweeds who has a tuft of hair on each cheek. He has a firm handshake. Apologies for death were obviously the code of the day. 'Very sorry indeed – your aunt was a good woman.' Apparently this is Geoffrey. Geoffrey looks like the sort of chap who smokes a pipe and goes on retreats where he never advertises his faith, but just lets it be known that if you have a problem and want a few quiet words, well.

'No, Alan, really, call me Alan,' the priest insists and introduces some dude, whose presence is never satisfactorily explained, guy in his mid-twenties with a handshake, that, by contrast, is like a bunch of wet lilies. He's garbed in a smart tailored all-black number and lisps his apologia in a spray of saliva that Jack feels on his face. And then, almost as an afterthought, he's himself now shaking hands with some pathetic little wizened old thing who'd fluffed around feistily with a duster the whole while.

He'd never realized that funerals provided more introductions than a marriage bureau.

Because he'd never been to one before.

'Matthew was a tax collector you know, Jack,' begins the vicar and blah blahs on about some of his wise words, throwing in a little comparative religion and all the usual stuff about sowing and reaping. Suddenly it must've occurred to him that he didn't have his visitor's complete attention.

'Ah, how well did you know your aunt?'

'Well, not really very well at all. But I used to see her sometimes. She came to see us one afternoon when my parents were over for Christmas three or four years ago,' Jack replies. Why is he interrogating me like this, he wonders, and feels disconnected from it all. So when the vicar finishes his next little speech ('A release . . . can't imagine the joy her soul must be feeling now . . . free at last from the painful shackles of the sufferings of the mortal body'), he says nothing.

The silence is difficult, embarrassing.

The saliva-sprayer mutters something about flower arrangements.

Something here ain't right. The twee décor. The appropriately sincere expressions of concern. The gratitude for past favours Beela had done, the remorseful flaunting of the good times they'd had together – the deeply meaningful spirituality they'd discovered over the counter in the sports shop she'd run. All this automatic micro talk. Oh, trite on.

'I don't really read the Bible very much, I'm afraid,' Jack eventually concedes. And, he thinks silently, there is nothing that would give me greater pleasure than to take an Uzi machine-gun and blow all of your stupid fucking heads off.

'Would you like to share some tea with us?' Revd Alan suggests again in his reedy voice, as if to implicate Jack in the fantasy that the frontiers of morality are lubricated by hot drinks.

'No thanks. I'll see you in church,' he says abruptly.

He walks down through the council houses towards the shops. Inside the newsagent's he buys

Doublemint,

a fresh pack of high-tar cigarettes

and a Judge Dread comic

from the grinning Pakistani proprietor. Then he's in the pub up the road and banging back a couple of stiff brandies.

Working people, mostly male, sit around wreathed in everyday expressions of frustration and deep-set gloom. They wear drab, dirty industrial uniforms and laugh occasionally, bitterly it seems, at things he knows he's forgotten how to understand.

'Such nice, clean, crisp photocopies,' said a colleague of the man who'd just been turned into ectoplasm by the rampaging swamp-thing on page 46 of the comic. Jack feels tears well behind his eyes. He tries to shut it off, to cut if off from his mind. He drinks another brandy. He smokes the cigarette. He chews the gum. He'd scarcely known the woman. And already it's creeping towards 2.00 p.m. 14.00 hours, Beela would've said.

He'd left the sling-over-the-shoulder blue suitcase at the priest's house. The flowers had already been arranged by his parents in a rare gesture of generosity to his father's long-despaired-of sister. So all he had to do was throw his leather jacket over his pin-stripe and go.

He takes a deep breath as he approaches the church. And spits out the gum. Show-time! He walks past pews full of strangers, conscious (he thinks) that all eyes are upon him. He sits at the front, on the right. Graham's family, the people who'd been looking after Beela, introduce themselves in hushed tones. It might've been uncomfortable any other way.

He stares blankly at the oak coffin, its gilded handles, as it sits there in the aisle on this peculiar tray supported by criss-cross metal lattices. It was distressing to stare at Beela hidden away in this box like that. The box was so very small.

OK, she'd barely scraped in at five foot two. But that anyone's entire life could be reduced to such a so-what speck seems heartbreakingly cruel.

Not least because another's death is always an intimation of one's own mortality.

The organ plays. People sing hymns. He hates hymns. Behind him he hears the lily handshake pillow-biter boy pipe up mellifluously. Graham stands next to him and sings fortissimo. Jack's voice begins to crack.

The first funeral he's attended in his life. He feels he ought to cry and knows he's going to anyway. He wants to cry. He is the sole blood relation in the congregation that fills the depressing little church. The priest, the Revd Alan Bluegenes (can that really be his name, he wonders, repeating it like a mantra, Reverend Bluegenes, forever in blue jeans), mounts the pulpit.

The sky-pilot shuffles some papers around and the microphone picks up the noise. Jesus was a techni, oh yeah. He is in your headphones, your mainframe computer, your semi-conductor chip circuits, your pop vids, your minicams, your business dreams.

'Julia, or Beela as she was more widely known to her family,' (quick, knowing glance there at the front row) 'her many friends and all those throughout the community she came into contact with, came from an old-established Jewish family. It was this that made her contribution as an evangelist – not only by her lay preaching but by her very presence with us here . . .'

Jack's world stops dead. Flip the card, freeze the dream in the valley of the dolls. The words come right back at him. '. . . from an old-established Jewish family . . .'

'. . . an old-established Jewish family . . .'

It was like a missing person being run over by a road train and seeing twenty-three years of life in a flashback in one moment on impact. But all those years belong to somebody else.

Only he is the somebody else they belong to.

And that somebody else wants to scream like a wild thing and tear down the walls of the world. For twenty-three stupid years there'd been something missing. And now here it was. A mystery all of his very own. Do you want to be an enigma – or just seem like one? Do you want to trauma – or just discover one? Another dimension – the tears in the onion ring, the dream in the jam jar. Then the reality of it hits him all over again.

Oh God, he thinks, I have this in my blood, this is my blood, this is my family. We are all refugees, I have been wandering, we are all wandering, and I was alone in this strange place but now I have come home, I never knew there was any home. But there is. A home, a real home. Here in the hole in our heart.

Come home, come home.

Now he understands why he talked a little faster than the others, why the kids at prep school had asked, 'Are you American?' the first day he got there, why he'd always roomed with yiddisher boys, why he'd enjoyed haggling in markets, why he'd always fallen for dark, sultry Japy girls with sad nagging eyes. He remembers his first day at secondary school, when he'd told Jewish jokes to the other kids to ingratiate himself – to belong. Everything blurs. The oration, the pallbearing, the walk down the aisle, the hot tears.

'But I just never knew, I just never knew . . .'

Graham glances at him, embarrassed.

'Why didn't they tell me?' he sobs out loud. 'Why didn't they tell me?'

'Whose car are we going in?' asks Graham.

'WHY?' Jack asks.

8,000 questions. No answers. The answer's another question.

'Come along now, dear,' murmurs Betty.

More blur.

And right on cue the heavens open once more and the limo takes off like the driver is an angel late for the apocalypse.

Betty, Graham's mother, sits in the front. She's a middle-aged woman whose bobbed red hair sits uneasily beneath the black veil that tops out her mourning dress, beneath which she looks like an over-bolstered cushion tottering on two overwrought legs. She picks up the messages. They make her nervous. She's been dreading this occasion and it exceeds her worst expectations. She rubs the hem of her black nylon dress with her spongy white slabs of finger. Bob, Betty's husband, sits uncomfortably in the middle of the back seat, and looks at the crazed person beside him with the total emotion of lard melting in a cardboard factory. This is more excitement than he needs in a year, let alone an afternoon.

Jack scarcely knows they are there. He sees flat land and dead chimneys. Grey clouds and dirty grass. God weeps and rain runs down the back of his neck. Betty talks of sandwiches, what-a-good-woman-she-was-giving-jobs-to-all-those-boys.

And thinks secretly about the will.

The crematorium. It murks. The party shuttle through. Only now there is an air of urgency to all this. Run to schedule, things must. Otherwise: bodystack, grievous relations go biswaz, letters to local paper, municipal inquiry and jobs lost. Bad business when things don't run to schedule. So run they must.

Everyone's milling around aimlessly. And there's clearly nothing going on here on the launch pad.

'Where is she?' Jack asks.

'I'm terribly sorry,' Bob says. 'They've done her.'

'Eh?'

'She's gone.'

'Too late?' asks Betty.

'Too late,' says Graham.

'Oh.'

The final fuck-up, he thinks, looking at Bob's flubby cheeks, tiny paralysed eyes, button nose and blubbery lips.

Jack walks sadly out into the Garden of Remembrance. The rain is just soft tears now. The grey clouds still roll over and over crying, 'The earth is falling in, the earth is falling in.' He looks bemusedly at the wan wreaths and the dumb-dumb flowers, spent cartridges of life. They too are destined to disappear into anonymous smoke. The sky shifts, creating and destroying, creating and destroying shapes of conceit in the breeze. Change, change, everything must change into something else – something new. The dreams in your jam jar, the holes in your heart.

POODELICIOUS

I KNOW.

Know what you're thinking.

That there is no possible way to turn a penguin, that stocky groundbird bird so often pictured toppling into snow during high gales, into a poodle – that snootsome pedigree height of canine fashion dog, which very much enjoys temperate climes where it is pampered and attended to, and knows nothing of any stubbly wings or icebergs or gales or toppling over.

But this would be to misjudge the situation. Because what we are talking of here is not some cheap skate dramatic switcheroo to wow the ankle-biters of an overlong school holiday afternoon at the zoo, but real spiritual metamorphosis.

Poodle arrived in this city as Christina Ivalliovitch from some hokey, hickety-stick industrial backwater the wrong side of the Mistral a few years back. Quite a few years further back, in fact, than she usually cares to let on.

Her old man is this brunty industrialist of the old school who is well in with the government when it chooses to make its face felt up-country, normally round about election-time. He uses this influence, such as it is, to attract all manner of hideous smokestacks – which the young Christina, precocious rug-rat, is prone to call cloud factories – and other types of manufacturing businesses up that way to keep the dully vapid citizenry out of the bleak hard-drinking bars for 8 to 12 hours during the week and, in the process, make a shake for his cronies who own said massfac plant and so-called light industry and cloud factories and all. So, as you may imagine, her old man is a big deal in that depressed and depressing land. He's also quite popular with it. He makes a major production of keeping the teeth-grinding cat's-claws-over-the-blackboard accent in which the locals are wont to chatter up there; and also goes positively Hollywood about a covey of homing pigeons he keeps in, dig this, an allotment he picked up 400 squillion years ago when just a whippersnapping research student and all-round local wide boy. Papa I. is bazonkers about pigeon-racing (a popular recreation among the indigenous malefolk) and is always up billing and cooing at these dumb birds, feeding and mucking them out, breeding and ringing them, and hanging out with the lads (as said males are apt to term a posse of their mates), flying the grey pigeons hither and thither and putting the stopwatch on them, not to mention having the odd wager about which will come home first in such and such a tournament. In fact, his only child, untouched by anyone except her mother, since she screams her head off when papa accidentally snags her skin in her anorak zip, age three, cannot help remarking to herself *sotto voce* in later years that her papa is looking increasingly like a goddamn pigeon. And this is not entirely inaccurate, as his chest sticks out remarkably, and he takes to strutting from place to place and looking around and about at his various investments and interests with notably more beakiness.

Now Mr Ivalliovitch is so busy playing flyboy with the pigeon fancy fraternity, attending certain meetings with various governmental desk-jocks and, in addition, keeping his own far from trivial industrial plastics-moulding business tripping along, that he has very little time to spend with Mrs Ivalliovitch, who is neurotic like dinosaurs are dead. She is the kind of lycra-curtained aspire-to-twinset woman who has year-long spring cleaning programmes and rises around five each morning for the first vacuum of the day. She is prone to telephone her husband at work to have him come back and kill a bug on the wall – and then bawl him out for leaving a mark on the paintwork. She is the daughter of a fishwife and, supposedly, not a bad-looking dame in her day: but now, having ascended the giddy social inclines way beyond her wildest fantasies, due to Papa I.'s business pre-eminence, finds herself thrown into a tizzyspin by the prospect of hosting a coffee morning and other such amusements as are available north of the Mistral. Understandably, Papa I. spends much time attending to his pigeons and his business, both of which duly prosper.

Now Christina has a very hard time at school, with her father being this big-shot identity and her mother that ratbag whacko-weirdo, so age nine, she starts stamping the tiny foot and pretty fast the parentals get the message that their little princess is not exactly copping royal treatment from her peers. At the first possible opportunity, age 12, they ankle her out of there to attend some swankypants local convent for young ladies, where she receives the elocution lessons that leave her talking a dream and gets harnessed into braces that do less than nixety to alleviate her prominent buck teeth. Also, she learns to write stories and the general opinion is that she writes pretty well.

But, age 15, she is seduced by Laurie, the local Lothario and wild card who sneaks her into the cemetery during her first school dance – and screws her stupid on some ancient worthy's raised tomb. Christina falls in love. He does not reciprocate. Laurie is basically a moody, tall, dark and handsome Italian stallion type in the traditional mode. But Laurie is putting it out and about a bit because he reckons himself stacks and stacks, and sees not why such a fabulous thing as himself should limit his exquisite favours and formidable prowess solely to members of the opposite sex, when playing with both feet would conceivably double the amount of attention he receives around town – which is already humongous heaps of monolithic masses and, the way some citizenry tell it, arguably much too much for any one 16-year-old dude, however studly. The upshot of which is Laurie runs away with a fashion tutor at the local poly and, for a while anyway, they live miserably ever after.

So, first chance she gets, Miss Christina footstrikes down to the Smoke to study drama at Realito Park Academy of Fine and Performing Arts where, within two terms, she falls head over heels in leurve with her English Lit tutor Harriet Sheridan. Simultaneously her music lecturer, a pointy headed beard-breathed baldy on the verge of collecting the O A P, leaves his wife and three because he is so smitten with Christina, now pretty watchable herself. Her eyes look dark and deep; her tresses raven, superfine; her legs are the length of luxury; and the plunge of her firm décolletage grows increasingly breath-defying. And then there is her skin. She has the bleached pallor of an arsenic-eater: her complexion is white, gothically blanche as a photo of a ghost. Her movements are delicate and fragile almost to the point of frailty, as if her bones are splinters of white crystal bound together in a tight, constricting dress like a shroud.

So she becomes an adultress to the sounds of Mozart – but all the time Christina is still carrying the torch for Laurie.

And here in the city, she hangs with a faster crowd who are constantly asking the 8,000 questions and finding the answers in the bottom of a bottle or on the roach of a joint, on a mirror or in the lavatory at a nightclub of the type Papa Ivalliovitch's pigeons would never return home to lest they discover themselves making an unscheduled appearance on the table around dinner-time.

So overexcited by the big-spend probabilities of metropolitan life does Christina become that within a very short space of time she accumulates 102 penguins of various sorts in her room. There are china and porcelain penguins; fur penguins; penguins which are lights; penguins which are penholders; penguins on mugs; penguins which double up as hot-water bottle holders and cushions; ancient velvet penguins; severely PoMo penguin stationery and pre-millennial penguin wrapping paper; penguin patches, watches, lighters, puzzles and torches; penguins both clockwork and remote-controlled, penguin coats, summer shirts and scarves; a v. small penguin on a medium medium key ring; a pengy bedspread, a black and white birdy clock and some chocolate penguins, not to mention the penguins you find when you put your feet in the freezer to cool out your heels and hit: the penguin ice-cube shapers – you start to get the picture here?

But despite the fast-breeding of this well-down crew of black and white ornithological talent, all is not well with their keeper. There are, for starters, many arguments with Papa I. on the vexed question of the penguin debt bomb. The English tutor ditches her in favour of another girl. She discovers she's pregnant by the geriatric muso, who's now deserted his job to pursue a freelance orchestral career and compels her to have an abortion. On leaving the scrape-clinic (their jingle jangled 'We'll Take More Care of Yewww Do Do Do') in a less than tip-top frame of mind, Christina returns to her apartment to find that where her pink VW convertible was, there is now a space. What's happened, it transpires, is that the trick-cycling student she's been playing off against both of her academic lover-mentors has stolen the car papa gave her for her birthday and is in Morocco already with her best friend. Then, upon entering her apartment, she discovers a flat-as-a-pancake letter informing her that Laurie has fallen off his motorbike, wrapped it around an oncoming touristo-coach and is little better than strawberry jam. Poor pengy-chick hears on the grapevine, later that arvo in the snoozer, that her musical squeeze has returned to his wife and three. So it comes as no surprise when later that week Christina, who has much to her disgust inherited much of Mama Pigeon's predisposition to irrational anxiety, decides she's been asked one question too many and answers by curling up with Viscount Valium and a bottle and a half of cheapo 117 degree Japanese melon Scotch liqueur. Now at this period Christina is living in this low-rent gaff on the northside with a girl called Bee Melrose, who is hustling antique threads, and a guy called Joe who is a scribe on the local rag. Joe has been covering some deathless thrillaminute fête and decides he could use the rest of the afternoon off to chill his excitement somewhat. He strolls in to find Christina sprawled all over his bedroom, having a big nod. And being a conscientious sort of bloke, he checks her pulse and whatnot and concludes all is not well with this Christina and telephones the ambulance lickety-split.

And every day Princess Penguin is in hospital he visits her and brings a selection of flowers and chocs, and listens patiently to her kvetching about her mother's constant naggety nag and smuggles in liquor and cigs, for which she is most grateful, not to mention the small matter of saving her entire life, which she doesn't. So neither does he but makes his feelings known by his quietly solicitous attentions and small but significant gestures and entreaties of assiduous devotion. And the upshot of this is that three months after she gets off sick row, she and Joe get spliced.

But it's only a matter of weeks later that the novelty of playing with her very own washmach has worn off fractionally, and Christina is starting to think that this is the worst mistake she ever made in her life. For one thing the marital state curbs her sexual activities. And for another there is, she rapidly susses, a fundamental mismatch here. Joe (a tall, rangy dude whose looks are academic, whose disposition is studious and whose idea of

Nirvana Central is indeedly-doodly to sit down of an evening with his Integrated Circuits X M Z2000 computer and do a little bugzapping or dropping of the logic bomb) is superficially very phlegmatic and all control. But underneath his jovial matterafact exterior lurks an emotional masochist. No problem. But Christina and her penguins seem to wanna hit The Scene, grabba gabba way show off and out see and be seen here there in all the high-fashion nightspotting groovoid fun palaces. *Seem* – that's the problem. 'Cos some time ago Christina I. recognizes that beneath her funster penguin persona is a chick who wants to be stepped on.

'It's traumatic, it's really awful. It's like two people talking in different codes and there's no code book,' she confides to Robbie the Mad-Hatter, a tubby fag-ash blond who is a fellow Realito collegiate drop-out, one afternoon when the latter pops in to the second-hand dress shop she now runs in a smart mid-town hypermarket with friend Bee Z. (a.k.a. Melrose) who is becoming something of a big wheel herself in the dealing of old high-fashion wares. 'There's no communication at all.'

'Well,' says Roberto (who's now, as his handle suggests, in the millinery), after pausing to consider this snix-up for all of two seconds. 'What I'd do if I were you, dear, is have an affair. Even if it doesn't make him change into the Prince Alarming you desire in your heart of hearts, it may alter your perspective and perhaps even eventually alter your situation, so that you find someone who'll give you what you want and what you need.'

So Christina the Penguin is going out lots more and not always returning to the roost too soon. She runs around town in the low-cut dresses which give her cleaverage maximum leaverage, and the stiletto heels which display her long long legs to the best advantage. She's accumulating many dresses with bustles to emphasize her tail and one day in Bee Z.'s clothes shop, betwixt customers, she is trying on such a dress with a bustle. It looks not at all bad and she notices her tail wagging in the mirror. At this moment it suddenly strikes her that penguins wag the tail only to balance – not in fun. And it strikes her that she may be changing, ready or not, into some other type of animal altogether. And all the time she has this increasing miasma of untrammelled vulnerability breezing around and about her person like the Guerlain perfume she wears, just waiting for someone or something to latch onto and melt all over.

So she drifts further and further apart from Joe, who keeps blatting away on the old QWERTY, and she takes to hanging around with Bee Z., who knows many of the most weirdsome and arty-crafty characters. Types like Sailboat Eddie, who is the first man in the city to pick up on the Loons craze and advertise same in three revolving colours on the back pages of the music rags, but now runs an informal importation business of certain controlled substances.

Also she is seen at Tokapi – which is this dingy basement afterhours run by a nefarious character called Capt'n Jonas who is nothing but a red-rum-and-black lush and reefer maniac taboot – along with Morty 'Big' Kinsella, the high-fly fat-money legal eagle with an over-developed taste for low-life. Also Joe runs into her on more than one occasion in the arms of various rocker types who are far from freckle-punching pillow-biting fag-boys and, in fact, have the reputation as being bad bed notchers. Individuals like Ziggy Shondelle (of the famed purple pineapple haircrop) and groupie-vulnerables like Bruce Dior (of whose landing tackle scenester chicks murmur to each other in giggly gurgles of intense respect) among others. And Christina is also frequently spotted shooting into nightclub lavs with a miscellaneous jubilee grab-bag of disreputable boy louts. Invariably they take advantage of her sweet disposition and Come Fuck Me shoes to borrow sums of money from her which they seldom return, steal her drugs, sometimes screw her stupid bad and even beat her black and blue. She loves it. And it's about this period that Fat Tuesday observes that Christina the Penguin is becoming Christina the Poodle. And Fats, having spent the afternoon in the company of Marie Antoinette, says as much to her one night at White Jaqui's place and Poodle turns right around by the bar and says: 'Yeah, what of it, biggob?'

Fat Tuesday is greatly surprised. Firstly, because he's unaccustomed to catching backchat from any chick on The Scene, since all are supposedly savvied as to the wicked whiplash of his tongue and are scared shiftless of his rep as a gossip monger and credibility broker. And, for another, it is usually v. difficult to hear what anyone is saying to him over the din of the random-stack funkarama discs he spins at his various clubs.

'Poodles are wondrous animals,' Christina tells him at the top of her lungs. 'Do you know of any other dog that died on a battlefield during the English Uncivil war? Furthermore poodles are companions to the great and good. Churchill was one of many such poodleowners, and not only are they smart at doing tricks of one sort and another, but are also very funny, and loyal and extremely ferocious when necessary. So no more dissing of the poodle, fat boy, or you get some of this.'

At this point she emits some unearthly growl, which sounds to all the world like a hunting dog snarling up a blue blue streak, and then – much to the delight and surprise of White Jaqui's clientele – she drops onto all fours and, with one movement of considerable alacrity, springs at FT and bites him on the ankle.

Fats shrieks something most hideous and wails at Blackjack and other assorted acolytes and scenesters to get him an ambulimo *stat* since he is afraid he is dying of rabies and needs treatment this second if not sooner. So now all across the city of night, from

Jaqui's Whitetrash to Boosterfish, from Tokapi to Rififi and Le Hot Club de Now, from the swankiest kissy-kissy drop-dead palaces to dank basements full of torn armchairs and rat-talk faces, everyone cops the word: WHO IS THIS POODLE?

Meanwhile, back at the kennel – as Poodle has taken to tagging her eternally devoted's apartment – Joe remains v. calm and collected about these goings on, despite the tattle surrounding Christina's increasingly egregious behaviour, which becomes proportionately voluminous and exaggerated among chattering scenesters and scandal-swapping celebutantes. Not that it needs much hypewriting.

One time she turns up at a pop group launch party for Eddie Sweetabix clean sheet blasted out of her noggin and pelts the act with small pieces of cheese from a metal spring-loaded catapult she carries in the frilly velvet bag that she calls four dollars ('cos that's what it cost) until the quartet flee and she storms the stage and plays chopsticks on the sequencer to the cringing embarrassment of the assembled company.

Another time Joe surprises her giving a colleague of his, on the national rag where he now toils, a full-on blow-job behind some anorexic bushes in total view of 3,000 liggers at the Flamingo, a well-known swanky mode roof-top nightspot. But he keeps very very chill about this. He is reckoning that all the liggers are preoccupied – with their own wild witticisms and (natch) the snatch-up of as many freebee argon-coated Japanese laser-writers with variable sensotorque precision brush-stroke as they can possibly lay hands on – that they won't notice much, and perhaps he's not wrong at that either. So he just ignores the whole palaver and keeps churning out the unauthorized biogs of various stars of stage and screen and makes a minty lolly by so doing.

But one day Christina tips up at the launch of *Motive*, the freshest newly ultra-happening super-fashy style rag of that moment. It's at some converted school on the borders of Stewartstown, which is the rough tough tumbliest and most viciously cred area of the city. And the proprietors of said new rag hand out throwaway video cams to all the celebrants, and also champagne cocktails. And many people are puffing away at the exotic cheroots and pounding out the long long lines of Marie Antoinette, when Christina captures something in her camera and falls in love with it instantly and takes it home.

What it is, is Tony Burgoyne, who, in addition to being a very famous artist in his own right, is also the older brother, that is very much older, of Laurie, her teenage crush and cherry snatcher. And what it is about Tony that puts the Good Spousekeeping seal of absolute irresistibility on his bag of bones is that he is married to someone else. Christina is the kind of girl who not only cannot resist a challenge even where, strictly speaking, none actually exists – but also takes such challenges very personally indeed.

Now the affair between these two characters is not so much hot as a raging inferno. Tony is, charitably, the wrong side of 40 and no oil painting – his hair is grey but not so much distinguished as extinguished; and his bod is scraggy and gnarled with years of licentiousness and rad behaviour. The problem is that Tony is unwilling to relinquish the household he keeps with his meaning-of-wife, Eleanor, who is this very fierce formerly blonde artlaw accountant thing. In a good looks and youth contest she'd be beaten into the back of beyond by Christina, but if it came to being the leatheriest suntanned lairey on the street, EB would win at a canter.

Ellie is of the firm opinion that it is she who has supported Tony through thick and thin, but mostly thin. That being the kindest possible interpretation of the very many lean and mean years she is on the wrong end of while Tony screws around waiting for his daubing career to get the old vertical lift off. And

Eleanor takes an understandably dim view of this Poodling person moving in on her turf, because she hears this is no bimbo candyfloozette of the type her significant other is wont to dally with for the purposes of massaging his ego and other private parts, but is, in fact, the genuine 24-carat home-wrecking trouble-broker from hell.

At the same time, Christina is always conscious of the fact that were it not for Joe she would not be drawing breath let alone social security, and thus also finds it tricksy to blow him out totally. So the compromise is reached where the sweethearts rent a third apartment along the lines of a lust-nest down near the sleazebag section of the Strip. They have same most swishly decorated by one of Burgoyne's friends with many exotique animal prints, expensively imported materials, black and white artefacts tastefully slung together in the highest of styles. And these two are the bright lights of the beau monde and a magnet for jaded thrill-seekers around the metroplex since their antics and attitudes are wild, to understate it slightly.

One night the couple decide, after a 1970s dinner-party at which the genuine Vesta chow meins are dished up, the incense burnt and the startling fur-lined bomber jacket and platform shoes displayed for viewing, that they are heartily sick and tired of their sexual thraldom to one another and go out and pick up two total strangers and do them with an appetite and disregard for inhibition bordering on the rapacious; and then come back and film each other describing their experiences in excruciating detail. To celebrate, they drive down the road to Jim Jam's 24-Hour Video Tattoo Parlour, where Poodle pays for Tony to have a black rose inked onto his cock, and on her lower bosom she – how did you guess? (Will you tell?) And this, believe me, is just the tip of the spiceberg.

And somewhere during this blur of telephone trauma,

bofforama à go-go, present-giving, mutual adoration and intense jealousy, Christina divorces Joe. But this is all most amicable because they still run into each other here and there and she still keeps both her penguin collection (now static) and her poodleabilia (now expanding apace) round at Joe's place, there not being much room for either on the Strip. The lust-nest's cramped, what with all Christina's new clothes and Tony's old canvases and the constantly changing character parlour of peripatetic international flotsam jetsome who drift in and out, perhaps on the pretext of biz, but somehow often end up staying for three months or so at a stretch.

Anyway, things are generally pretty much on all fours between Poodle and her former owner, as she comes to think of him. He is now feeling stepped on to the requisite levels and used and abused no end since, when she has a spat with Tony, Poodle spends the night at Joe's, and this is helping his career greatly since he is now driven like a man repossessed and appears on chatshows and gabfests as Mr Showbiz, which he finds not uncongenial. Also Joe, not three vouchers short of the proverbial pop-up toaster, realizes that being married to that Poodle is like trying to keep an angel on a leash, and has taken to hanging around with a pacy hareem of most devious doxerallas and fast-talking flygirls, curvaceous starlets and silken bimbettes, being v. careful not to get too tied up with any one of them. His true pash lay elsewhere – in his room. It was glass and plastic, silicone and metal, garbed to the unseeing eye in a drear blandness of creams and dullard browns, enlivened only by occasional flashes of electric green or flecks of deep red and gleamy silver.

Joe was obsessed with the elusive heart of his computer. On one of its many meaningfully interfacing disc-drives he'd affixed a promo sticker saying YOU CAN'T BEAT MY SYSTEM, PAL.

Religiously, he'd pass many hours in narrow, sepulchral book-lined corridors of research libraries where he pored over and absorbed all points germane from the very latest manuals and abstracts. He supplicated and paid homage to the cold soul of the machine with offerings of fresh software and ever sexier peripherals. He had, by corresponding with like-minded on the net (inconspicuous and thus wrecklessly brave behind their fabuloused call-signs like SCARLET LADY, D'ARTAGNAN, RUBBERMAN and BUGZAP), learned how to hack inside his self-created system and commune with its imperial interior. He felt a sense of reverence during such sessions. Other times he would play games like DOUBLE IDENTITY, ALICE, PRISONER, BREAKOUT, NEUROMANCER, KISS CHASE or MOTOR NEURONE SCARE, safe in the knowledge that eventually, by the grace of this greater intelligence, he would triumph over the software writers and win the game. Though sometimes he suspected that the only reason he was granted victory was to ensure his continuing participation in the Cybernetic Love Ritual.

When not deeply immersed in the exciting new graphic possibilities of some esoteric modem or adrift in the fantasy haze of Curmudgeons and Dragons, Joe nurtures the secret dream that one day Poodle will pop back and live with him full-time. He is the sort of guy that must always have an elusive ambition to enliven the workaday round of celebrity lunches, farflung freeloads on Concorde, outtahead tele-highs and many other impedimenta that detract from his ability to enjoy being deeply and utterly miserable.

And for a time everything is funkydory, except that Poodle and Tony both have to hustle like crazy because the expense of maintaining two households apiece is driving them solid nuts. Poodle, by turns, is a literary agent, blowing prospective publishers for her memoirs like Hurricane Charlie; an unreconstructed narcotics merchant and fugitive from injustice wanted by two different banks for two entirely different reasons – one bank manager she introduced to Marie Antoinette, the other she took for a red Porsche, a vodaphone and miscellaneous poodleabilia. She scammed and tricked as a personal energy consultant working the lucky dip both at the Church of the Mystic City Sign and hustled justifiably obscure indie-pop bands up-country to relieve the tedium of the dull and vapid citizenry there. She sells her old dresses to Bee Z. after her own concession goes broke following slight extravagance in the matter of buying Tony presents and keeping the poodle collection up to scratch; works some afternoons with Bee Z. on her new fashion store and, finally, becomes so desperate that she moves into her ex-spouse's field of endeavour. She taps not just her new chums from the afterdark but also old up-country cronies such as Two-Dinner Skimmer (who hit the jackpot bigly big by scrawling the authorized hagiography of the Unknown Rocker and other leading lights of modern mythology) for day-to-day data about doings in and around the pantheon. And what with her native writing ability, intuitive smarts, ruthless *modus operandi* and scenester connections. Miss Poodle is a big hit in this field.

And it's at this point that Tony and Christina become a really hot item. He takes to putting her on a gold lead when they go out together, and sometimes lends her to random faces in bars and clubs for a couple of hours while he goes walkabout elsewhere on designer drugs jags with some disgusting old mucker from his psychedelic wheyheyhey days.

And this gives Poodella a most mischievous idea.

Who (she wonders when, at a party in a penthouse at Xanadu Towers thrown by a hipster merchant banker who'd just cleaned up in supertankers, she finds herself on loan to a not entirely unattractive young property maven) is poodling whom?

Oh, she really wants an answer.

For it occurs to her that when an owner is walking the dog it would seem, to the naïve, that it's the owner who calls the shots. But, reasons Princess Poodella, this ain't necessarily so. The dog is as much leading the way as the person on the other end of the lead, since if Muttly – say, hypothetically, a poodle – decides that it desires a change of direction, it can simply sit down or make with the small stamping foot to produce the desired effect.

Afterall, she thinks as the property maven (who is neo-neat if you scrunch your eyes up and pretend he's on TV) repeats for the third time in 15 minutes the total seven-figure summation of his net worth, perhaps it is really the animal on the end of the lead that calls the shots since, if it exerts sufficient force and strength of will, it can lead its owner any goddamn place it wishes.

Later, back at the lust-nest on the Strip, she reappraises blow-jobs in this light. Superficially the blow-job is an act of female subservience. And yet . . . Poodle muses as she says, 'Feed me an almond, Tony' (for she is most attached to same) . . . and yet reality is that the blow-job is a situation where the female's overpowered her mate. She can withdraw the privilege or enhance the act of oral sex at her whim and further, during the phase of his supposed peak puissance while his member's in her mouth, the man is actually at his most exposed and vulnerable.

She cracks the nut in half with her teeth.

She closes her eyes and savours it: the taste is good. Better than good – it reminds her of her lover's seed.

Bittersweet and poodelicious.

So it's soon after this that she begins to tug at the leash a little, somewhat, a lot and then a more than somewhat whole lot of little lots. She starts setting up situations in which the discussion rolls round again and again to the question of Tony scramming on Ellie, who has by now become deeply peculiar and spends much time in dark rooms with various dubious characters at the Church of the Mystic City Sign – of whose *modus operandi* Poodella's only too well aware – in table-tapping letter-rapping olde-stylee seances during which Ellie claims she has reached some long-time toe-turned great-grandmother for the inside dope on what's going down, and exactly what kinda inside fast-track moves to make to resolve her vexatiously worrisome *problem de coeur*.

'Ellie's lost the plot,' Poodella advises her all-in-all from time to time. She's good at advice, but, like the divorced marriage guidance councillor, seems unable to heed her own wise words. 'Why don't you declare bankruptcy, give me your money, hand the silly sow her cards and be exclusively mine?' But life is not a bowl of cherries, chérie, and that Tony is more than somelot reluctant to do this. Especially after Poodella, as she is now universally dubbed among the city's deepest-grooving scenesters and most ostentatiously vivacious celebutantes, announces she is pregnant. The telephone traumas increase; the shouting and barking step right up off the graph. Even neighbours on the Strip, citizenry not renown for their prissiness or prudery, take to complaining when Poodella spends nights outside the flat scratching on the door, cocking her leg in their doorways and howling at the moon.

It all culminates when the dynamite duo go, stirred, shaken and totally heartbreakin' (once again they have spent too long in the court of Marie Antoinette and feel their heads are likely to blow off any second), to the Metropolitan Museum of Beauty and Culture for the unveiling of Christina's portrait – 'Young Lady with a Poodle' – by Tony. Out of the cornea of her paranoid's paranoid dark beading eyes, Poodella spots Ellie, labelled like a human billboard, canoodling with her husband and totally loses her rag. Poodella starts barking very loudly, growling and waving her forepaws around somewhat threateningly in the air. Harsh words are traded and suddenly someone slaps someone and the next thing the venerable trustees of the Museum know Ellie goes blapsolutely and radically biswaz, screams and, tears running with the mascara downdown her cheeks, tears a bloody great clump of poodle fur off the top of her rival's noggin, which never ever grows back again. The whole incident is captured on tape by TV2GO and splashed all over the morning rags the next day (ARTHEADS GO BARKING MAD the *News* said in a page 11 photo caption that spelt everyone's names wrong), which is most embarrassing for all parties concerned.

Christina has another abortion.

And cries weepy buckets for what might have been.

Poodle begins to refer to herself as the mother of dead baby whenever she talks to Tony and their affair winds down. Although she's got the high-octane butter and Russian furnishings, he top spins her and cool bruises the translucent skin of her ego maybe once too often even for a masochistic ex-penguin. Sure, she's Poodella – but the dog's only half the show, so when she bites back and plays dead no tricks, he goes walkies. And Poodella slinks back kennelwards and, for a while, her tail hangs between her legs.

But soon she gets a new clipping. Joe takes her for walks and buys her many bijou bijou bones and finely turned sparkly trinkets, and she pom-poms her coat, deeply delves into the acquisition of many new fur linings and is seriously investigating the possibilities of establishing a poodle parlour.

So it happens that one day Poodella, by this time now engaged to a character called Eddie whom she meets at the ballet (Eddie is a multi-squillionaire who frequently sends her orchids, first-class plane tickets and other small love tokens), mooches around the Barrio, keeping an eye open to sight her canine couture, coiffure and grooming joint. She has Prince, her real-life black standard poodle whose very smart new lion clip and blow-dry she has just personally supervised, on his very smart spangled lead when who should she see trotting towards her?

It is none other than Ellie, looking murderously smug, and, fancy that (she still sort of did), Tony. Ellie's consort's mien is much downcast and his posture crys, 'Pussywhipped.' His work, she's noted during recent months, has not been as prolific or of such quality as the dealers had come to expect of late. As the pavements in the Barrio are notoriously narrow, and filthy dirty digging ops are in noissome progress on the opposite side of the road, there is no way either party can avoid giving some ack to the other.

Poodella fortuitously notices that Ellie wears a Madame M' Rocas original creation, an exemplary red satin dress with much front-loaded corsetry and detailed needlework on it, which she recognizes as costing not two bob short of three-gee bucks, since this was the price she herself (more accurately, Papa Pigeon) paid for it from the couturier when she first acquired it four years back. And, because it is such a remarkable garment, she remembers well the miserable afternoon when she was forced to trudge along the Strip to sell same to Bee to turn a buck and raise some loot to buy a crate of Château Bagaweewee to lubricate several of Tony's more filthily rumbustious arty-crafty friends.

'Ah,' says Poodella, casting the fish-eye over her one-time rival. 'I see you're not content with my cast-off men – you have to have my cast-off dresses too.'

And she sticks her schnozzle in the air at 90 degrees and walks on by, leaving Burgoyne and his wife badly bitten, and herself with the satisfying feeling of knowing that she's not only got it like the best of breed, but that when she wants to be, she can be a real bitch.

Poodelicious!

Get Radical

GLORIOUS SUMMER DAY. Cressida awakens to the sun stream through her window like songlight. Click: clock-radio floods the bedroom with the mellifluously couth harmonic strains of Rachmaninov.

For a moment she gazes out through the bedroom window at the blue blue sky.

Andiamo!

This moderne model gel flings aside the snug yellow patterned duvet that's wrapped her bod most nights since she was three. She puts her right foot down on the thick grey carpet, her head abuzz with a chequerboard dream where cartoon people explained the crucial strip comedy of life in frames between white squares.

Her life?

She pads on the quiescent carpet through her bedroom and its votive sensurrounding St Marilyn memorabilia, through the living area, packed with the black, white, grey and silver trophies attesting to her accomplishments. Objects. Items compact and synthetic; consumerability manifested digital and electrical, designered to the power of *n*, all very quiet, very hard but rubbery to the touch.

She knows the meaning of the dream will change as the day progresses, will metamorphose to refranchise new layers of significance as she peels back the hours like an onion.

Insight without tears.

That mirror in the bathroom tells her she looks good.

But she's going to look better.

She mounts her Flextel-coated chrome Toturcise™ machine and cues Shane's Total Bod off remote. A read-out on the bottom of the black matt flat-screen bathroom TV measures her pulse rate.

Play for it.

Play to win.

The sweat breaks as she pushes, bends, twists and pulls. 'C'mon,' urges the ridiculously healthy Australian full-contact karate champion from somewhere within the tube. 'Work that body to death, chick, work that sucker to death.'

She power-showers with Florabella transparent orange baby soap, cleans her teeth with the green gel from the pumpy tube of Shine cosmetic plaque-pulping toothpaste. She applies minimal Designer Life make-up from the terracotta and jade toolbox which unfolds on lattice hinges, to reveal its tranche of compartments and hiding spaces for powders and paint, that can artfully make a face appear what it ain't and push the fizz on who she is. This is her arsenal, this toolkit of the professional visageist. She applies St Laurent, Clinique and Chanel. Then spends 14 allotted minutes on her long blonde mane.

Pace.

Back in the bedroom Marilyn's framed all over the wall.

She dons her dress-for-excessive-success Quite Quiet grey silk suit and the match-from-scratch grey Crocodillo Khamen Marino court shoes that show she's no pussyfooter. Residual thought: the sell-out. Fade to grey? No way – raid to grey: the Monochrome Highwaywoman steps out. Check that look – say it once, define the terms, tell the world what colour it is today. Then, and only then, does Cressida D C pour into her Marilyn Monroe mug the fresh decaf her sister (who usually rises 40 minutes before for her aerobic self-defence class) has left to hubble bubble in the new chromo-aluminium anodyne-coated Cellini Futrismo cappuccino-maker. The in-car variant is on order at one of her Galleria mall department charge-it accounts. She sips the hot black liquid in tandem with the contents of a prepared chill-swill that's festered overnight in a Waterford crystal glass. This pale pink elixir is her wealth of health breakie-blast, all power-yoghurt and tiger's milk, dense-packed full o' fruity, nutritionally enriched brans, ergonomically bonded with organically chelated trace minerals and extra added time-released energizing enzymes in a vitamin boosted zero liquid suspension.

She breaks her fast, her slender fingers tip tap tick tack toe touch hold switch along the data-stream of multi-channel to zip and zap there and back 'twixt tele and text so she may pick up on perky points, interesting information and feast among the fact-tracts: oh facts, you are sacred, we worship your tributaries, your very varicose veins of verity. Facts, facts, fun to know, fun to tell, survival knowledge in pulsed nuggets that put the edges on the creative interaction, heart-warming humour and richly rewarding adventures of the day ahead.

She sips from the mug and drains the glass. She watches.

This is what she watches.

The satellite weather report ('Looking for a top of 29 degrees with a south-westerly wind-chill factor mellowing out of the smuggy 30s'); the fine-tuned horrorscopes ('So all you Geminis start smart to check that trend – and remember that today it's most propitious to talk to Scorpios and Capricorns wearing reflector sunglasses'); the hard-hitting news stories ('We've got an up-date on the five-year-old little boy we were telling you about earlier who looks like being the planet's first space shuttle stow-away'); the germane colour ('If you're worried about a relationship problem, write in and work it out with Dr Dog – the only canine relationship counsellor in the country') and up-beat socksy pop ('Na-na-na-na-na-na-na-na-na-na-na'); the cute-shoot bits ('But that's not a real DB6 – it's a Japanese replicar, isn't it, Ed?'); the personalities ('This morning we're talking about male lesbians – the question is, why?') and cool bite data-bullets (talk is cheap – bullets cheaper) that send her skipping insouciantly along the corridor past the splashy blooms in the redwood tub tended with love – not forgetting the care, which she doesn't – outside her front door with a song in her heart, a swing in her hips and an infectious smile that plays around her lips.

Cressida D C pauses. Pauses only to look in on Mrs Ezeikial, her disabled but dignified 86-year-old next-door neighbour, with a cheery greeting. Does she want anything out?

No?

Senescents Autonomous.

Move.

Cressida D. Crane jumps into her two-tone grey Merlin XTC GTi sports soft-top and gets her AM antics off to an audaciously auspicious debut by cutting out the bottleneck at Van Damn Drive. It was a hunch – and it worked. She finds the small feeder road she's always expected would short-cut onto the Von Alvensleben Interchange. Less stress: less mess.

She hits the unfold-roof switch and, as the top creases, crumples, doubles over and tucks under, her long, clean fresh-blonde hair flys out behind her in the sun and the breeze blows just so and the tweeters-upfront system pumps out the Beach Boys' 'Good Vibrations'.

She arrives at the art-rococo city offices of Hennessey Kinsella Partners (successors in title to the original Attorneys at Law since 1752) twenty minutes early, frazzle-free and with a pathologically planned schedule. She clutches a drop-dead two-tone carrier-bag full of a new Gazelli party dress she couldn't resist impulse-buying when she passed the Melrose Shop on Bernini Boulevard.

'I want this outfit! Buy it for me now! Now, now! Now, now, now!!! Now, oh – please, sweetie.'

A little weakness. Wouldn't life be dull without it?

'Love, work, contrast – and something to hope for,' Cressida says to her secretary. 'What do you want from life, Sal?'

A voice cuts in on the squwarkbox.

'Miss Crane – may I have a word with you momentarily?'

The voice belongs to a portly man in a dark super-safe Rieves Revell suit. She walks along the carpet, it is corrdior; surveys the lushness that is floor beneath her feet and now it splits 50/50: one office is transparent, see-through. Post-millennial it's all-business glass, décored up to say up-front!

Bloody up-front! Bloody fucking up-front! The animal within believes, 'This is mine because I protect it.' He is of the Get Real school – he requires your ass or at least a severe touch of bank roll for preserving it.

She pauses and sees Morty 'Big' Kinsella in action inside.

Watching him puff his huge cigar as he simultaneously flexes his finger muscles on the microsciser and bellows into the squwark while welcoming a client with hand-gestures.

Cress pauses to observe the enormous bulk of the pig-faced tyro. In that instant, she speculates the scenario.

'So who's hangin' with who? (Motions siddown.) Are they tight? TEHRAN BOYS? Woa. Hey! Troy? Troy Donahue! Huh – so tell me about it – look I know dat muthafucka from way back when. Guy usta make me slammers in da Wah Wah Bar. Listen, I know fuckin' everythin' about that cocksucker. Heez edited porno vids mit three machines, two slaves. Heez copping attitudes an' pulling strokes. Heez a plastic-money arts grad, what a joke. Ya tryin' ta make me laff, uh? I wanted humour I'd check the Comedy Store 'scume that'sa hot-line: hi how are ya princess now about that publishing . . . OK, OK, you know we'll lunch it anyways. (Slams down receiver.) Heya Scroop haba Habana whydontcha? . . . (huff puff smoke signals) . . . youse gotta prob, Scroop, bit of a worry. Lemme tell ya I just bin talkin' to . . .'

But Cressida walks the other way, to the other office. She knocks. She pushes the door open. At the far end of the room, Bleeker, silver-framed half-moon specs in hand, is completing a conversation with some unknown party. As she enters the room, she again absorbs the details of Bleeker's statement-makers. Even though it's full of heavy furniture the room seems light, airy. Contrast Morty 'Big' K.: land a dust bunny on his runway Fun-C-Tion glass desk and he'd go claustro with the tension.

Bleeker.

Mr Bleeker, the firm's only senior partner who concentrates on law rather than city politics, has the sort of grey hair that's usually described as distinguished. He's the father everyone wanted to have: his expression says tough-but-fair, his movements signal fire in his heart, his speech an ice-cool mind that'll never need a calculator to know where the chips come down.

His room is mahogany panelled, carriage clocks, antique tea-chest converted to a table discreetly showcasing the most exclusive up-scale gizmology, the old globe in the corner, the mantelpiece crowded with invites that say IN CHAMBERS. It all whispers the same message: reassurance, tradition, *gravitas*, respect. Power. Leave it to us. God bless. In one corner the Louis XXI drinks-cab jokily festooned with postcards from up-country, Torquemada and other glamour coastal destinations: in the other the totally empty partner's desk that once belonged to A Founder. The space – big, the emptiness – wow. Just one small paper pile discreetly on a mirror-polished corner table tagged with action notes. Power!

Money! Success! Now! Every time she enters this inner sanctum, she still feels like a fraudster on a small-time game show. Twinges of intimidation tweak the pit of her stomach as it sinks to the souls of her shoes.

And he sits down at the empty desk and removes his glasses. Their silver frames rest on its pale-blue leather surface. Bleeker swivels in the chair he sits on, which is old and wooden. He looks distractedly out of the window for a moment or two, beyond the quills in the antique poison-pen glass inkwell that stands on the windowsill, out into the scantily clad city where a million litigants lurk, perpetrating all variety of interesting and potentially most profitable torts and actionable behaviour on one another. Bleeker reaches for his glasses and replaces them on the bridge of his nose, takes them off again and sticks one end in his mouth . . .

What is this with the specs, Cressida muses. What gives, old sport?

. . . leans forward, and then (power is making people wait: all's late in love and war) and only then does he begin to speak.

And what he's doing is congratulating her on her finely judged defence of that cut-up-rough contract compliance case on Friday. Does he know how pompous he sounds, like an incontinent judge slumming up, or is it all a slick and mannered ploy? A tangential rad *obiter dictum* breaks sudden spring turf.

'They put their cock on the table, Cress.'

Pause.

How to react? Lower eyes. A short, barely perceptible intake of breath. Glance back up from beneath tressed fringe. Suggest pout. Hold his gaze.

'And you chopped it off.'

Maintain, maintain, she tells herself until the moment – in time, at the right time, now – when she backs off the stare to eye flick flack around back around the room – bookshelves, leather tomes, ancient wing-backed armchairs, a table stacked with a neatly discreet pile of *Advocate and Attorney* (the corner of the one on top has the headline LEASEHOLDERS AND PERPETUITIES IN OUTER SPACE) – and tries to act as if this happened every day.

Smile.

She smiles.

One of the boys – a real cock-chopper. Demure lash flutter. She knows she could pole-axe him into signing up right now for Cyrogenics, but deems it smarter to play dumb. Not because she is a sycophantic creep or cissy bimbo-burlesque careerist – perish the thought – but simply because (Cressida DC reassures herself rapido) she feels a tad sorry for this sad old man. He says he wants to take her out to lunch later in the month to discuss her long-term career structure. In this context she recognizes a command to attend.

Merde.

She slips back into her fun but functional office, and tells her short-haired big-bustin' secretary, Sally, to firm the appointment. They smile complicitly – both know this means talking to Marion, the outrageously obnoxious old harridan who's worked for Mr Bleeker longer than anyone in this fascism-of-youth outfit cares to admit they can recall. Yah, boo and muck; the toilet-duck-breathed battlesack retires next month.

'Count the minutes,' Sally says when she puts the navy-blue squwarkbox extension down on her and pencils it in Cressie's big red leather-bound diary.

In that journal is a map of nation-by-nation international human rights violations. The map has a tiny vertical signature in the bottom right-hand corner. It is smaller than three point – minuscule. The signature belongs to one Kelly R. Guervitz.

Sally, pert, alert, short-haired and down in brown, was verifying this with a magnifying glass when Cressida returned, later, from her post-power-breakfast meet with an influential investment banker. He wants to headhunt her for a position on the coast – as well as whisk her away (he hinted in the sliver of post-prandial sexual skirmishing) to the v. verdant ultra private isle his father owns transpacific.

'Water-skiing, wind-surfing, coral, power-boats and clear water that never drops below 78 degrees. What do you say?'

She looks at him. Surely he's not serious? It's a wind-up, isn't it?

'There're even security guards, like a private police force,' Bank Boy says. 'They're all telepaths. My father trains them in karate.'

Cressie throws back her head and laughs.

She shall not go. She has a reason for not going.

'Oh, it's personal.'

Can't argue with personal, can never question that. She'd like to go but nods no.

'Why not?' presses her companion.

'Personal reasons,' repeats Cressida D. Drane and smils capriciously.

But now she's back back back and Sal gives her boss a list of in-coming calls calls calls that she's monitored on her behalf. Cressida scans fax, e-mail, telex in-bound and significant post: two items are marked 'Personal'. One is in a pink envelope. It's embossed with blue initials: NCKG. She feels disinclined to open it at that moment and puts it in her bag for later – pleasure deferred, as her octogenarian tutor had told her just after revealing that he'd spent the war playing the piano in a Soviet brothel, is pleasure compounded.

But there is also an invitation, It is printed on manuscript scroll.

'Sisters,' it says, 'the time has finally come for Maxine to leave our order. You are invited to her valetudinary party. Habits will be worn, relics venerated, wine drunk and bread broken. There will be an organ recital. New and old members are welcome.'

Whip-pan: let's active that.

Cressida arrives at the anointed hour outside the solid brick terraced house laid back on Brahmin Hill. She looks down the long, deciduous tree-line that delineates the avenue over the hill and far away. Onto the horizon deep into the heart of Belleville.

She locks the car door, and stares up at the tiny window of the attic flat atop No. 55. It's early evening: the light's unique to the city in August – a wan brown, almost translucently liquid.

The door opens to reveal the most elegant nun on seven continents.

'Watercress!' whispers Maxy delightedly at the top of her lungs.

On the table in the hallway: a candle illuminating photographs of old boyfriends. On the T V in the bedroom: a hardcore porno-vid. In Cressida's pocket: an unopened letter.

The girls have dinner. With the plates from the last course (banana, bisected apple, fresh cream: picture the subtly arranged placement of the fruits) still on the table, they smoke the grass Katy had dropped off – before leaving to pursue her relentless delivery schedule – and play after-dinner games: Botticelli, Ultimate Sexual Trivia, Diseases.

Stories unravel. Long, strong, all-night-long fables. Here facts are no longer sacred: never mind those stupid facts, feel the myth.

The time Knocker had fallen asleep when Maxy was giving him a blow-job in the back of a car and she was so drunk she threw up all over him. The time Charlie Burroughs, Laverda's brother boy, had bunked up with Maxine when they'd gone skiing at her parents' villa on the coast. Charlie had drunk soooooo much that he'd crawled outside and chucked his cookies. In the morning Maxine's mama, a large-boned, grey-haired woman with big blue eyes, who dressed in go-faster stripes and other apparel unsuitable for advancing years, called her daughter into the kitchen. In her hand she grasped a lump chunk of discoloured ice.

'Darling,' she'd asked, 'why did you leave this frozen pizza outside last night?'

Nick's shirt: Maxine had bought Nick a Sir Um Rocaz silk chemmy from some debt-bomb boutique on Bernini. It was striking, expensive, rakish – a fine shirt. On its red background were pictures of American eagles and European emperors in shades of yellow and hues of blue.

Nick wore it for the first time three days later to a studio party which had been appalling because – there were no women there! All men! Pillow biters and freckle punchers! All fags! (His project subsequently encountered inexplicable operational difficulties and actually dropped right off the roster for four cuticle-crunching months.)

The next day Nick washed the shirt, pulled same from wash-mach and blanched. The colours had run. Silk suicide.

At the dry-cleaners down the road he'd asked the old crone behind the counter if anything could be done.

'Typical,' he muttered as he examined the schmatta. 'Expensive threads ruined because you went cheap on the cleaning.'

'It wasn't like that,' Nick protested. 'I was just terribly excited about getting the shirt and, well, didn't realize it had to be dry-cleaned.'

Eventually they did a deal. The old man with grey wispy hairs agreed to write Nick a receipt that said, 'Garment damaged – faulty manufacture.'

He drove back to the boutique and showed both shirt and note to the assistant who'd sold it to Maxy, unknown to him, at an under-the-table discount.

'Huh,' he said. 'This is what comes of using a nickel-and-dime dry-cleaner.'

'I didn't,' protested Nick.

'Please,' the guy said, all biz. 'There's no charge on the receipt.'

'That's because they didn't charge me,' Nick riposted indignantly. 'My lawyers would've killed them if they'd tried to make me pay for trashing it. It's my favourite shirt and I've worn it only once.'

The assistant, early 30s with a meticulously trimmed brown beard, rubbed the material between his fingers and looked at Nick for a sec longer than was comfortable.

'Are you sure you didn't wash it?' he asked, his blue eyes suspicious.

'Wash it?' Nick looked horrified. 'No way.'

'I don't know about this,' the assistant said, inspecting it again carefully. 'Hold on a minute, will you?'

He returned eventually, accompanied by a blonde wasp girl who introduced herself as the manager.

Negotiations ensued.

'If this shirt is faulty we've got to send the whole lot back,' she finally thought out loud, weary in her concession.

'But we've sold three,' her sidekick protested. 'No one else has complained.'

'I think we'd better get them out and check them anyway.'

'Look, there's no need to do that, honestly. It's probably just this one.'

'No, no, I rilly appreciate you pointing it out to us. Phil, dig 'em out of the stock room and pack 'em all back up for the Tuesday run,' she replied imperiously. 'Phil'll give you a credit note,' she added and swept away to some invisible sanctuary of boutiquedom.

'Look, I don't want a credit note,' Nick said. 'There's nothing else I want to buy. I just want another shirt.'

He'd got it.

Cressida knew because she'd seen him wear it. Last week. He'd put it on after they'd made love.

'So he said, "Give me a blow-job, then".'

'What did you do?' Emma screams.

'I sort of grabbed it,' Miranda screeches back, 'and blew over it.'

'Excuse me,' says Cressida as she rises from the table.

20 minutes later Miranda's banging on the door. 'Cressie, Cressie.' Bang bang bang bang. 'Cressie? Are you OK in there?'

'I'm fine, fine,' Cressie manages to mumble.

'Well bloody well hurry up, then – I want to pee.'

'I'll be out in a minute, OK?'

'Oh Lawd,' Miranda moans from outside in mock-cockney.

Cressida returns to the mirror.

She has to hit this last one – has to. She can sense the sebum pump beneath the skin, feel its negativity, its ability to block, its grunge-power clogging everything. It will be disastrous, she knows, if she doesn't take it out. The spot'll erupt like a small mountain on her face, will daily accelerate in its disfigurement, the blemish silently accusing her, pressing against her flesh, and she'll guiltily feed it more of what it needs to survive and thrive and the mini-mottle will embolden as it distends, gradually asserting its secret identity upon her own – like a child, it will behave badly to get attention, demand to be fed more regularly, to be included in conversations; it'll require a seat at the opera, at the United Nations – it has to go, has to.

She squeezes – a pinch-grip that uses the hard flesh of each middle finger. But both skedaddle ineffectually over the target zone: the monstrous unrelenting lump nestling beneath her pale, tensile flesh.

Not good enough, she tells herself.

She is a benign but cruel dictator – the scarlet pimple a criminal, a scuzzy low-life dissident a terrorist pinned dow by her ruthlss military machine in the last no-go area on the chequer-board of her nation face.

So, employing her thumbs, she pulls the skin right back until it tautens unbearably tightly. Drum skin. It has to work, it has to, she thinks. At the moment she adjudges it to be at the epiphany of stretch, she push-piles the pressure full-on back into the tiny hillock that pulses submerged below the flesh.

I've got to get the poison out, she chants desperately to herself in silent desperation. I've got to get the poison out.

She has it now and squeezes hard, pushing furiously with all her might, willing the concentration of her energies into the small red patch of skin one last time.

Zit Zen.

Zit Zen 4 Citizens.

Pop!

Satori.

Hit the mirror!

For a moment, she stands stock-still in total tranquillity, marvelling at its speed and trajectory, and her ability to nurture and control such natural pressure without having to visit a gynaecologist.

But here comes pay-back time. She dabs at the straggly spurt of white grease and staunches a red speck that instantly becomes a bubbling torrent, gushing like a geyser as it transforms itself into a flashflood of blood.

Quickly, she snatches more Kleenex from the box on Jane's grey marble mirrorsill, and covers the offending blemish. She looks in horror as a fresh surge of red burbles up through the paper, recalcitrantly refusing to clot.

'Cressida,' nags Miranda from the other side of the door.

'What are you doing up there?'

'Won't be a mo,' she replies, and flecks a swab of Zit Zapper No 4 from her handbag over the battered red battlefield below her broad nostril.

'Oh, come on, I'm desperate,' Miranda whines.

'Shut up, Mira – I'm hurrying as fast as I can.'

She concentrates the Zit Zapper on her facial gulag, layering it like cream on a pavlova.

Why oh why does she torture herself this way? Is the self-mutilation a punishment her conscience imposes as the price of sluttishness? After all, she's the only person at the table – probably anywhere on the planet, come to that – who can truthfully say she's slept with both parties in the up-coming nuptials. She swiftly dusts her face with a final thick coating of powder.

Do they know?

Of course not.

Of course no one knows. They couldn't, could they?

She picks up Nick's letter (which she had left at rest next to the Antiseptic Minti-Fresh Deep Cavity Cleanser by the basin) and stuffs it in her pocket. She scrutinizes herself and grimaces. The thin blonde hair, the heavy make-up. The big blue eyes, the picture-perfect pouty red lips. The lurid romantic, old Charleston demi-diaphanous dress, overlaid with relucent black-bottom decals, formerly the property of some fly flapper girl. Actually her great-aunt. Who'd willed it to her when she was a tiny ankle-snap toddler.

Hell, she'd do.

'Cressida, please, I'm BUSTING,' Miranda pleads.

Cressida opens the door.

'Sorry about that.' She smiles. 'You know what my periods are like.'

When she returns to the table, everyone's playing the Truth

Game. Charlotte is describing the deadly details of virginity. Maxine tells of the time she discovered Nick *in flagrante* with a duck.

'We ate it for lunch the next day!' Maxine says. The staccato laughter separates – and stops.

Mira says, 'Cressie, come on – your turn.'

She feels heady, slightly drunk.

Conversational fragments from last week's Nick knock-off revolve in an inane brabbling babble of taunt and tears.

He'd rubbed her back.

'Tell me again,' she'd said. 'Tell me how clever I am. Mmmmmmmnn – that's good, just there, yeah. Oh. Tell me I'm smarter than they are. Say the bit oooh yeah, mmm about how they'll, mmmmnn, about how they'll all look when I pull it off. Tell me, Nick, tell me again.'

She can't. She can't do it. Fortunately, there's no shortage of amusing anecdotes that can serve instead.

'When I was 16 I met a man in Louis's Patisserie who owned a big house in St Cloud. Really enormous, a mansion – he was a tycoon: a grouchy old Turk with crackly skin and knobbly knuckles. He invited me and my friend Rep to come and visit him. One Sunday afternoon we had nothing better to do, so we went.'

She embellishes key details extravagantly – Rep wasn't there to contradict her – but the story she tells is basically true: after a ritualistic preamblette, the pervy nabob told the girls he'd pay them 50 notes each if they'd remove every stitch of their clothing and tell him, in considerable detail, of their sexual fantasies.

'So we did,' Cressida concludes.

'Wow,' whispers Miranda. 'What happened to your friend?'

'She died in a car crash three years ago,' Cressida D. Crane lies fluently, with a loud, brittle laugh. Why had she lied? To protect Rep? Why had she told the story in the first place? She doesn't know, she cannot think.

'What happened to the man?' Lotti wants to know.

'He's like the left-handed hitch-hiker: he's all right.'

'What do you mean? He's all right?' Maxy asks, toying suggestively with a banana slice.

'Nothing. He's OK.'

There's a pause.

Cressida studies the group.

Maxine, like herself, assumed blonde – but her blue eyes were clear (Cress's own were clouded from ciggie-smoking and miscellaneous life-abusage), and her fine bone structure was like a china-doll's song-bird save its enormous cavern of dangerously sensuous mouth. Lotti, plump white skin, fine dark hair, pug-nosed with anxiously neurotic broody brown eyes, had never been the same since she returned from China. Miranda, coltishly rumbustious, her plainness foiled by her happy, freckled smile and high-spirited vivacity. Until recently she'd worn an eye-patch to disguise a dreadful attack of shingles. Emma: buxom, ginger, asthmatic, giggly, deep as a fortune cookie. Jenny with her hair in a bob, her intense face and its sad little mouth, her perfect make-up, her practised pose to hide the artificial latex arm beneath the table. Zarah: tall, big-boned, practical, horse-faced and spoiled rotten.

She had told no one of this before.

They're all looking at her.

'I saw him last Sunday – he's fine.'

She wasn't quite clear why she was telling them now. Intuition?

'I don't believe it.' The disapproval bristles through Zarah's flat disbelief.

Cressida savours the shock waves. She realizes she's enjoying it.

'Of course things have moved on a bit since then. I mean, these days I've got him up to 200 bucks, but I have to do it with this enormous black dildo and pretend to get off while I'm telling him the stories. It's a real sweat coming up with fresh stuff every week, believe me.'

Miranda stares at her, open-mouthed. Jenny looks at her disingenuously, her face masking whatever cold emotion she feels. Zarah clearly does not approve – she squirms with embarrassment, shifting on her chair, unsure where to look – here? There? Cressida realizes, at that moment, that she doesn't like Zarah and never has. In some strange way, this comforts her. Maxine smiles appreciatively. Emma bursts into a giggling jag that quickly leaves her wheezing.

'So if any of you've any suggestions – answers on a postcard, please.'

There's a long silence, punctuated only by Emma's gasping fumbles within her big brown bag for her blue and white inhaler. Mira gives a low whistle. 'Wow,' she adds when she's sure it's registered.

Yes, thinks Cressida. It's the Last Supper. Wine into vinegar. If Leonardo da Vinci was alive today, he'd be drawing posters for Daz. And I'm hip to that.

Hip to what? Hip to the word. The word is wisdom. And the received wisdom is Cressida's intuitively hidden agenda, the subtext of which is – we hate yuppies. The perceived attitude: the dignificant citizenry who rank some kinda cultural kudos in this metropolis are

boho art music counter-cult junkies;

dreadrock hairdressers with hot gloss-up, cool party stiffs, unlimited chill pills;

gang-banger whores who can shake down funkytown when they feel they're kicking too close to the edge as they tread on the egg shells the pimp sells;

close-cropped hard-way wiseguys who surf;

lonely concrete tramps seeking new-found Rolls

and schizoid beat-free rhyme me me me poets whose state of the art is fresh from the heart because it's this *problème de coeur* can you dig it can you dig it's a love affair with life.

She can see the faces of her friends around the dinner table who, emboldened by her disclosure, have begun to discuss a visit to Mr Rabbit, a boybar down-town.

By the time they are 30, or before – could it be so fortuitously arranged – they will all marry a lootworthy investment banker or an aristoprat with lots of old cold lolly. They'll do pretty much what they do now:

work as a joytoy in the city,

a P A to a commercials director,

an esoterica expert in an auction house,

a go-get bimbette in a polysyllabic ad shop,

a dotty jeweller constantly re-casting pieces with Persian princess over interminable cups of tea.

For a few years they'll live that life, two-income groovy, buy a house in the country.

Then?

Baby-time.

Meanwhile the guy gets promoted, inherits, whatever. They've got their kids, they've got their house, they've got their teeth, they've got their cars, they've got their dogs, they've got affairs, they've got their cash. They've got pet names and their hands in each other's jeans pockets and, of course, they've kept up all those fascinating and funny contacts from when they were both young, single and photogenic. And that's their life, it's a comfortable life, it's a wonderful life and life goes on.

Yus.

And on and on and on and on and on and on and on and on.

Like a motorway.

And one day something snaps. Cut the crap. Bring it back.

Same girl, same flat, next day.

Morning.

Cressida drags her wrinkled underwear out of crumpled sheets in a cold sweat. The radiostatic's interrupted her instantly blanked-frightmare: she was trapped in a tower with a pale dreadlocked man. He was a prophet and he spoke of the moon. The image and the fear dissolve in Mr Deejay's blah blah blah before the break to a commercial for low low low unrepeatably low once in a life-time bargain shopportunity give-away on u-build polyester furniture corner dining units Scandinavian Viking style natural pinewood-look bedroom suites and more more more all available at zero point credit 'ats right nothing to pay for three months at a swampside warehouse just 90 minutes down the Western Highway this Sunday this Sunday only. And then cha cha cha cha more papped muzak interrupted by synthetic-fun anti-black gaybash glee-coated hoax jokes.

Cressida looks at the grey sky outside – an Islamic Airlines 797 cruises criminally low and shakes every shonk-built prestressed split rivet in the concrete block as it scrapes over the building, dropping its rollerskates with a cacophonous screech that sends her bleary bod reflexively grabbing for a fag to kick-start her lungs. She coughs and lurches for the kitchen. Cressida pauses to wipe her face on the back of her grunged-out dressing-gown and cops an instant earful from behind a door, half open on what could be Hiroshima 1945, some kind of indoor demolition-derby or skip surprise blown in overnight by bad building fairies. But it's none of these things. It is her sister's bedroom. And the noise is ripening, and rising, instantly recognizable as the orgasmic operetta her sibling shrieks in moments of grinding passion. Cressida squints through the crack – the bitch bonks the boy with the split-level hair-cut and for God's sakes the arsehole's left his dirty Doc Martens in the fridge and there's mud in the milk and Cressida screams,

'Turn that fucking record down.' It doesn't help. It makes it worse, her morning-after comes on radical now, a really bogue lobe-pincher, a humorous meta-paralyser, and Cressida DC starts to cough again and just for a moment everything's constricted, her eyes screw up in pain and she could swear she's going to die.

But she makes it into the bathroom to throw up, except it's only a hideous dry heave. She stares at her face through the crap on the mirror, stares at the discoloured stain inside the glass, that grows minutely larger every day; and looks again at the bloodshot eyes and the straggled tresses and the pale blotches of puffy skin and the yuck-barftermath of dead spot and thinks, shit – I look horrible, really fucking horrible.

She looks so old, she can't believe it.

The time-check before the news galvanizes her: there's one pip too many. She's gripped by a febrile sensation of damp ineluctability: she's gonna be late, very bloody late indeed.

So she forces herself back into the kitchen and turns the TV right up to drown out the squeals and screams from next door and hurriedly pours warmish water into the Marilyn Monroe coffee mug and feels ratshit, kakky as a four-dimensional oil painting from hell.

Back in the bathroom she flings make-up on her face from the pile near the cracked sink but the scab on the zit still shows, she knows, and she can't even think about a tit-check because they're depressing: too small, leadenly gravity-bound. If St Marilyn had had tits like that, she would never have left home. Aggravated domophobia: double-binding the victim in slow limbo; can't stay in, can't go out.

'It looked like a kind of monster, it had a mane like a lion, its feet were scaly and it had wings. I'm sure it had wings . . .'

The alien AIDS-IX scare. Far-out.

The grubby brown linen suit still has the tear at the back and the flat shoes still have run-down heels and she couldn't care less as she slams the door.

Then she makes a mistake.

She stops moving. You know the rules, she knows the rules: KEEP MOVING – NO LIMITS.

Too late.

Stops to wonder whether to go back and put some tights on. And in that second next-door opens and – that awesome smell of piss hits her full in the face. It makes Cressida reel every time, it's an even worse environmental hazard than the flight-path or the psychopaths, those sickos upstairs who play the same scratched Thrash Sabbath album-side night after night till 3.30 a.m., and on top of the tights trauma and morning-after brainblast, it's just much too much, threemuch altogether. But Mrs Ezeikial, her incontinent neighbour, insists on spitting a babble-curse of angry hisses and cackling venom her way. Cressida backs off, she can't cope with this, not now, she knows she owes her money but she has none. She spent it all last night, after she and Maxine and Mira had gone to meet Katy and Fillet at the boybar.

The solitary functional memory from that night was a supersite on a lonely Mantran platform. Had it been at Brandenburg? Byron?

Or – no matter. What it said was: CANDOUR THINKS IT'S TIME TO TELL THE TRUTH.

The poster showed a grainy graphfreak of someone who might've been a barmy derro or a hi-style mannequin, a ginormousity of steal-this-face, sharp-shadow of chiaroscuro. And underneath in minuscule print simply that line. CANDOUR THINKS IT'S TIME TO TELL THE TRUTH. But no explanation for the woman's hungry animalistic eyes, nix that suggests what her lippy cross-patch o'gob is selling or telling you me and she not to do, nuthin', ace, nuthin'.

A tickler vote-me for the First Citizen? Or an opposition ambush? A magazine? Make-up? An anonymously donated ethics break?

Maybe her boss's office had paid to place it there.

Only she no' thin' bout that.

LEARN ANOTHER LANGUAGE OVERNIGHT
WITH AN INFORMATION IMPLANT
EVERYBODY'S SCRATCHING SCRATCHING
SCRATCHING –
17 FLAVOURS, TWO TASTES –
WELCOME TO THE DREAM ROOM
KEEP TELECITI PRETTY – DESIGN AGAINST
CRIME
NOW ANYHOW* . . .

Appraising it now in slow-time as she fumbles with the car keys, it strikes that she's beginning to bring personal meaning to the bloody subway ads. Media details chatter round her head, along loud, little life paths of their very own.

Goddamn key.

She wonders if she is becoming an emotionally disturbed person – an inappropriately traumatized humanoid dead-set cert for Attitude Adjustment – or, if others felt the way she did?

But she had no one that she could ask.

Just herself.

'Oh for God's sake.' She looks at the key, slides it back into the door and forces it open.

Sitting inside the car, she cues the ignition, remembering how last night she'd reached out for the vitamin-C shirt that'd flung itself over by the bedside light. And chewed on it.

But no sooner had she torn into the munchsome, blandly flavoured, fizzy synthetically mandarin impregnated cottonish fabric than she heard the ricochet of answerback: IT'S VERY CATCHING CATCHING CATCHING.

Outside the grey sky's turned to drizzle. Now the damn junk-machine won't start. As she grows more frantic, the car, which she suspects is inhabited by some malicious sprite who's been awaiting just such a day as this to work its mechanical malevolence, becomes increasingly recalcitrant and trixsy: a dashboard light flashes at her, warning of techno-error, and then another. She slams the door, leaves it and waits 17 drippy wet minutes before eventually flagging a taxi that isn't water-soluble.

Inside there's a THANK YOU FOR NOT SMOKING sticker and more. All messages. Metro-data: input for the city's half-life.

The driver jams up, stuck bumper-to-bumper on Van Damn Drive. Oh Gawd, she'd tried to tell him about the feeder but he'd said, 'Hey bitch, I'm the fuckin' pilot here, OK?' Cressida interrupts his crass cross-chat as he attempts to pick up a passing pedestrian ('Hey, come on, baby, tell me – you're with Models One, right?') to ask the time. 10.50. *10.50?* She wills the jam to break, she curses the driver, blames her car, herself, her mother, Nick – and then realizes yaaaaah, jolt-shock – she has no money to pay the fare.

At 11.35 she finally arrives at work. A drenched, exhausted hellhag with a hole in her shoe, she collapses in her chair. Sally is suddenly very busy on the telephone. Zero eye-contact. Cressida D. Crane looks at the scrawly mass of illegible messages. Her own line begins to ring. It's Excess. An auto-voice tells her she is over-limit and her card has moved into status of doubt. As the preprogged Cassandra-loop drones dire-doom wails *re* incremental penalties incurred for financial sin that accumulate, yea, even as she speaks and snarls the precise finality of payment instructions, a familiar face presents itself.

'Mr Habgood wants to see you,' sneers Marion. Her primly filled fatpig features betray a smug smile of the petty satisfaction to be gained by putting the hob-nailed bossyboot in. 'Now.'

Cressida D C peers down the abyss – an edge – of urban frenzy. She riffles through the mail pile mechanically, her hands shaking. Hang on. Here is one interesting piece. It is in a brown re-used manila envelope marked 'Personal'. She opens it with the standard office-issue paper knife, its serrated edges rounded out from hours of tedious usage.

Ri-iiiip.

Inside are two smaller envelopes. One is white. It contains 500 smackers in 50s. She knows what its twin holds and stuffs them both in her pockets because she now realizes the grief-motivator: she's left her handbag behind too.

'Sally,' she says. 'I think we'd better drop the conspiracy charge on that Fullford case.'

'Drop it?' says Sally, plainly surprised. The city port authority was the only prosecution work the firm handled.

'I was thinking about it last night . . .' Cressida begins, but a great wave of nausea overcomes her. She realizes she doesn't even have the energy to dissemble plausibly. 'Yeah, drop it,' she finishes lamely.

Cressida hurries down the narrow, dimly lit corridor with her crinkled plastic wrap in her hand. She nearly trips over the rip in the lino as she goes into the bog. She locks herself in the fluoro-lit cubicle to put on the tights she's shoplifted from the Paki shop next to the garage after poncing the cab fare from the security guard.

Now she enters Habgood's office.

Rain streams down the windowpane. She sees: stacks of legal papers; a cheap dust-rusted print-out calculator; buncha mould-culture-topped coffee cups Fat Marion won't move because, as a qualified paralegal, it's 'not her job'; scuzz-printed diplomas on the small walls to reassure any paying client foolish enough to inquire within that this office is indeed occupied by one Nigel Arthur Habgood, technically her boss, realistically a wussy thug with a valid licence; strewn piles of files documenting the details of others' misery; an obsolete digital clock stuck on 13.37; scruffy brown carpet tiles; two burgundy vinyl seating units from swampland pushed together to form an impromptu sofa. And Mr Hapgood, thin, worried, sideburned, twitchy inside the ill-fitting blue suit with its too-wide pin-stripes. He's a chancer; she knows it. But how much does he know about what she really does?

'Mr Bleeker wasn't entirely happy about the result on that Midlothian gas board case,' he mumbles, his lips quavering. He does not look at her directly: he sits behind his desk, shifty eyes flicking from paper to paper.

'What do you mean?' Cressida demands angrily. 'We won, didn't we?'

'Uh, yes,' Habgood pulls at the hairs in his ears, agitato. 'The client's, uh, complaining about shortfall – erum – some, ahem, monies that have disappeared.'

There is a short silence.

'I don't know what you're talking about.'

He looks at her for the first time during the interview.

'Huhhuhuhu,' he begins. 'Achoooo.'

He wipes his nose, coughs and starts raving incomprehensibly about time-per-hour charges, operational deductions, the pittance that the almost invisible Mr Bleeker kicks Cressida's way in lieu of a proper salary. She becomes conscious of strange messages – now he keeps looking at her equivocally, as if he's examining some piece of radioactive plankton from outer space.

My God, Cressida realizes suddenly. He's scared of me.

Enter Marion with a mouth full of boot polish – she asks the legal beagle if he wants some tea, pointedly ignoring Cressida D. Crane.

'Aware of the highly, ah, entrepreneurial *modus operandi* of certain of our clients,' Habgood continues to mumble at her, through a filthy snotrag, in his lugubrious voice. 'Degree of autonomy and individual responsibility obviously necessary in these, ah, ad hoc situations – but the possibility of a criminal client, that is, uh, a client using our services in a criminal action, ahem, ah such a client um, in the heat of the moment going to a huhuhuhuhuchoo, excuse me.'

His voice thickens by the moment. Rain belts on down outside and he blows his nose noisily. Then he opens the handkerchief and momentarily inspects its contents. The interview continues, 'Yes, erum, such a, ah, client going to the appropriate or even, herumph ahem, an inappropriate professional body and taking up a complaint could be, herumph, ah, extremely embarrassing for uh, all concerned.'

She looks down at her new tights. They have a hole in them. She feels monstrously cheated. She feels suddenly, it is imperative to obtain another pair immediately.

'Look, what gives?' she snaps.

Habgood pauses. Tweaks left ear as if he's about to produce a rabbit from within.

'I don't know how to say this,' Habgood says. He seems to have developed an extraordinary facial twitch. 'There's a rumour going around the office that uh, ahem, uh.'

Oh God, Cressida thinks. This is it. Habgood gets up, turns his back on her and looks out on the breaking yard outside like it is the Sistine Chapel.

If Michelangelo were alive today he'd be banged up as a vandal. Rembrandt would be moonlighting as a Dutch masseur so he could paint by numbers in the afternoon. Salvador Dali would be a hairdresser in a nightclub. Andy Warhol would ride a motorbike in a jacket that said SUICIDE DISPATCH. He blows his nose as if it's a couturier's clarion call, then turns round again to face her. He looks a man in desperate need of a truss.

'Rumour, going around the office that, uh, ahem.' He actually shuts his eyes. 'That you're not, em, really, uh uh uh uh not really, uuuuhh, uh a woman at all.' He looks at her now as if he's just had an enema. She is totally gob-thwacked.

'WHAAAAT?' Cressida DC rises to her feet and bears down on him. 'See these?' she cries, and tears open her white cotton blouse. 'You want to check them out? See if they're silicone? Or is it this? Is this what you want? You want some of this?'

Want some? Thirty days on, thirty nights away, a new day dawns.

'Back off – don't try it guy – I'm not kidding.'

She smiles at the man before her. She hopes she looks cool, in control.

'But you such beautiful girl . . .'

'Then put the money down.'

'Deborah – such a beautiful girl, such beautiful eyes,' he says and grabs at her. But Cressida's one step ahead and he's grasping air.

Frantically she looks around the chi-chi penthouse suite for hostages. She picks up the compact vid-disc player, snatches it – bits of wiring fall out of the back.

'No!'

She stands by the window in her diaphanous, filmy party frock, her make-up loud and harsh in the morning light.

'Give me the money.'

The player hovers perilously close to a 26-storey ride down pavement-side. The man looks at her evilly, his eyes hard.

'You . . . ptah,' he spits on the carpet.

'I have no other trouble with the agency girls. None. I take them out, I buy them dinner, present, casino, we do fucky-fuck, no trouble. You –' His dark eyes narrow as he counts the money out onto the table. She doesn't listen – she watches him count. For a moment there's a stand-off: she's going to have to put the player down to pick up the money – he might try it again.

She throws it at him. The unit hits him, THUNK, full on the chest. She snatches the cash and moves.

He shouts at her as she retreats down the corridor.

'Miss Deborah, Miss Deborah, come back – I take you home with me, marry you, make you very rich, very happy.'

She thinks of nothing until she reaches the hotel foyer. She catches the sidewinder glances of the staff as she swans through the glittery lobby, but she doesn't care, they can't touch her. Outside she hires a limo, tips the flunkey-joe doorman with a really appalling knowing wink born of sheer fatigue – and tells the driver to take her home.

She stretches her long legs in the back of the obscenely vroomy vehicle. Through the smoked-glass window she sees faces trudging along, some hopeful, some fearful, but most simply dimly resigned to their lot. Suckers, she thinks, and mechanically begins to tear a hole in the leg of her tights.

Back inside the apartment, Cressida picks up the lipstick and writes on the mirror with bold red strokes the single word: ME. She looks at her face for a moment: are the crows feet deepening around her eyes?

She sits on the toilet and cooks up her morning smoke. She finds it too bothersome to inject. She inhales and reads the letter for the hundredth time.

> Dear Cressida
> I am sitting down to write this letter with a heavy heart. As you know, Jane and I are soon to be married,

> and under the circumstances I feel it would be for the better if we no longer saw quite so much of each other . . .

Doors close, Cressida muses as her world comes back into a more palliative focus – but they rarely lock.

She drinks some camomile tea from her Marilyn Monroe coffee cup. If she's selected again in the line-up tonight, she'll have enough money to put down on the first instalment of her breast implants.

As her figure passes the glass, she sees an aeroplane sweep across the cloudless blue sky. In its wake it leaves a clear white vapour trail. She wonders about the people on the plane, what traumas, dramas, dreams and fantasies they nurture. She speculates on who they are, where they're going. Next week, she reflects, perhaps I'll be one of them. She examines the figure on the coffee cup and wonders if she too has been through this.

As she starts the car, she repeats the prayer she'd bought from the seer in the Church of the Mystic City Sign: 'Protect me as you protect all vulnerables who come to you seeking aid and assistance. Help me to discover the power in my weakness, the good in all the evil that we do. Help me hold back the ravages of age and decay from my body, my mind, my spirit. Liberate me from the shackles of visual crime and reflect the eternal vivacity of your anima that is beyond all price, all place, beyond all time. Now and forever more.'

As another jet roars overhead, Cressida Deborah Crane tumbles deep into a world without edges, where perfumed circus clouds billow in candyfloss citadels. She sees the shape of a face of a man who flies. She cannot distinguish any features, nor any colour in his face.

Yet how fervently she wishes he was with her.

Welcome to the Dream Room

VISUAL CRIME – SEEN IT? Doc Martens, air soles for air heads; bulletheads with try-me-I'm-well-'ard crew-cuts, trans-neck tattoos that say CUT HERE, GENE VINCENT RIP; drongo bumper stickers ('Messa with my car and I messa with your face') on cheap old chrome; the starched white doilies that witheringly prim fossilized neighbours serve their dry afternoon pastries on; the acrylic sunset as the smile goes down on the face of the far-too-fat sweating no-businessman in the pink suit and stupid gold chains who's dropped his wallet and has to touch his toes to pick it up; the wine-boxed derros in cardboard shoes and dirty stink rags dragging bags full of yesterday's papers and hard-luck stories in smeggy rovercoats from one end of some bitter-litter street to another and the trashrags inside the bags that blew up the car-crash picture to detail the kid's face drippin' black blood so bloody big that the headline doesn't fi

Cheap old chrome.

Let your eye roam in the chrome, catch a distant mirror image: that girl, five nine, blonde hair, long legs in fish-net stockings marred by a hole in one.

Guy: 'You've a hole in your fish-nets.'

Girl: 'Yeah. How observant.'

Guy: 'The one that got away, huh?'

Girl: 'Excuse me, I've just seen a friend of mine.'

How will she develop? Is that Debbie a negative girl, do you think? Terry Kinkaid would definitely have something to say about it. He'd ask questions like – does she watch television? What drugs does she do? What clothes does she wear? Can she speak Bimbo? Has she got it like that? Is she a fantasy person or a known fact?

What no one asks is how Cressie DC got to be this way. Because who gives a fuck? Negative girls always have boyfriends who aren't very positive about loving them.

Cressie has . . . other motives.

Visual crime? She lives it. It's not that she's a frumpbag, a gross-out fat chick occupying more than an entire another half human being's fair share of space, air, water and food. *Au contraire*. Cressie as in watercress and the short form of her second name – which she's taken to using these days as there are one or two people she isn't overly anxious to run into for a while – is bed spelled backwards. There's strings of guys who want to go there and do that, heels over head in deep lust with this chick. Yeah, she's got it like that. The way she dresses emphasizes what she's got to sell: these gam-glam pins in those fish-net tights with the hole separately placed in each and every individual pair, the pert little ass in the cute drop-dead crinny-bubble skirt, the perky bosoms with nipples like micro-rockets – even though none of this is on sale at all any more and that's reality. Still, C. Debbie Crane lives visual crime. Yet believes only she can see it.

The Interior Vandalism of The Soul.

She presses the entryphone button marked HUTTON. Nobody knew who Hutton was – she'd asked around. She'd speculated on the existence of Hutton. Was Hutton a real person? Did H. really own the place, or was s/he just another transient moving through Lonely Street? Was s/he dead or alive? Was Hutton some rank genetic engineer or a wealthy person's blond plaything? (Hutton was blond/e. Somehow, she felt pretty sure of that.) Where was s/he now? What would Hutton think if s/he knew what she did in their apartment? One time she'd asked Linda – but her friend was quiet for a beat, gave her what the pulpies describe as 'a meaningful look' and ostentatiously changed the subject. Debbie stopped asking after that. Recently (everything was recent, consensual, synchronistic, karma-colic since she'd finally split up with Nick), recently she'd had to come to terms with the fact that she found it easier and easy-peasey-Japaneseier not to ask too many questions. Once Cressida had gauged the intelligence of the motley migration of clients who'd tramped through her office by the number and quality of questions they'd ask. Recently, she'd taken to assessing Other People's stupidity and vulnerability by the same criterion.

As she locates the keys in her velvet purse, the one with the hand-painted butterfly that Arturo had bought for her just before he took off for the coast, the door buzzes open.

Which means Jean Paul is in. Since she'd really moved in on the place, he'd taken to staying out later at nights.

Sometimes he wouldn't return at all.

Two years ago, Jean Paul had helped her. She'd had no place to go and was getting there fast. He'd met her on the aircraft back from Skios – the only time she'd ever been abroad, the happiest time of her whole life – and put her up in his flat behind Electric Avenue. But two months ago the tables had turned – and now he was the one who was helpless. Increasingly, she worried about him.

It is dark as a womb in the hall – the shonky chandelier still hasn't been fixed. Perhaps it's Hutton who's responsible.

Visual crime: the deprivation of light.

As she reaches each of the three landings, she hits the brown deco time switches which protrude from the landings' walls in the darkness with deft familiarity.

At the top of the block, she unlocks the flat door with the other key, opens up and there, smack bang in front of the fetching expanse of the facing fuchsia wall, it is.

Unquestionably, you couldn't miss that bed – the very first thing you saw. Napland: in-scale and in place in front of your face. It was tiny. A runt-bed. She was five foot nine, whippet thin and hyperactive; whenever sleep finally had her on its knock-down tenterhooks, she could always wobble into a bit of a crash-landing.

In sleep she'd fly through dreams of paparazzi obsessed with the lines that had written a book across faces that hadn't got too rich but were rapidly becoming too thin, on-the-beam dreams of blurred features and circuses, telephoto dreams of aviators and diplomacy. But when she awoke, it felt as if the city was closing in on her.

Jean Paul pulls himself up from underneath the blue-black and red patterned wool blanket and rubs his eyes. He wears a black and white acrylan sweater with stripes that run the wrong way across the thin, chalk-white pallor that covers his scraggybag o' bones.

'How are you feeling?'

'OK.'

He runs his thin fingers through fine messy blond hair.

She sits on the edge of the bed. Television's on. She looks at him – maybe the horizontal stripes were right. She constantly schemed protective strategies to shield his shrine of pure pain. She defended him against outsiders who said he was hopeless, lame, parasitical, a loser. He looks so thin, soooooo emaciated. Poor poor Jean Paul.

'Anyone call?'

'Yeah,' he says. 'Dan.'

'What did he want?'

'Nothing. He just said he might be coming up.'

'When?'

'I dunno. Maybe this evening.'

'Didn't he say?'

'Nah.'

Dan owes her money. She owes Linda money. Sometimes she understood why romantic protagonists inexplicably leaped into dark doorways, suspect stairwells ('don't go in there Frank, it'll kill you') and passing sedan chairs whenever a convenient opportunity presented itself. They were evading their creditors. She could sympathize. But sympathy didn't cancel out Dan's debt – 700 bucks. He'd owed her a thou for three months, but two weeks ago she'd obtained, not without a little difficulty, a first instalment payback of 300 goldies. He kept telling her he'd take care of it. But he was negligent.

And she could use the wedge – she really needs it.

She puts her head in her thriftily gloved hands, and lets her bare arms repose on her knees so she can't see the hole in her net. And she stares at the stainless steel sink and the gas burner near by (the doing of blond/e Hutton?) very near by, stare stare stare stare underneath the window maybe 10 feet away. Yes – the sink's clean, she's checkered it out, deodorized the dust bunnies to death, purged the stains so the sink is stainless.

'Where are my papers?'

He leans out of the bed slowly, reaches across the floor, hands them to her.

'Anyone else call?' she asks, as she begins construction of her three-skin T-joint.

'Nah.'

'Arturo?'

'Nah.'

'Linda?'

'Nah.' Jean Paul scratches his right forearm with his left hand and stares disinterestedly at the TV.

'What is this?'

'Golf, I think,' he replies. 'Gotta cigarette?'

She gives him one. Two left in the flip-top box. It's the Now brand. There are billboards and supersites all around the city that feature this brickie in an asbestos jump suit offering the viewer a lux-length snout from his larger than life soft 'crush-proof' ciggie pack.

And all it says is 'NOW, ANYHOW* . . .'

. . . like a stoker on a square-rigged triple-decker man o' war at battle stations, loading up a dark gun-metal cannon for the show-down, she ramrods the tobacco down into what would become the spliff's flame-on end.

'John came round.'

'What did he want?'

Her speech is clipped, precise, and fast. It's as pointed as the four-inch black winkle-picker stilettos that help her look down on city life.

'He wanted to see if Lisa was here.'

'Lisa?' She lights up. 'That girl is poison.'

She offers him a smoke. He declines politely.

'Poison.'

'Why d'ya say that?'

'I know,' CDC asserts.

She has feelings about things. She trusts her intuition. It springs from her inner sanctity, the moon, her period, somewhere out there something very clear that is still part of who she is.

On the TV screen a golfer arches his ball high into the air and puts his hand over his eyes to watch its progress. The camera follows its trajectory across the sky. All the tiny screen shows is grey fuzz.

'What did he say?'

'Who?'

'Danny,' she says, cross, now emphatically cross-patch.

'Oh, nothing.'

'Where was he calling from?'

'Uh, I don't know. I think he said he was on the train.'

'He can't have been phoning from the train.'

'Yeah, yeah, I think so.'

Jean Paul scratches his right arm with his left hand and sniffs listlessly.

'They've got phones on the trains these days, you know.'

She puffs the weed.

It assists, she believes, her cerebral clarity – and that clarity is so important because more and more of the time she feels positively exasperated by the Islamic maze that has developed within her life.

12 weeks ago she'd had her flat in Realito; Arturo, her new man; and her new 'modelling' job with the agency. Now she's lost them all and, she sometimes muses in moments of desperate despondency, her way in life.

So she keeps busy. Has to. These days C. Debbie Crane seems to have so much to do. Find a new flat, shift more Spectre, look after Jean Paul, listen to Linda, run around after all the flea-bitten ratbags who owe her money and hit hot pursuit from the flint-skinned bastards ready to ambush her with hassle flack about the stupid dosh she supposedly owes them. So much of her activities benefit other people, support them – people like Jean Paul, Arturo, Dan – they all rely on her, depend on her. They're her friends and they're in trouble.

Trouble.

It's everywhere. Even when you weren't hauling someone else out of trouble, you were probably piling up a future tranche of aggravation because the world was a maze and there were mad things marauding within it, wild spirits that had no place to rest.

Like the avarice of the people Arturo had hit seriously ugly-time with, double-trouble because he owed them money and now, unjustly but (she reluctantly conceded) understandably, they expect her to repay the debts.

All the fun has evaporated from her life: it has become uglier – a dreary drudge relieved only by awful lurching sensations of imminent encroaching danger. Sometimes, when Jean Paul is out, she sits and cries for what seems like hours on end.

The only satisfaction she has from life is derived from her Marilyn memorabilia and her library, a collection of paper-covered novels. Nothing after 1920. She keeps them in cardboard boxes piled on top of each other in the bathroom. Every day she spends at least an hour taking books out, checking that they have not become damp or soiled, patting them like small children before safely returning them to their lodgings. Catherine Earnshaw, Madame Bovary, Scarlett O'Hara, Emma, Becky Sharp: these are her true friends, her inspiration, her lovers, her life-line away from the dizzy edge of the cold black vortex that every day she feels whipping and whizzing and biting, penetrating with each passing hour deeper and deeper within the Islamic maze. If only, she thinks, my maze's walls were made from glass, I could see where this dark wind was and blow it away.

Her bleeper buzzes. She is a slave to the bleeper.

She presses its orange grooved READ-ME button and obediently the dot matrix flashes its message across the mini-display.

'See you in Court at midnight, Dan.'

She turns it off, rises from the bed and takes one pace. Directly in front of her now is the wardrobe. Inside: the trousseau of her life since Nick'd married and she'd split from Arturo: clothes for the negative girl. Clothes that are all black, that always look right for first nights and funerals, for nightclubs and nine to five, for any sort of naughtiness, nihilism and nightmare you'd care to name or maybe not, clothes that never show the dirt, that absorb burns and spillage like a vacuum cleaner in a black hole, clothes that always match into instant outfits, outfits that can dematerialize into a crowd so suddenly that their wearer would just, literally, disappear; dark fabric outfits of anti-atomic quasi-matter, few of which had been designed to live domiciled on these bent, cheap old chrome triangular hang-on thin-wires.

Immediately to the left of the wardrobe is another door, also painted pink. She picks it up and moves it aside, pushing it back into position behind her. The bathroom is a cerise colour, like the wall opposite the tiny window above the bed in the other room. There was a giant inflatable banana taking the air in the shower. Also five or six record covers and a coupla battered beer cans. The shower doesn't work.

Lovingly, she looks at the meticulously author-alphabeted labels on each of the seven large orange plastic crates stacked on the dismal yellow lino floor. How strange that one's life could be packed up in this awful way.

As she puts her make-up on and teases her long blonde tresses into some semblance of come-hither in the mirror with five light bulbs round its frame, she wonders why Dan wants to meet her at Court.

It's a newish afterhours club down a dark side-street at the snake end of the Strip. She'd asked Kinkaid who went there when she'd run into the granite-jawed scribbler at the old-fashioned ambisex lavs behind the VIP room of Rififi two nights ago.

He'd said he'd seen a cop he knew hang out there, undercover, and thought that soon they'd get up a full court press to shake down Knocker, who ran the place – how smash-landed are the once-fashionable.

'Hell, he should worry,' she'd said insouciantly. But now she realizes it was just another thing for *her* to worry about. She is becoming obsessed by security.

Wall-to-wall worry in the maze – one she's afraid to demolish– – fear is a wall, but at least it's solid.

I wish Arturo was here. Or Nick. Or someone, she thinks as she'd thought too many times before – and stops herself short.

Briskly she looks at her shnooky Big Time watch that tells her no time – make your move this minute. She paws the door and replaces it in the space that is its rightful place in the scene of things in the bitching L-shaped dog-room. Jean Paul lies on the bed, hollow as a cartoon ghoul, sicker than a deaf Dalmatian that has been drop-kicked across town and, somewhere along the way, has all its spots knocked off.

'Have you eaten?' she asks him as she checks her purse.

'Nah,' Jean Paul says. His eyes stare unwaveringly down the low-def zilch-resolution black and white tube in its el-cheapo cheapo plastic casing. He scratches again.

'Not really very hungry.'

'Have you had anything at all today?'

'Yeah. Had a Big Mac.'

She gives him a 10-buck brown spot from her purse. She glances quickly round the tiny cubicle. Has she forgotten anything? Her eyes take it in at a glance:

the two-tone walls,

the window with no view,

the ancient, early 1960s two-tone plastic transistor radio,

the noisy metal wall heater,

the mini-mound of runt litter surrounding the bed with its unwashed blue-black and red blanket,

the thinly grimed white telephone,

the stained brown carpet,

the chipped wooden bedside table with the sticky bottle of cough medicine on it,

the hingeless sliding door,

the kitchen cupboard on the wall with the same window at the other end,

a whole ragbag of intrinsically valueless artefacts she could not yet dare to hope would one day be consigned to an obscure drawer of their own, trash-ready future memorabilia of her present misery.

No, she has forgotten nothing – on the contrary, she remembers it all too well.

'Oh God,' she says – she'd found herself recently coming around to the idea that God must exist, must exist because she talked to him so often – 'I'd do anything to get out of all this. Anything.'

'DAN!' SHE CRIES as she grabs the back of his white jacket. Its owner spins round at her touch. He looks surprised. And he isn't Dan.

'Oh God, I'm sorry,' she stammers. 'I thought you were, I thought you were my friend.'

'Could be if you play your cards right, young lady.'

Young lady?

'Why don't you let me get you a drink?'

'I'll have a beer.'

She digs her elbows tight into her bod, and reaches into the velvet butterfly bag. Would she ever, in time, be able to forget the day Arturo had shop-lifted it for her, ever be able to erase the moment when the invitation from Maxine had arrived and she'd opened Nick's letter with its pompous printed head and she'd realized this was not a rehearsal, it was not a joke, it was not something she could shrug off any more? Even now as she absorbs herself in the babbling noizak of hell-is-us around her, the needle in her mind still burns bright as it tracks on the fine edge of her memory with its repetitious white-hot intensity.

'No – please, my treat,' the man in the white suit insists.

'Oh well, in that case I'll have a glass of champagne.'

'Champagne? OK.'

She pulls away from the scrimmaging scrum that mêlées around the bar (by day Court is a dodgy Greek restaurant designed to accommodate maybe 70 covers; now it's packed out by more than 400 teeming screaming funsters) and returns to reclaim her seat in the bamboo booth. But Georgina, the black model who'd cameo'd in the *No-Frank-Don't-Go-In-There-It'll-Kill-You* vid, has snitched it.

The girls stare at each other.

'So where's loverboy, hotlips?'

'He didn't like all the flakes here so he split – hey did you go to the hairdressers today?'

'No,' Georgina says. 'Why?'

'Noooooo,' Debbie counters as nastily as she can. 'I thought not.'

Earlier, Dan had bought her a drink and then hit her with brand X ratpooh craptrap about his mother making him pay back the cost of his rehab treatment. When she made it clear she wasn't buying that, he'd just walked off. When she'd pleaded with him, he'd told her that he'd driven down to a party on Friday with a guy called Nigel he'd met in some hotel at lunch-time. He'd been a Hell's Angel until he'd smashed his legs up in a bike crash. And this Nigel, which Cress Deb Crane thought was a peculiar monicker for a Hell's Angel if ever she'd drawn breath or social sec (and she still did), this Nigel knew some outtatownie party happening. They'd stayed until the wine went flat, and over-refreshed revellers had parked pizza and collapsed throughout the house and gardens like dead fall leaves.

'It was great,' Dan'd said. 'Henri Enriques was there and crashed out into this metal bathtub full of champagne and ice on one of the terraces.'

'Who?' she'd said, determined to remain unimpressed.

'The racing driver,' Dan'd replied. 'He won the Torquemada 24-Hours eight years ago.'

Dan had poked his snout in the trough too so, just before they hit the Western suburbs, he let Nigel drive and halfway up Shakespeare Zoom, the plastic muscles in his legs suddenly conked out and the car careened very slowly right off the autostrada into a passing lorry-load of illegal immigrants. And he had to tell his mother because, of course, it was her car, and she cut off his allowance, so now he didn't have any money for the payback.

Cressie'd promised herself en route, on the train, that she'd be tough with him.

She'd tried. But when he dropped his sportboy pose and snapped his smile like a garter-belt, she found that easy grin was charm incarnate, sucking her into the weeny roast of memory.

They'd reminisced about the time they'd been to that Japanese circus with the red pagoda where Arturo'd been so smacked out he'd nodded off on the big wheel. And she remembered how Arturo had beaten her thwack and blue that night after he'd overheard her leave a lascivious message on Nick's office answerphone. And every time she saw the smile that played around Dan's pout-couture lips (he was a sometime male model, this boy. He had no home but drove a red sports car with the glib rationale that you couldn't drive a house but could always sleep in the car), she found she just couldn't fling the verbal acid she'd brewed so painstakingly as the silver machine had belted, earlier, through the dark, labyrinthine tunnels and vertigo-inducing skybridges of the city.

But now, she remembers sourly, that the cocktail she'd bought him was financial death compared to Dan's offer of near-beer. He'd even tried to borrow more cash but she'd refused, she realizes glumly, not from any late-surging courageous rise of the heart, but simply because she had so little left. 'Remember how you got that place, that's all,' he'd sniped.

The liar! she thinks indignantly, that wasn't all at all. All it was

was major leverage. She'd been able to rent the L-shaped room only because Dan had signed the lease: it was a corporate let. Of course Dan's corporation is a completely baked bottom-of-the-harbour swizzloid husk of pure fraud, but it's the only way to rent accommodation in the city now: the market has dried up and so outsiders have to be super rich, in on a corporate let or get out.

Dan had moodied off in huff-huff storm-clouds of sulkily threatening retribution and recrimination. Now, two (or was it three?) drinks later, she'd sussed it was a dog's-breath ploy to prevaricate about seeing her again. A surge of angry trouble wells up inside her – he'd bamboozled her again by shadow-boxing.

Linda had some friends, well, her boyfriend, who was tied up with Alex Culver, and that mob could probably break Dan's face with all the thought she'd give to choosing which dip to have on junkfood chicken chunks.

Visual crime, visible time: its imposition of ugliness. The beautiful and the innocent have no enemy – but time.

So what good would it do? Culver's mob might scare him, but considering for a moment the complexity of the plan that would have to be put into effect, she nixes it. Dan was slimy, wiley-guiley and sneaky-deke sly. Even if he shifted into the bottom of his spare brown trousers, there was no guarantee he'd ante up with cold cash money. Whereas, her intuition tells her, the rogue, bogue little creepoid might well grass her up to Arturo. They're best friends, those two, closer than a dead-heat, blood brothers like no others ever since they'd been slung out of art school together.

Arturo, nominally a hairdresser, lies low somewhere secret on the coast. It narks her that though he'd always talk to Dan, sometimes four or five times a day, Arturo'd cut the lines of their communication.

It's so unfair – Dan wouldn't reveal when or say what they discussed (although he'd drop tantalizing little pearls and curls of information so she knew they were still in touch) – and that, she realizes, is his most powerful hold on her of all.

Now here is this guy in the white suit with her glass of champagne. It is pink.

Mnhuhmm, she thinks and checks him more closely with a once-all-over, aided by the low-slung basket-light that hangs on a long wire over the adjacent formica table top.

It was always a telling moment in her paper-covered editions, the bit where the heroine sizes up the man she's just met as a potential life-time partner or, at least, a part-time paramour.

Now she is Jane Austen, 21st-century housewife; she is Sylvia Plath, suburban mother of three and walker of a big dog; she is George Eliot counting the days until her salary check comes through while she paints eggs for Easter and plays the out-of-tune piano for the music and movement classes; she is Elizabeth Browning, traffic cop; Colette the bus conductress; Becky Sharp double-parking her second-hand compact outside the department stores to catch the sales on Bernini Boulevard; Catherine Earnshaw delighted to find her Magi-Mix exactly where she'd left it after all; Emily Brontë, snacking on the banana 'n' cinnamon natural vitamin E enriched pore-opening cream, who notices nothing amiss or awry as she waits for the familiar sounds that signal her husband's cheery arrival back from another hard day at the office. The simplicity of submission to this man, any man, to comply and collaborate in the fantasy of a happy life.

And this one isn't even terribly nice-looking. But perhaps, she speculates, he might have some interesting drugs. He looks the type. Otherwise he wouldn't have any reason to be in this place – he'd be selling plant insurance over the telephone or something.

'Thanks,' she says, accepting the proffered glass. They're almost pressed together and she doesn't feel comfortable. But then, looking over his shoulder, she sees Georgina get up to go downstairs and dance with her spotty beau in the Greek sailor's hat.

They manage to sit down opposite each other.

'What do you do?'

'I'm an air hostess.'

'Who for?'

'No one. I used to fly for Mantran but I jacked it in. All these creepshow businessmen kept treating me like a bimbo.' Appalled by the easy routine regularity with which she tells the lie and anticipating the next move, she turns the question round.

'What about you?'

'Well, I'm a sort of photographer.' She can tell from his long o's that he's from up-country.

'What do you take pictures of?'

'Pretty girls,' he shoots back salaciously. 'No, heh heh, just my little joke. Actually I'm working on a book about cars.'

'Cars?'

'Well, number plates, really.'

Number plates? she thinks. Lame!

'Have you ever noticed all the personal plates going round in the city?'

'What, like 4MYEGO and things?'

'Yes, that sort of caper,' says the man in the white suit. 'My name's Brockie, by the way – Brockie Haslam.' He makes to shake hands and then kisses hers. Creep factor 4: she shudders.

He asks her what her surname is. 'No, just Debbie,' she replies. He looks as if he might press the point.

'Back off,' she warns. He shrugs. She smiles.

'Why are you taking pictures of number plates?' She'd heard of this somehow, somewhere around the maze haze.

'If a person's sufficiently extrovert to wear an identifying plate on their motor-car, now that's some sort of statement, isn't it?'

'Yeah.'

'It is,' he affirms, 'a statement in a medium that hasn't been available before, so it's a completely new thing. Well, it occurred to me one day that if people were that outgoing, not only to display the plate, but to pay 120 bucks a month to lease it for the privilege, they may also be of the same mind to be in a book which'd be more or less an extension of what the plate was saying. The plate, you see, reaches a limited audience, obviously in the circle where the motor-car goes.

'I thought, hallo, these chaps will certainly be in the book if I make a nice one, photograph their cars, pander to their egos, obviously, and possibly publicize whatever business they're in.

'I did a bit of research, went to the Department of Motor Transport, who told me that there were nearly 70,000 of them issued, which was amazing because I was thinking in terms of a few thousand.

'After a few problems that I managed to, uh, iron out I was able to get the low-down, if you like, on the plates I wanted. And most of them were owned by some sort of entrepreneur or other. So I thought, right – I'll do a book.

'I decided to go to a publisher, Carbottle & Lightowler, who had a record for doing slightly off-beat things. We decided that if a person's willing to pay a fee to go into the book, it'd cover the cost of production. And we were right.

'With very few exceptions, everyone I've approached – and I've been very selective about approaching people, because bear in mind that a lot of the plates are either Christian names or surnames or initials which um, while they may be very interesting to the persons that own them, aren't really very thrilling for anyone else – Well, everyone's responded very positively.'

He tops up Cressida D. Crane's glass; perhaps he'd read that article that said champagne lasted longer that way.

'People are intrigued by them, Deborah, they've seen all sorts of strange ones. I've been asked, literally, many thousands of times, "Have you seen this plate? That one? Who owns DEALER? POSEUR? 4MYEGO?" All that sort of caper – it's an intriguing business.

'You see, if you see a plate going down the road with EI EI O on it, you think, "Christ! His name must be McDonald." And of course, the car does belong to a fellow called McDonald.

'You haven't got a car, have you?' he asks her, suddenly. His face looks slightly worried.

'No, no, I don't drive,' she lies. It was absurd, habitual, inexplicable. Or almost. Because, as they continue their conversation, C. Deborah C.'s intuitive system begins to send messages. And she realizes she's standing on the edge of a gap.

It's exhilarating.

And, within her, grows the conviction that she knows something about this Brockie Haslam that even he himself does not.

All around them people mill and swill; dead-head dudes in flat-top hair-cuts; James Dean thinkalikes who're chat-attacking baldies of three sexes or chicks with bare midriffs and saccharin-sweet smiles; funking lock-tonsorial B-Boys seeking dream roles in A-list fantasies; mess-tressed femmes hanging on, hanging in, toughing their stuff. Here's the girl who, glad-ragged in her fly fifties specs, glittering silver plastic top and glitzy patched red quiltwork dress, looks like a def siren, an MTV mermaid. Every kind of demi-couture and tricked-out costumery to encode fantasy and engage identity is here, among the pill-popping joy-boys who blow big spliffs as they shout across the room at each other, and play the backgammon tables off which Knocker makes most of his moulah.

'Who else is in on this?' Debbie asks.

'No one,' Brockie says, pulling at his champagne and refusing her offer of a Now from her crumple-proof pack. He seems to hesitate for a second or two.

'I do it all. I go crazy with it sometimes. We're only running . . . I'm only running two cars at the moment – the Quaasar and the Crusader. John Crawford from GDMC lent it to, uh, me, as a goodwill gesture.'

His sip becomes a quaff.

'Very decent of him,' he says.

'Has it got a plate?'

'Yes. SHOOT.'

She smiles.

'What do you hit them for?'

'Pardon me?'

'How much does it cost to be in it?'

'A thou. Actually 90 per cent of the people have said fine, probably 30 per cent of that 90 per cent have said, "It's far too cheap, it's ridiculous." We're getting people in fashion like Bee Melrose or the Grey Boutique in St Cloud who'll regularly take a page in *Belladonna* or *X* and pay them 10 K for it, then pay to produce the material to go into it. We don't charge for the space at all, the space is there. We charge a fee to cover the cost of producing the pictures and everything.

'I've knocked back more than I've accepted, it's in our interests obviously, because we want to be as intriguing as possible, because we want to sell the damn thing. If you get every damn TOM 1, DICK and HARRIET in it, well . . . but THE RAT and SPUNK BUNNY and SNOOZE, you know? Everyone who goes into the book will derive some sort of benefit from it. It's amazing, Deborah, really astonishing, how many of them are the number one or the most successful in their chosen field. There seems to be some sort of co-relation there.'

She realizes he's paused and might be about to start probing her. Hurriedly she fills up the conversational blank with the first question that pops into her head.

'What plates have you got?'

'CLASS, 0000000, Carlos Jacquenelli's PENI 5, EPAISAN which belongs to Alex Culver, WOW 007, WIN 999, GAS 000, BARON, MR 119, PUNTER, ZZZZZZZ, gosh – there's more than 700 of them. It's intriguing, Deborah, intriguing.

'NEWCAR belongs to a GDMC concessionaire – NUDO 4U's a hairdresser on Sheepy Island, KREEPY KRAWLEY are those people who manufacture those strange devices that clean out your pool as they climb the sides of the walls. I FIX UM is a motor mechanic in a red Ferrantti who specializes in supercars. KEPT is a blonde woman from Realito Park who now lives in St Cloud.'

Flashpoint! Debbie's mouth drops open like she wants to catch a fly, which is extraordinary, really, because she's always hated insects, and, as she has her glass in her hand, she hurriedly pours the champagne into her mouth and pretends to swallow it the wrong way so the chokes and splutters and his back-slaps and solicitations after her health cover her surprise, distract him, and buy time to recompose herself.

'I bet there are heaps of really interesting plates,' she says, dissembling enthusiasm.

'JAGGER is on a small red GDMC. A is Jimmy Hennessy. RATBAG also owns POSEUR. Now he's an interesting boy. A 19-year-old totally inarticulate brat from the Stewartstown housing estate projects who has this plate on an extremely expensive Bolero Turbo Vendetta for which he paid a great deal of money. One wonders, at the age of 19, how he got it. That is open to speculation, though, funnily enough, his brother drives a Mondiale Bloodhound which is plated DEALER. Make what you will of that.'

'Wow,' says Debbie.

She speaks Bimbo.

'ORATOR is Carol King-King, the public-speaking champion. Flick Colby, the trainer, has WAY2GO. HIHOAG belongs to a chemist. THERAT is Marc Ratt of Ratt records. SKYTOP manufacture sunroofs. LEBELT is Kashif Osiro, the designer. PITS is the drive-in gas station/restaurant people.

'Oh Lord, I'm sorry,' he says suddenly apologetic and attentive. 'All this is business talk – it must be so dull for you. Let me get you another drink.'

'Sure,' she says. Her mind is engaged in developing a mental picture, glossing it, concentrating on something positive.

And indeed a picture begins to emerge, a picture in a developing tray, 'synchronistic developments' as the tarot-reading hippy at Mystic City Sign had said. And suddenly, like an engine engaging first gear, like her this-goes-with-that wardrobe, like the moment when you remove the paper from the tray and shake off the dev and turn it over: clickety click. Everything says yes and for the first time in a long time she sees a light somewhere inside, illuminating the labyrinth.

She remembers the evening 48 hours ago now, when she'd run into Terry Kinkaid and they'd talked about Court – got it like that chic-chat and miscellaneous mutual moaning and bitchery – when the bleeper had squeaked bleakly. Yeah, it was just before she'd bought the new batteries.

First time she'd called back Linda's line had been busy. Yeah yeah, she remembers now, very clearly.

Linda often went on frenetic telephone jags, calling up everyone she knew at three in the morning when her boyfriend Paulie hadn't shown. These no-shows were freak-quent events: full-on ticket-only theatre of trauma. Linda was the sort of girl who was like a mirror, reflecting the breath of the last person who'd been near enough to make an impression on her. Her language had really crashed through the gutter since she'd met Paul Casales at the Grey Boutique, the drop-dead shopportunity spot where he habitually picked out bijou rinky-dink designer trinks for his Jappy little wife. Contemporaneous with Cressie's separation from Arturo, Linda's lifestyle had become not just yupwardly mobile but totally stratospheric: she'd zoom-boom-boomed clean through the ozone layer on clouds of Dior into a charge-it world where her own apartment had paid-for staff, whose duties included cleaning the sports Merc with the number plate that said KEPT where Paulie liked to get blown. She remembers it now with almost total recall, it's all as sharp as the blade she'd chopped the last batch of Spectre out with on the hard black surface in the telephone booth at Rififi's.

She'd tried calling again.

And this time Linda'd picked up on the first ring – a bad sign. Worse, her friend launched straight into a tirade of gob-blapping abuse dissing Paul. And right, right in the sites – she'd been rabbling about some twinkie who'd taken a picture of the car.

'What picture?' Cress DC'd asked. Vertical chop chop. As they'd conversed, she recalled admiring the handiwork of Hiro Kino, flavour of the month art-star, who'd decked out the nightclub's telephone booths like a miniature primeval swamp in mid-melt-down: toy dinosaurs with unnaturally elongated necks, warpo-weirdo trees, stretch fauna and flora of many mutations.

'I told you, numnuts. Pictures of the stupid cars. Mine, all of Paulie's. Alex's, and the cow's' (Linda couldn't bring herself to utter her rival's name: to name her enemy would be acknowledging her, and to acknowledge her would be to give her adversary power). 'Some wild guy's running around town hitting on everyone with this spiel that he's snapping VIP car number plates for a book or something. But Charlie or someone at the office noticed an invoice come in from the guy and, you know, Paulie just doesn't do business like that and he got really wired up about it. I think because of Ali Culver. He's on Paulie's case about the pictures and the invoice and blah blah. I mean it's gotta be that, ya know? He wouldn't just blow me out like this otherwise. He called me to cancel dinner because he said Alex wanted him to go straighten the guy out personally but he hasn't called or anything.'

Debbie had idled at the other end of the line (chop chop cross-ways).

Just then her knight in the white suit returns with another bottle of high-ticket, low-rent pink champagne nestling in a battered dull-grey ice-bucket. As the cork slides out, someone at another table simultaneously opens their bottle too. Pop pop go the corks and she flashes on a vision of Romeo and Juliet as the tragedy of two star-crossed mafia jukeboxes. What selection would Juliet jukebox play now?

One of the tip-top features about her bleeper is its stealth mechanism. Its function is to test that the unit is working. You surreptitiously hit a hidden switch and it yammers away until you shut it down to reactivate it another time. Like now. 'Excuse me.'

She checks the read-out. It says, 'Test Signal Only Test Test KO OK.'

'Oh God – I've got to move, I have to find a phone.'

'There's one right here.' He reaches into his jacket pocket and produces a matt-black punch-it portable.

'Brilliant,' she laughs nervously. She checks her horrology and realizes it's spilling out negative time that marches out of the clock face, all over the walls that surround the vortex. It elapses even as she smiles, grinning at him inanely, giving him a full-on jumbo-bimbo flash of pearly glitzkrieg toothrush, as she picks out Linda's number with her long fingers.

Linda picks up and she starts to tell her about Dan, as much to chill herself out as anything else.

'How's Paulie?' she asks eventually, listening carefully to gauge Linda's tone of reply.

'He should be round any minute. He just had to take care of some business – you know what he's like, always juggling 20 things at once. That cow was giving him a bad time at breakfast because he stayed with me mosta last night. Then there was some kinda hassle with a cigarette delivery or something. I don't know, Debs, maybe I'm too hard on him sometimes – he's under terrific pressure. The guy gets so wound up. I mean, I saw him this afternoon and it took me 25 minutes to get the knots outta his back, you know? I mean he was really fucking furious, lemme tellya.'

'What? About that guy?' Cressida D C says as she extracts the last cigarette and flames it, smiling sweetly at her companion just in case he unexpectedly stops his eye-ball tour of the surrounding pond-life.

'What guy?'

'Oh, you know,' Debbie replies, super casually. 'That guy you were telling me about.'

For a moment Linda says nothing.

Debbie toys with the empty cigarette packet.

'Oh, you mean Mr Numberplates?'

'Right,' says C. Debbie C. emphatically and almost bites back her tongue for coming on too strong.

'Well that's where he's gone, supposedly,' Linda says. 'Wow, there's been a lot of trouble about him.'

'Really?'

'Yeah, Paulie's gone to look for him. You know I get so worried when he goes out like that.'

'Out like what, what do you mean?'

She knows what Linda means. But she has to be sure. She stares momentarily at the empty crushproof packet – then crunkles it up into a tight little ball.

'Well he's gonna, ya know, whack him,' Linda says. 'You know.'

'Oh.'

Cress-Deb C. exhales the smoke with a barely suppressed gasp.

'Hey, are you still there?'

She takes a deep breath and forces herself to smile.

'Yeah, yeah I just dropped something.'

She's amazed at the timbre and richness of her voice. It pleases her – the modulation, the confidence, the control.

Brockie is glooping her, staring at her chest. Maintain, she tells herself, maintain. She indicates frantically she wants more sticks. But he offers her one of his Bunkum & Henrys. She jabs impatiently at her packet.

'Hold on a mo.'

'No, these you plank, get these – Now.'

'Right,' says Brockie and grins at her.

This is all quite natural, she tells herself, trouble-juggling in the mind-maze. This is a conversation with my best friend. Of course I'm interested in her boyfriend. Why shouldn't I be? She wants me to be. She wants me to be impressed by him. And I am.

'How does Paulie know the guy's a flake?' she askes Linda, blowing two kisses to Brockie as he leers over his shoulder at her and begins to fight his way through the crowd.

'Listen, Debs, you don't get to where Paulie is if ya still think the Xavian Brothers run a seminary y'know? This geek's trying to burn them. Can you imagine? Some outtatown hick trying to rip off Paulie, wow, that's dumb, that's really lame. I mean he's gonna wish his father and mother had never met – you know what Paulie's like when he gets mad about something. And Ali's really on his case about the guy.'

'Is he?'

'Believe it. It's business. Ya can't let freelancers burn ya – everyone looks stoopid and that's very bad for business. It's a real fuck-up.'

'Alex is blaming Paulie for it?' Debbie asks in pseudo-gothic tones inlaid with mock horror.

'Mmmnnnn – *cosi cosi*. Culver lent some cash to the guy on Paulie's say-so to go get a new engine for his new Bolero, but it was, you know, cold cash on the deal and this jerk musta put it through his books. So they went round to the guy's office to straighten him out and he's ankled.'

'How does he know where he is?'

'Paulie knows everybody, honey, and the caretaker in the block told them the guy was catching a plane outta town tomorrow. So Ali's adging Paulie and Paulie's adging everyone, and he's gone out to look for the guy and whack him.'

'But you could just pick him up at the airport.'

'Geez, Debbie, you can be really dumb. What if something screwed up, like one of our guys isn't on the rota or he catches another flight or something? Those engines cost 70 tax-free. I mean if Paulie let the guy bite Ali, well, hey that wouldn't be such a smart move, you know?'

'What's his name, this wiseguy?'

'I don't know.' There's a beat. 'How come you're so interested anyway?'

The man in the white suit is returning and Debbie can foresee an argument with the over-animated sportboy in mirror shades and too-tight leisure wear who's slid into Brockie's place.

'Oh, excuse me. I'm just interested, that's all. I know how much you care about him, I just wanted to see how it all was. You know, if I'm being nosy or something, just tell me to back off. I don't want to get into your business.'

'Well, you wouldn't believe what that cow did this morning,' Linda begins but Debbie cuts in. 'Hey the money's running out – gotta fly, love you.'

'Did you get them?' she asks standing up.

'They didn't have any,' he says, crestfallen. 'At least not that brand. But I've got a carton back at my flat. I could drive you over and we could pick them up. Want to spin along?'

'Just try and hold me back,' she whispers, and clasps his hand tentatively. For a moment she considers kissing him. No, she tells herself. Make the bastard wait.

'FUCK ME, FUCK ME.'

He pauses. He looks up. His piggy eyes beg from narrow, deep-set sockets. His sebaceous cheeks heave: porky, rotund, wet from pleading. His mouth is tight with want-you-now.

'What colour is love?'

'Blue?' he ventures, seeking some sign of approval. He stares across the room at her. Glances around the black, white and grey décor of the flat as a pancake, as if the over-polished black leather director's chair or risky lithograuve investments in their cold chrome frames might provide him with comfort and inspiration.

'Blue,' she repeats tonelessly.

A wasp has flown into the room.

It buzzes.

He gazes at her as she stands there, another strip-cartoon kid all blister-Magoo and goggle-boggled by her big blue eyes. Pale and abstracted, blue, enormous blue hyperspheres that wander nomadically through alien dimensions of whicky whacky what? Perhaps they even now pondered some abstract philosophical conundrum he could never hope to even glimpse – let alone comprehend.

He drinks her up like a rare unblended Cognac.

The bodice. So tight it skinny-pinches every miraculous curve of her perfect shape. The peculiarly scrupulous, churnful lust suggested by the functional, restrained organization of its hook-and-eye clips. The black thigh-high boots: dark, sweaty hell for leather, hooked up to the snappy give of the fresh latex suspenders via the medium of her fishnetted legs: long, lithe shapely legs he'd die for. Her pale face, her delicately blemished skin. And the skin stretches over the cheekbones, cheekbones that could stop a desperate man jumping off a tall bridge. The hair, so perfect, wild-style pretty-frizz candyfloss tied into a top-knot by pearls with a scarlet bow.

In one corner of the room one of the Samsonite suitcases has been opened. The clothes she wears actually belong to his girlfriend Melena, who'd walked out this afternoon. She'd cracked.

Brockie suspects she'd found those Amex receipts from Sinderalla, the justifiably famous Belleville bordello. Melena had been such a fool – it was all so trivial.

Nothing, for sure, on some of the stunts he and the boys had pulled with those two hookers they'd picked up on the Strip the other night: bees, goldfish, harnesses, vacuum cleaners – the works. Now if she'd found the wicked polaroids that'd come out of that, well a chap could've understood. But she'd just done a runner. Flake Out. He hates her for it. But perhaps, he now reckons, it's all for the best.

As consolation prizes went, this wasn't too bad. Brockie'd given it a whole lot of charlie and a few lines of smack and kapow – she's worked out what he needed as his pre-flight relaxant straight away. Actually going to bed was, of course, right out of the question. He was much too tightly wired for that.

'Please,' he whimpers, and as he shifts his weight fron one knee to the other, the wooden boards press against his bones; for a moment the absurdity of his worship of this movieface and its perfect body, his devotion as he'd spray-polished her outfit after she'd talced herself into it and got it on; the manifest stupidity of what he was doing strikes him. Could she ever learn to love him? Could he trust his lust? The handcuffs jangle behind his back.

The wasp buzzes again.

'Oh, oh please please,' he implores ecstatically.

'YOU FUCKER!'

She screams. The sound of the whip ricochets around the sparsely furnished room like a bullet in a hospice.

Now see the Negative Girl move. Predatory in Kill City. Fast. Shuts down the space between her weapon and the prey.

But at that very moment, all the way to the top along the apotheotic arc in the grace of her cruelty, one of the high, pointy tips of her stilettos snags unexpectedly on a small, gnarly hole in the polished pinewood floor. And instantly she's sprawled all over the deck in an ungainly mess of kick-kick limbs.

Ms Crane picks herself up and staggers forward, an over-reaching extra in Jack Dante's Rockin' Beach Party Inferno à Go-go, drop-deadly determined to catch the public breath with seven seconds of glory in her cameo role. In one movement, she swings her arm right back around behind her body. For an instant within that moment she freezes there. Only to suddenly thrust her entire weight behind the ferocious, forward propulsion with all the might in her right.

KERASH

'I can't stand you fucker, fucker, fucker.'

And the girl in the rubber tutu belts it again and again and again and again and again and again and again.

Sounds rush in through the broken window. Somewhere in the distance the sound of an opera-singer practising her scales cuts through early morning birdsong. Jagged fragments, shards of glass, have scattered across the stripped pine floor.

She breathes hard now. Tiny, light down is still raised on her forearms as she turns to him.

'Fucking insects.'

She's trembling, but that rage has left her voice. Perhaps he hasn't given her enough smack? She's bearing down on him.

'I hate fucking insects.'

Her face contorts with disgust and she spits at him.

'I'm sorry,' he cows, abject, skull gravity bowed. Oh feistybug flaw, how could he have so foolishly humiliated himself in her eyes by this failure to anticipate such an obvious need?

She takes two steps in his direction and staggers forward as she twists her ankle.

'Oh my Gawd,' she wails and collapses awkwardly over the new grey sofa and its subtle white dots. She seems smaller, fatigued, flabbergasted, dog-tired as, disconsolately, she examines the black boot's broken heel.

'Well, that's Goodnight Charlie for a kick off,' she says matter of factly.

He wonders if he should perhaps point out that the broken window will act as open messwithme to every winged beastie within the city limits. He begins to speak, but she curtly cuts his verbals dead.

'OK, I'm fed up with all this crap now anyway.'

She mechanically unfastens the suspenders and laboriously begins to unroll the leather off her left leg.

'If you want to play stupid games, go back to Tag.'

He looks at her. She's so watchable. He feels that if she didn't drive him mad first, she'd learn to love him. They would go out together and she would only have to enter a room for the furniture to become invisible, and the people to vanish. For when they were in the room, he would see nothing else.

'Will you fuck me? Jesus. Please.'

'She looks at her watch.

'I said, "That's enough,"' she repeats coldly. 'What I want to know, Mr Haslam, is where you've stashed the money.'

His face looks puzzle, bemused. And for a moment he almost believes him. But it is 5.20 a.m.

Wall-time.

'Come on,' she says wearily as she grapples with the boot. 'Where's the money, honey?'

'What money?'

The boot's stuck.

'Just give me a hand with this, will you?' she snaps.

He doesn't. He can't move.

She sees and laughs out loud.

'Give me a hand, give me a hand, oh God that's funny.'

She realizes it's the first time she's laughed properly for months, which makes her laugh more with relief, and longer with her joy in the exultation of sheer happiness.

'You-look-so-stupid,' she manages to gasp. She wants to share the joke, but of course he can't see it at all. He is powerless – and it's his own naffing fault.

That makes it funnier. And since, she realizes, this is no time for laughter – because any second Paul Casales or Alex Culver (or, more probably, a couple of their goons from the Armageddon Wrecking Company) or the Metropol or Brockie's girlfriend or maybe an enraged DEALER and his brother POSEUR might put in an appearance – but she can't stop laughing, she rolls around on the floor with the broken-heeled boot half on/half off, and looks at him trussed up like a plump spring chicken and laughs and laughs and laughs a whole lot more, lets it all go and allows herself to roll and coast on the rapturous surf of mirth, roaring until her sides hurt and her eyes gush as if she's an hysterical schoolgirl again.

When it finally subsides enough to allow her to move, she

reaches over to the clear, low-slung perspex coffee table above the white fluffy rug, and picks up a pack of cigarettes.

'If you don't tell me where you've hidden the cash,' she says, scrambling for the lighter, 'you're dead, guy.' The refillable moulded plastic red and white packet carries but one word. He stares at it morosely.

NOW.

Anyhow . . .

. . . click goes the lighter and disgorges some flame.

'Oh god, where did I put the keys?' she mutters. The laughing – and the shock of it – like a downpour breaking a drought, have drained her.

'There are some spares in the bedroom.'

She wedges her boot into his mouth. He grips like a crazy man and eventually, between them, they work it loose enough for her to pull it off.

'The bedroom,' he repeats. She thinks she can just detect an edge of panic in his voice. 'There are spares in the bedroom.'

Oh God, she thinks, sniffing up the last line on the mirror by the bookshelves, suppose he's come in his shorts? With a supreme effort she sublimates the neo-irresistible urge to giggle into a series of smirks.

'What time's your flight?'

He looks at her sneakily, and then stares into space. He says nothing: he's trying to work out what to do. Somehow he has to persuade her to take the bracelets off without revealing where the money hid.

'Brock-ie,' she sings out.

She comes over to him and leans down so her eyes stare directly into his.

'I know all about it,' she murmurs as she strokes his face.

'What flight?'

She slaps him across the chops. Hard.

'Culver's mob are gonna get here any minute, you stupid cunt, there's no time for any more fucking games. Now where is it? Tell me where it is.'

'Debbie, I don't know what you're talking about.'

'TELL ME!'

'Money? What money? You're crazy. Completely mad. I don't know what you're talking about.'

She slumps back into the sofa. Outside somewhere, a police siren winds out its baleful wail. Trouble.

'OK,' she says calmly. 'Let's make a deal.'

He looks at her suspiciously. His face gives away nothing.

'I'll fuck you, I promise I will. But you have to tell me where you've stashed the dosh from the book. Just tell me where it is and I'll release you, we can go to the airport together and everything'll be fine. Don't you see how fine it could be?'

'And if I don't see how fine it could be?'

'We haven't got time,' she shouts and stands up to tower over him again. 'And you especially have no time at all. 'Cos if you don't tell me where the cash is inside the next 60 seconds, I'm just gonna leave you here and Alex's boys will do you like a dinner. In fact – I'll do better than that – I'll tell them where you are.'

She walks over to the broken window and leans outside. She feels a stabbing shock of pain in her arm.

'They'll pay me too,' she says, rubbing where it hurts.

She puffs on the ciggie then stubs it out, grinding the butt into the plank of the floor, glances at her watch marking out positive beats of negative time on the walls of her soul.

'Not as much – but enough.'

She picks up the black telephone from the table.

'They'll kill you. That's for sure.'

She puts her finger on the button.

'15 seconds. Go ahead – Brockie, call my bluff. You can either fuck me. Or die.'

She hits the voice activator and says, '555 62 –'

'When will you fuck me?'

'When we get to the coast.'

She holds the telephone. Its function light winks at her.

'We can't, we can't go to the coast – Melena booked the flights out to Sheepy Island.'

'94.'

He hears the gizmo click.

She sees its red light fade to amber as it searches for Linda's line.

'OK, OK – it's all in the bedroom.'

'Where in the bedroom?'

The light turns green. The 'phone at the other end starts ringing. He can hear it. But he can see blood on the table. He looks at her. She hasn't noticed.

'In the top drawer. The top drawer,' he says. 'You'll find everything in the top drawer of the drawers.'

'Hallo?' Linda answers grumpily.

Deb C. looks at him for a moment.

Then she replaces the receiver and goes into the other room.

Brockie is still on his knees. He is thinking as fast as he can. In the other room, she opens the drawer. When she sees what's inside, she thinks she's ascended to heaven.

Heaven, full of angel-people with bodies made from glass, exactly as she'd always imagined it. She checks his wallet, sees the civilizing comforts of clipper class on the Mantran tickets, but picks up just the key and one other object that lies in the fusty-smelling Victorian pinewood drawer.

As she comes back out of the bedroom, she's swaying slightly.

About four feet away from him she stops and, using both hands the way she'd seen Clint Eastwood do it, when Nick had made her watch those endless spaghetti westerns, she raises the machine-pistol unsteadily in the general direction of his harnessed form.

She smiles broadly.

They both hear it at once.

The police siren sounds again – much nearer this time. Nearer, faster, louder – it's right on top of them. Outside. It stops. Car doors slam.

'Let me go.'

She glowers at him.

Doors open downstairs.

Footsteps.

'Where is it?'

Her smile is really animated now. Light dances behind her eyes.

The footsteps are coming, climbing the stairs.

Something distracts her – she looks down.

'Oh my God, Oh for God's sake.'

She is staring at the blood on the floor.

Visual crime.

'I'm bleeding.'

'OK OK OK OK – in the safe behind the picture on the wall.'

She's taken three, four paces towards the safe when the gun drops from her hand.

'I've cut myself,' she says, her voice rising an octave. 'Look, I'm bleeding.'

He is screaming something as the cops burst in.

Debbie doesn't notice. Her body is made of glass – and now black blood from its walls seeps out into the world. She only looks up when Casales starts shooting.

'What about her?' the dark-haired cop asks Paulie, who's still wearing his blue business suit.

He's a lean man with very short, close-cropped grey hair and features that are long in the vertical but compressed on the horizontals of his face, giving him a hard, predatory look. Tight lips; shifty eyes; long neck; bony capable hands: everything about Casales, right down to his plain, polished black shoes, seems both unobtrusive to the point of anonymity and unequivocally supremely functional. Nothing in body or mind is fat, superfluous, showy or wasted.

'That's tough,' he says, rubbing his chin, feigning concern. 'Shit, did I wing her?'

'Nah,' says the other patrolman. He's younger, fair haired.

'Look.' He picks up her arm and holds it out. 'She's got a great big bloody lump of window stuck in a main artery. We better get her to St Vinnie's.'

'Come on, sweetie,' he says kindly and starts to pull her towards the door.

But she's staring at the ID plate on his blue cotton short-sleeved shirt.

HUTTON, it says.

She starts to snigger again. She's still laughing light-headedly when they reach the hospital.

She's still there in a dark, poky little room in a different wing.

And every time they catch her burning a hole in her tights, Cressida D. Crane laughs in their faces.

Now she has all the time in the world.

Welcome to the Dream Room, baby.

Welcome.

LA WHEELS

PRIVY IN THE LAV CUBICLE, Jean Paul buttons h'self back up into his fading black jeans. He's about to unlock the door when, zipedy do, he notices something on da loo-lav floor.

As he stoops to retrieve the black animal-hide package, the page that Katy had torn two and a big bit hours before from the back of her address book – hit the deck.

Inside the wallet is a thick wadge of credit cards and 80 bucks free money in cold cash. But already, the blue paper of Katy's bindle (No – *his* bindle!) has turned pink as the urine from the floor swamps the delicate crystal alive within the ritually folded tear-sheet. Inside: the Spectre is dying. It had fallen out of the top pocket of his shirt as he'd bent down to swoop on the loot.

Jean Paul doesn't know whether to laugh or cry.

He does neither.

Instead, he quickly retrieves the wet bindle, drops it back into Crane's shirtpocket, extracts the notes from the billfold and slips it separately into his back trouser pocket before opening the door.

Outside hang a couple of good-looking jocks.

One is a blond fellow, very tall, pro-tanned, some kind of a body builder. The other is more wiry, be-blazered and dark haired, his high cheekbones set in a feline face whose tired eyes have seen too many early mornings through the bottom of a cocktail glass.

For a moment everybody stands off to check each other out.

'Ride?'

The dark guy lights a Ranliegh Mellow cigarette in the corner of his long, thin-lipped mouth with an electronic lighter, puffs languidly, and flicks his reptilian eyes back probingly at Jean Paul.

'Sure.'

They don't seem two bits like the usual clientele at all.

The troika makes its way through the steaming, subterranean back alleys of the Power Exchange. The venue is predominantly gay. But tonight is hardcore – a club within a club that attracts all manner of fetishistic fanatics and devotees of marginal cults.

There's a lot of interesting action in dark corners. Other People: pure visual entertainment.

Outside the valet delivers the car with a flourish, and Mr Urbane Suavity stuffs a couple of bucks in the back pocket of the car-jock's purple satin boxer shorts.

'Want to sit in the front?' Blondie asks.

'Sure.'

Jean Paul slides onto the bench seat. He's forgotten to hand the wallet in, but hey, that can wait.

'I'm Petey,' says the dark-haired guy piloting the car into the traffic stream. 'And that's John.'

Jean Paul turns round and smiles.

'Hi.'

Blond John smiles back at him. He has a big, friendly open-featured face with a firm jaw and warm, clear blue eyes. His fair hair has a natural wave; he has a deep tan, and easy smile which reveals flawless white teeth. His movements seem effortlessly athletic. Even as he sits still in the back of the car, he radiates a natural, happy energy.

The Cro-Magnon shape of the carefully restored Davino Strato-cruiser swings left into Atlantic Avenue.

'Where are we headed?' Jean Paul asks.

'You'll see,' says Petey, and half turns to his new companion. His mouth is slightly twisted, and his smile is like the punch-line of a sick joke.

'You guys do a lot of cruising?'

John mutters something from the back seat.

'Not if we can help it, let me tell you,' Petey elaborates, clashing the gearshift. 'That place is getting arse-paralysingly dull. I can't think why we still go there.'

'It was your idea,' John reminds him and Jean Paul catches the blond boy preening himself in the passenger-door mirror.

'Take no notice,' Petey tells Jean Paul. He leers slightly. 'He's very vindictive, dear, that one.'

'Are we going far?'

'All the way if you want, dear boy,' Peter quips. 'Why?'

'I'm hungry.'

John seems to brighten.

'Let's go to Harry's,' he suggests.

Petey rolls his eyes heavenwards but makes a left onto the parkway feeder.

'I love Harry's,' John says.

'I'm just wild about Harry's,' Petey lisps back at him sarcastically.

A few minutes later, they pull off the Von Alvensleben Interchange at Reichold and stop outside the city's most venerable mobile fast-food vendor: the awesomely legendary Harry's La Wheels.

Petey parks the Stratocruiser fussily, fastidiously distancing the vintage vehicle's bodywork from the mass of other cars.

John jumps out, one foot on the running board.

'Whatdya want kid?'

'Hot dog?'

'No sweat.'

The big-boned blond bounds off to the stand, where the usual quota of hoods and no-goods on the deadhead beat chew the bratwurst and put each other down with vinegary wind-ups as they bray off, trade wisecracks and shoot the fat, while their faces snout down on into La Wheels' Monster Hot Diggety Dogs, served with Harry's Special Hot Sauce.

You always had the sauce, even though Harry (or, more probably, one of his acolyte familial sidekicks) would, as a matter of courtesy, offer you alternatives of mustard and ketchup in homely unmarked white squeegee bottles with red caps. The hot sauce's ladled out from a special metal canteen next to the grill. Harry left the trailer, where he sat watching movie re-runs while he chatted on his portable telephone, less and less frequently nowadays – but when he did he'd inevitably chastise the kitchen minions for their over-abundance, super-stinginess or foolhardy neglect of the simmering delicacy hidden from view, bubbling in its square aluminium vat. People still said Harry blended it himself fresh each night from some special type of lizard that could be found only in some remote and secret area of the Western Hills. Whatever it was, from which the piquant blood-red liquid derived its unmistakable bouquet and flavour, it certainly had more kick than a mule-train. Throughout the length and breadth of this city, it is universally agreed that Harry's hot dogs possess a taste and texture second to none.

'You two an item?' He has an idea that they'd bought something from him one morning at Plaza de Soto market.

Petey scratches his head and looks out of the window.

'I suppose so,' he eventually replies, wistfully. He looks back. 'You know how it is.'

'What's your name anyway?' he asks in a friskier tone, lighting up another stick from another flip-top box inside the polished walnut veneered dashboard.

'Jean Paul.'

'I prefer John.'

'I don't.'

Petey peevishly exhales the smoke in puff-rings.

'Would you mind if I . . .' Jean Paul begins, then realizes that it doesn't matter if they mind or not . . . 'Excuse me.'

He zips off towards the corrugated metal stall on the other side of the site, slamming the door behind him in his haste as John returns with more nosh.

'I'm just going to spring a leak,' he explains as they pass, buys some cigarette papers from a Harry-sprog and goes to the can.

The door doesn't lock – this irritates him.

He fishes the bindle out of his pocket to examine it. The pink tinge has spread. Jean Paul moans loudly through tight lips. It's still wet. He wastes no time and sets straight to work, using the blade of his small Iraguan Air Force Knife to carefully scrape the precious powder remnants into the cigarette skin on his knee. The Spectre has already begun to decompose into scroggy yellow lumps.

There ain't much time.

He lights it and inhales. The smoke is vile, acrid.

This is so bad, he thinks. It's fucking degenerate. It's like smoking the toilet floor or drinking other people's piss.

Then the rush comes on. Colours run into each other in rivers of molecular paint. He feels that warmth, an empathetic integrity, a sensation of belonging. It surges and then the familiar, yet always fresh, totally dazzling white flash as his sensory system overloads and shuts down. The world stops. He sits on the lavatory, solid gone for three totally braindead minutes.

After a while he hears someone rattle a metal door.

'Awight. Coming, coming.'

As he eats the hot dogs and popcorn in the car – they've

finished, but John has gone back again, saying, 'A boy's gotta eat you know' – the city assumes its night-time plumage. Hookers hang about on Second Avenue, gaudy birds of prey. As the trio motor down the Shakey Zoom, and take exit 45 out of the city limits, they see a hapless stranded reveller on the hard shoulder and, backdropped behind him, the suburban streetlights that say it's all quiet tonight.

Suddenly it begins to rain – one of those unexpected neo-tropical downpours.

But the car drives on relentlessly.

'Where are we going?' Jean Paul asks again when they hit a patch of relatively open country about 20 minutes later.

Blond John burps.

'We're nearly there,' he says.

'Nearly there,' repeats Petey. His eyes concentrate on the wet wet road.

Jean Paul remembers a conversation he'd had three nights before with an architect, and starts to talk about the way that Sally Laverne, the Pre-Millennial urban planner, had skilfully managed to arrange the tree-line on the motorstrada so that it was impossible to see the surrounding light-industrial buildings.

Suddenly there are hands around his neck. Powerful hands.

'You can't even see the trees,' John whispers in his ear, soft as baby's breath. 'Realax kiddo.'

The grip loosens almost imperceptibly and John begins slowly to massage his neck.

'Strong hands,' Jean Paul says.

'Believe it.'

The car slips up another smaller road – almost a track really – into the blackness of the night. The fields are filled with pylons strung out through the countryside like a giant human chain.

'So whatdya guys do anyways?' Jean Paul asks, tilting his head back towards John, who is still neck-frotting.

'Well, not a lot really. I keep busy. Go to the gym. Do some afternoons on Lancaster Beach.'

'What about you?'

Petey grimaces but keeps looking straight ahead.

'I used to be in publishing.'

Jean Paul feels his nerve endings send messages that say relax – John had done this neck massage number before: it's professional. Jean Paul knows – he'd worked as a masseur in the frot frat too.

'Now I'm in the, uh, food business.'

'Distribution, you know, that's the ticket,' Blond John echoes.

Petey turns the wooden steering wheel round to the left and the car bumps along a gravel path and stops outside a large, dark building 200 metres away.

He hits a switch and the window whirs up.

It has chilled out.

As they walk round to the side of the immense concrete and steel boxy structure, Jean Paul notices how Petey's buttons shine in the dark, and how bright, how luminescent, John's loose white mid-town Fit-U-Up sweatvest appears against night's black blanket.

Petey stops at a door and presses a complex sequence of buttons. A red light flashes on and off. He repeats the procedure and eventually the door eases open.

'Wow it's cold in here,' Jean Paul says.

Then someone turns on the lights.

They are standing in a small reception area. There is a Securi-cam mounted on the far wall. A nondescript u-build coffee table neatly stacked with dog-eared supermarket junk tabloid mags:

KNIT YOUR OWN ROYAL FAMILY
CAT EATS PARROT – NOW IT TALKS!
LET ELVIS CURE YOUR BACKACHE PAINS

EXCLUSIVE PICTURES – MOM GIVES BIRTH TO
SIAMESE: ONE IS BLACK, ONE IS WHITE!

All this on a table in front of a cheap black leatherette sofa against the wall. Petey slides behind the receptionist's desk, bends down to examine something there and picks up something else. Some kind of black box. It nestles in his small, manicured hands.

'Good?' John asks.

'Three,' Petey replies cryptically and makes a follow-me arm gesture again.

'What is this place?' Jean Paul asks.

'Don't ask so many questions, stupid,' John chides with a soft murmur in his ear.

Now they go through another reinforced metal door, through into another dark area. Now this is cold, really cold, the kind of cold, it suddenly occurs to Jean Paul, you'd feel when you kissed a deadie.

Jean Paul follows Petey, and Blond John walks just behind him.

It seems to be some sort of factory – he can make out irregular shapes suspended from what he takes to be some sort of airborne production-line. The floor is hard – concrete? Their footsteps echo but then the echo dies, disconnectedly disappearing somewhere deep inside the building's deadweight inertia. There is a smell. A really rank smell. But Jean Paul, who'd smoked too much too long, can't place it. Two weeks ago Harvey had unloaded a bad batch of readi-mixed Dr Modesto (a speedball brand) on him that had all but floored his remainingly functional nasal nerves, leaving him effectively smell-dumb.

Petey has forged ahead of them. He has gone on into another room – there's a bright fluorescent light on when he opens the door.

They troop inside.

'Jesus wept,' Jean Paul gasps.

All around the room are animal carcasses. They hang from meathooks. The white lino floor is covered with old blood stains. Nausea rises inside him.

Steadying himself, he looks round at them.

Blond John is tying a mask over his mouth. Petey does some reverential gazing at the object in the centre of the room.

It's a table. A long refectory table. Converted, after the hi-tech style fashionable during the late 1970s, to industrially functional furniture with a clean, stainless-steel top.

'Lie down,' Petey says very quietly.

'Look guys,' Jean Paul begins. 'I'm not a charity.'

'C'mon, kiddo,' John cajoles pleasantly. With the index finger of his left hand, he pulls down the top of the mask to show that his tanned face has fallen into its natural, easy smile.

'Loosen up, hah?'

Then Jean Paul notices that in his right hand Blond John holds a ferocious meat cleaver.

'Take all your clothes off and lie on the table.' Petey leers. 'John boy's a veggie – can't stand the sight of blood.'

'S'true,' John avers from behind the mask.

Chockers, dildos, harnesses, rings, straps, buttplugs, specula, whips, handcuffs, shackles. He'd dealt with all of them. Jean Paul is pretty sure that he could handle whatever they'd got. Earlier in the week he'd had an Arab who'd gone warpo-weirdo on him, but he'd put the brakes on that by pouring brandy over his clothes during lust-play and – under the pretext of lighting a pre-coital cigar – had set fire to them, triggering the apartment's security systems.

Punters – whatever next?

There's no way he can run the strongroom door – Blond John has locked it with a heavy-duty industrial chromium-bar. He reckons he's going to have to talk his way out of this one.

There'd be someway out of this. He's very calm – he can still feel the Spectre suffuse through his nervous system.

Then Petey hits a switch and concealed bolt-clamps spring out to pinion him to the metal table top. Jean Paul shifts. That he hadn't banked on. Blond John has been doing him for about six or seven minutes when Jean Paul sees Petey's face bear back down on his.

'The thing is,' he says, his face up really close to Jean Paul's now, his breath smelling like a bar, his voice wheedling, pleading, quasi-logical. 'Even though John Boy's a veggie, I just love blood. I love it to death.'

He splits the boy's head cleanly down the middle with one downward thwack. He watches for a minute or two, then turns away. He pulls out the black box from his pocket and flips it open. He hits the autodial button and waits.

The party answers at the other end.

'Harry?' he says, and before cutting the line Petey Casales adds just one word.

'Four.'

24 Hours in Torquemada

JACK HUMS ALONG with the jolly tune on the car radio. He rates this funky hunk of rented azure GDMC Merlin junk metal which pelts well-mell along the dark, narrow lanes and chicanes of bandito country.

Its headlights don't discriminate. They illuminate oak and ash, larch, birch, beach and cedar; surprise freaky-deky chinless cows; hit the epigrammatic messages that glower cryptically on crucial roadsigns and wow sleepy villages that have more virgins than café-bars alike with glare as justly random as it was ferocious and surprise!

Eat tarmac, baby, suck my carbon mono, let these tyres tread each and every inch of your tender soft skin. Catch the dirt, mud in your face, get out of my space.

Economy compact car from hell!

Miraculously, the rent-a-bomb has clocked merely 0000097 klicks and the reading-light still works. Had he so wished, he could've tackled *War and Cheese* – the new hardback he'd picked up in Venice about the role of food in military history – full of armies marching on their stomachs, flanker fodder and gourmet pincer movements. But instead he deploys his Enoch Baden-Powell map-reading skills. Jack has a graphic black and white sense of direction. The fascism of finding the right road. This way is right – that way wrong.

Sometimes it's that easy. All roads lead to home. Others, not. When all roads lead to home, navigation's simplicity because a pre-destined path is imprinted somewhere inside each of us like, perhaps, a miser's guarded scroll where *x* marks the spot.

But Jack is travelling without a proper map. The map is the landscape all around him.

Now as he drives he recollects Kelly. Kelly R. Guervitz.

Her travel was mostly vicarious: she'd discovered the secret of Zen and the art of getting lost.

Kelly was a thin blonde Californian girl with the large watery blue eyes of the irredeemably myopic.

She was good at maps.

They'd lived together in a poky terraced fag-end o' hippyshit hovel off Reichold Road. The kind of pseudo-squat where, before the y-word people had started to skip in and yup it up, there was usually at least one communard tuning a guitar, another selling drugs, and a third snivelling about holding a 'house meeting'. If you have ever come across such places, you may not be surprised to hear that one visitor had dropped by for tea three and half years before Jack had moved in, and had been there ever since because (on his way out to the backyard lav) he'd stopped to look in the hall mirror and wow it's like a flashback man he saw that he was really a dinosaur kinda trapped in a kink in the space-time continuum but you know it was cool 'cos dinosaurs are good karma they're vegetarian and they don't make bombs.

Another itinerant resident in this grimy hutch of a house, Jan, built small – but ingeniously fashioned – pink sculptures from the dental paste usually used in the manufacture of false teeth, which he stole from the surgery where he worked as technician.

Jack's friend, Tony, whose papa (a high court judge) actually owned the wretched dump, had a black pre-war Davino Strato-cruiser limosine with running boards and silver-plated handles above the dashboard which opened each of the split windscreens outwards to provide the contemporary equivalent of air conditioning. It was always parked outside.

He'd never driven it.

Neither had anyone else. It didn't work. No one knew why: Tony, who always wore his long hair unwashed and his brown suede boots scruffed up, had uttered not one polysyllabic word in his flat up-country accent since Mick Jagger died, well you know – like spiritually – and was universally deemed the demi guru of Zen Cool.

Kelly was the girl in the paisley-coloured silk smocks guilt-dressed from the ethnique box who'd long nurtured an ambition to appear in the yellow pages.

She had confidentially confessed it to Jack one summer afternoon. He'd promised not to tell another living soul. And to this day, he'd kept that promise.

Shortly afterwards Jack, the ambitious country policeman's son, had sold some hash to an incongruous blow-in teenage blonde. She was called Annie. And had just come down from secretarial college to work at an auction house where, she said flirtatiously, she'd soon be an expert. She had many hip hooray friends and a bedsit she shared with her collegiate chum Zarah, where she could hide from the incessant attentions of eligible suitors.

He'd married her before the end of that year.

Kelly had become a cartography-collector – and so billed herself in the phone book. She'd had 15th-century maps of Lincolnshire and 1950s maps of the solar system.

'I love outer space,' she'd told Jack as she unravelled her collection that afternoon in a focused moment during his distant blur of recollected past. 'Outer space is cute.'

She had maps of the world as a 2-D raggedy-edged flatland; as a sharp-angled, scrunched-up, sub-compact globe, like a cinescope production squeeze-zoomed onto the small-screen. Maps for hunting, maps for minerals; maps of mountains and maps which showed oceanic topography. Climatic maps and those describing the distribution of ethnic sub-groups on seven continents.

Yes, Jack always knew where he was with a map.

Tonight he needs to know where he's going and peers through fine lines of sheet wet confusion to follow the signs on the road to his overnight base. As he whizzes along, some peripheral corner of his emotional vision is unsettled as the rain drizzles down from dark sky above. As one part of him concentrates mechanically on the roads winding through the small towns that nestle, like windows on market day, between the hills and scarps – another eventually arrives at the reason for this disquiet. In all the years he'd come here, it had never rained before.

Not once.

Trip-time? 52 minutes. When then at last, there is a fork in the road. Behind which is what appears to be a stretch of black water. Atop a hillock lies – Les Arcs.

As he guns up the path to the house, gravel stones spin off the tyres. In his lights, he sees that his rendezvous is a rambling, old stone-built provincial farmhouse that, on closer scrutiny, actually comprises two adjacent buildings which conjoin in a grey, L-shaped protective proximity.

He jettisons the case on one of the smallest beds he's ever seen outside a doll's house. Another lies adjacent, both covered with identical red and yellow floral bedspreads.

The briefcase he leaves on the floor – he's very superstitious about putting briefcases on beds. For some reason he'd never let this personal idiosyncratic iggly interfere with suitcases. Intuitively, he feels suitcases don't count – even if they have hats in them. Stupid and irrational though it is, it's so ingrained within his behaviour that it has come to form part of his identity: memory trapped in trauma. A drama block.

Stealthed.

Again he remembers. Now how, as a small boy, he and his friends were wont to climb and sit in the branches of a particular tree which commanded a view of the village and countryside around. One muggy afternoon he was idling there when he heard a shot and clambered down to go for his life through the squelshy bog, chased by a farmer bellowing obscenities. Having made good his escape, he'd leant up against the old brick wall that ran around one part of the churchyard, panting to regain his breath. He'd ripped his shirt – but considered himself lucky not to have drawn blood in his hasty scramble to vacate the arboreal bower. He felt an itch by his right knee. He scratched it. Then he felt an uncontrollable urge to touch the corresponding spot by his left knee. And did so. From that moment on it became an irresistible impulse. He'd never consciously touch the left-hand side without also touching the right. Just to even up, so the right side didn't feel left out because it hadn't been itchy. It seemed to him to do otherwise might be to encourage whichever limb had been misbehaving itself, or indeed his whole body, to twitch and jerk as an attention-getting ploy, which would (oh no!) turn him rapidly into a tic-jerking tremulous pariah like fat, red-haired Alistair Laver who was mercilessly toughed up by everyone. To disturb this equilibrium, he remains privately convinced, is to tempt destiny in some unnatural way, to incur the wrath of the fates.

The dinner jacket is on top. Underneath lies the roused white shirt. He strips off his top and heads for the bathroom. Inside, his fingers search for the light switch.

The green soap on the clean white basin bathes his nostrils with a pleasantly verdant smell. It suggests a pot-pourri of esoterically rustic herbs and fresh-cut flowers, along with a veiled, but sternly carbolic, accompanying admonition to clean-up-your-act.

The tourist who aspires to be a traveller sniffs out the strangeness of places and attempts to quantify their many curiously individual smells, nasal clues and olfactory strands of come-hither wanderlusting big-joy.

But it can always, Jack reasons, go the other way.

The tourist who aspires to be a traveller, and so follows his nose, may well end up idly wacked off on the trough of some private idiosyncratic graph of quiet despair, lost in expensively confused sleep. Why? Wagga-wagga warm-wave that forces *el touristo* to retire to bed for the duration of the crippling face-sucky day-time hot-blast. Place-lagged and prisoner in any one of a squillion homogeneously decorated double-bedded luxury-class suites with identical room-service menus which serve repulsive club sandwiches in 17 languages and two flavours – gross and totally gross – while the radio that won't turn off plays a martial soundtrack to chuck cookies to in four-four time. And as *el touristo* puts his head down the pan again, he realizes he's sadly unable to pay for the privilege of all this, due to earlier smart fingerwork by dodgy taxi driver who knew 'best restaurant, my cousin's restaurant, you like very much, I promise'. And then there was maybe some man with a cutlass beating down the door; a stake-out with some vicious eight-legged funnelweb spider; an unpleasant scene with two big-breasted whores or 'misunderstanding' with the local police chief about his cousin's car, whatever. Such hapless homebods return from their big trip with a bijou-bijou selection of unfocused trannies of manhole covers from around the world, or sewing kits of many countries.

But this is merely the skin on the snake: all travel is hot yet also cool but rarely lukewarm – it is seldom wrong to explore, to experience the peripatetic reptile kick, to re-draw one's maps. To the traveller, the voyage's exterior crests and troughs run parallel with an expedition within one's own interior, an emotional shift into a foreign mind-scape of dark, of light, an adventure into a bigger world where there are questions in trees, hissing between the many burnished shades of green green and in-between. It isn't the buildings, it's the spaces between the buildings – such is the attraction of fresh architecture. Jack never fails to delight in the strangeness of other people's houses, the unfamiliarity, the otherness there. Like their owners, each terrain holds many different pockets of alien, unspoken history and concealed cartography.

He has to activate the lavatory with a switch to flush it. From a hole in the ceiling a slim, grey length of corrugated plastic tubing runs down one side of the wall and up another before plunging into the back of the finely cracked white porcelain lavatory cistern.

He realizes he's become so embroiled in developing his Theory of Soul Tourism that he's washed his hands before pissing – and so finds himself compelled to retrace his steps to the basin and start all over again from the beginning.

Twitch, tic, shimmer and shake – identity as behaviour that describes a circle.

Back in the bedroom, he wriggles into the white shirt, wiggles into the DJ, buttons up the black flies on the dark trousers Annie had bought on the knock with a spectacular bid some months before at the neighbourhood's shamateur dramatic society's fund-drive action auction jumble.

As he slips on his shiny black shoes, he notices that between the beds on the polished slats of wooden floor lies a small, distinctively patterned, predominantly red chinese rug.

He races from the bedroom, running seriously late.

At the head of the stairs he finds himself staring straight into the dim glassy eyes of a mounted baby fox's head. It had to be a baby fox's head. The mounting of the beast means the baby fox must now be dead.

BUMPETY BUMP. BUMPETY BUMP. Bumpety bump. Bumpety . . wheelspin! The blue-blazered man in Careera wraparound sunglasses bends down on the right. A sallow techi, with skin like olive oil, in the grease-smeared white overalls leans down on the left. They lift the back end of the car up away from the jutting, knobbly-gnarled tree-root and set the vehicle back on all fours, so the procession might continue. Bumpety Bump. Bumpety bump. Bumpety bump bump.

The drivers' faces, Jack notices, strike different attitudes. Some are proud. Some nervous. Others race with exhilaration and pure pleasure, while a few register screwed-up expressions of ferocious concentration. One small boy is animated in abject terror. He, Jack sees, wears overalls emblazoned with the logo of a processed cheese company.

Those little white replicars can't have been cheap. Even with their lawnmower engines, the pressed steel aerodynamic bodies alone must've hit the citizenry of Torquemada a pretty packet, full square on the hip-pocket nerve.

Jack heeds an urgent drive within him.

He keeps moving.

Milling auto-voyeurs now mooch past the GDMC display – the Euro car manufacturer's mini marquee which fronts their corporate orgy area. Behind the smoked glass of the prefabed pentagonal pagoda, the new GDMC XM3T24ST revolves majestically on a low-slung slow-show pedestal. As the platform describes its circle, it displays each glinting curve of the model's streamlined titanium body. Its trunk has been thrown open beaver-wide to grant those so motorvated a brief, tantalizing glimpse of the faithful facsimile representing the gleamingly awesome V-14 engine. The to-scale model replicates the result of nine months' intensive work and messianic research by a specially selected team of scientists, engineers, mechanics and Torquemada experts who had been isolated (Pam Tair had said) in conditions close to neo-monasticism to develop a machine that would finally – after 25 years of vanquishment – finally win back the coveted Torquemada 24-Hours Trophy for the motor vehicle division of the humongous giant global manufacturing corporation.

The three cars that would actually represent Team GDMC (sponsored by Long Life Ciggie Co.) in the race had been wheeled, some hours ago, into the trackside pits from the open tents where the mechanics had spent the last 72 hours frantically fine-tuning their charges into a state of pure peak of performance.

Hundreds of thousands of people annually converge on the coastal town of Torquemada in a hejira pilgrimage. Now it seems like every bloody one of them is moving towards the track simultaneously. A transmigration of strolls. Those with grandstand seats pre-reserved, saunter; those who must fight to ensure their viewing position get into gear with more velocity.

Velocity! thinks Jack. That's what's new under the sun.

Did Archimedes, he muses, discourse by fax? Did Henry V use radio telephones to call down a supersonic air strike at Agincourt? Columbus somehow discovered America, and Cook Australia, without the aid of satellite maps. Would Oscar Wilde have been wittier with a word processor?

Even beauty, he thinks sadly, blending into the crowd, isn't velocity proof. He is thinking of one of the Poodle pack, a tart called Cressida who's obsessed with cosmetic surgery – and she's just turned 27.

The Crowd. Other People.

Yeah, the weekend grease monkeys, the ratchet chewers, souvenir gear ball-bearing buyers, serious oily-nirvana types who've been staking out pole positions in the stands since 4 a.m. yesterday; daytrippers, sportsmen, support staff, townspeople, officials, dilettantes and chancy hustlers from around about all teem in the rough and tumble, mix and muck cavalcade of automobile pornography, corporate binge-out and a rising tide of expectant adrenaline and liquor-fuelled hysteria.

See the man in the crowd.

Here he is. He is six foot two, maybe six three. His face is thin, his eyes are grey, lively eyes. His beard is going grey, his hair hangs on the collar of the nylon easi-wash shirt beneath the GDMC pufforak, so generously donated by the car manufacturers in the distinctive purple and white colours of their toxic sponsors.

'The Long Life Ciggie Co., just in case you'd forgotten. You weren't going to forget that, were you Jack? I mean obviously we wouldn't dream of interfering in any way with your editorial integrity. But if, when you do file, you could actually remember to mention that it's the *Long Life* GDMC – well personally I'd be extremely grateful, Jack, extremely grateful. Great mileage out of these diesel micro-buses, eh?'

Pam Tair. Pam Tair the PR.

Around his neck, Jack wears an assortment of laminated kiss-my-passes that give him all-areas access to any and every inch of the circuit and its amenities. With informed interest, he observes the progress of the veteran and vintage hero-mobiles of yesteryear as they hurtle around the tarmac. He can name them all.

'That's an Alveria Cobra, wonderful classic Anglo sports machine.'

'What's that, then?' taunts the tall, blonde, but very slightly blowzy sex goddess at his side saucily. She points at a couple of freaky-deke vehicles with pointy fronts and elongated flipperlike back-ends which take off from the starting block with a rasping note in their engines.

'They're the old Prague 1500s.'

'They look pretty flash,' the blonde girl says.

It's Katy Montcrieffe. She still works for Dial-A-Drug. But now she's a nightclub room manager at Rififi, an agent for three thesps, a writer for Zeitgeist too. She's also investigating the possibilities of aromatherapy. This is the urban condition: to take on identity.

He sees warm bed-me blue eyes with long lashes textured like butterfly wings. More the masculine, that.

'Yeah, but it's just styling. They were designed about 25 years ago as exercises in fuel economy – they never actually won anything much.' He pauses, thought-ploughed brow. 'Though hang on, I think maybe a couple might've been placed in their class. Anyway, they're only equipped with 1,500cc engines. The Waguars and Ferranttis of the period made mincemeat of them. They were beautiful machines, those Waguar C-types – look there's one now.'

A racing green motor-car, with elegant curved wheel arches beneath a long, low inviting bonnet and air-slashing back-fin at its rear, resonates with a sweetly tuned engine melody as it whistles past.

Aging fame commands respect. Always, always.

'You really know about this, don't you?'

'I used to come here quite a lot. Almost every year, in fact, when I was a teenager. I used to camp out by the Palladio straight in a tent. I've always been into fast cars.'

She beckons him with her eyes c'mon.

'One year I arrived and lost all my money.' He chuckles. He finds his old mistakes funny: time dries your eyes, you rationalize, you synthesize and eventually history supplies the distance that makes it seem part of the plan.

'I borrowed a pony from a drunk Irishman I met at the fair. It lasted me the whole weekend – I had to hitch back. God, it was hell at the time – but looking back now I'm glad I did it. You know it's never the things you do you regret – it's the things you didn't.'

She looks at him as if he talks on water.

'It's weird,' he says and turns to her, the modulation in his voice changing like the engine note of the Aston Martin Volante Special, as its driver shifts a gear to accelerate up the short straight before them. 'But it seems odd to come here again. You know? All this VIP stuff – the dinners – access to the pits, all the hospitality, the interviews with the drivers.' He looks at her. He takes her hand. 'And being here with you.'

A red Ferrantti Guillamo XR tears past, twin-exhausts sparking to full throttle in a cloud of vaporizing rubber and hot burning oil.

They snog.

Faces in the crowd.

Now the geriatric steel gladiators have been dispatched back to their resthomes and trailers, and the leg parade of front-loaded bikini beauties (*'C'est La Midi,'* says the announcer over the loud-speak commentary system. 'Torquemada's the most on the coast!') has given way to the real deal. The cars are lined up on the grid, race cars. Fine-tuned temperamental snorty pieces of snarlo ultra-tech, 57 varieties of wheely groove sex-machine testifying to the mongerizing vanity of corporate macho.

A group of seven officials stands before the grid.

One man in the omnipresent white overalls carries a flag. He has a droopy walrus moustache. His team busy themselves with stopwatch-fuss and list-check lust from clipboards, or tote large signs. One of which is eventually produced for public display to the buzzing, burbling clattering chattering sea of faces packed into and around the stands.

5 MINUTES.

Paparazzi and TV crews scurry around, chased by track peons who shoo them officiously behind the white lines circuitside. As soon as the officials hurry elsewhere to pursue yet more naughty media miscreants, our original transgressors resume their impromptu interviews and merciless harry of the men inside those harshly functional cockpits.

Jack consults the glossy programme, identifying the various machines and their pilots. In the pole position are the two blue and white CZs. In the next three places behind lie three GDMCs. Then an ungainly rabble of Ferranttis, Nyghtbirds, Bell-Aviatronics, and tech-mech miscellania.

As he moves around, the droopy 'tached starter listens intently to all but inaudible instructions issuing from green, mufflerlike cans around his ears. Occasionally he barks terse instructions into his walky talkback. He signals. Another man holds up a new sign.

2 MINUTES.

A ripple of expectancy runs through the crowd like a wave.

Now see this crowd.

The crowd is a bitch. It likes death, fire, high-speed impact. The crackle of the engines. The bullet whizz of the vehicles as they accelerate past the pits opposite the grandstands. To them the sound's a tease. Because beneath all the intense reverential stat-crazed chit-chat about demi-mythic past heroics, lap records, drag factors, transmission crankshafts, gear-stick bearings, torque and compression ratios and race strategies, the crowd is a gloating pop-eyed vampire baying for fast blood, for searing metal which burns up flesh in a killing machine that ignites into an incandescent,

4,000-degree Celsius cellular pyre inferno as it hits top gear on the straight at 280, 290, 300 mph and then rolls over and over spitting fire and blood and screams and doom.

The sun is shining now.

Jack looks at the girl by his side. 8,000 questions. Pick one, Jack.

How the hell have I got into this?

He remembers the way 48 hours before the First Citizen reached forward and grasped his hand to say, 'But didn't you want to ask me another question?' Death in Venice. Death in Torquemada. Death – everywhere: just add gasoline and fuel the fantasy.

The smell of it – everywhere.

In your eyes, your hair.

Now a white-coated figure parades a new sign: START YOUR ENGINES.

The noise is a punch in the ear. It is a wall of sound. But just as a wall of brick contains any colours that make the whole, so this sonic wall has many notations, variations and crochet-humming tonal demi-quavers that soar and mutate within it.

'Are you ready to race?' he asks her, fortissimo.

'Are you?' she shouts back through the passage between cupped hands.

For an entire day, absolutely incessantly, the noise will continue.

The sound of the fury of the will to win.

From this point on there can be no escape from the screams in the balls of the beast. This is what's happening for 24 hours in Torquemada.

New sign: 30 SECONDS.

The starting crew move to the right-hand side of the track, and the stewards now urgently hustle a lone paparazzi with a flyaway beard and brown leather jacket from the tarmac.

'Do you always answer a question with a question?' he shouts in her lug.

'Whatever makes you say that?' she answers back.

The starter drops a green flag and the noise is like the water breaking over a sea wall in a typhoon. The cars move off in a slow-mo dreamy blur of sheet metal that roars. But by the time the last ranks are away, they've picked up speed. And even these back-ranked monsters, for the most part smaller class III machines, move very zippily indeed.

For an hour or so Jack and Katy watch all their speed and colour whizz by in a thrash mirage.

'I don't understand this, actually,' she complains. They've now adjusted to conversation conducted in raucous bellows. 'How do you know which car is on which lap?'

So he takes her to the press box on the other side of the track, where there is a teletext display, diligently updated. This is part of the apparatus of media-cool: it shows the precise positions of the cars in relationship to one another. Their fastest lap; the number of laps completed; pit-stops taken; their current driver and much much else besides. Cars 17 and 16, the team CZs, are in front. Two GDMCs are half a lap behind. Then a privately entered CZ. Then a Ferrantti. And then the pack. Somewhere in there is a vehicle sponsored by Telcom, somewhere else a machine liveried in the colours of a group of Sunni Muslim fundamentalists.

They watch cars stagger pitwards, observe the various crews tackle their limping and perky charges both, hear the percussive nuhnuhnuhnuh of the automatic screwdrivers. They see smoke pouring out of the pits, see one car, then another, abandon the chase. Already disaster has struck a privately entered Ferrantti on the recently altered S-bends preceding the Palladio straight – the Pace Car is out.

'If' – para 23, extracted from the *Official Rules*, Torquemada

24-Hour Road Race – 'during the progress of the race, the Race Marshall decides that some extraneous factor – such as blockage of the track by debris – renders conditions dangerous, the Pace Car, identifiable by the orange lights on its roof, will drive onto the circuit and progress of the race shall be halted immediately. Competitors' positions remain static from the moment of its appearance: drivers must immediately form their vehicles into an orderly procession behind the Pace Car and not attempt to overtake on pain of automatic disqualification. When the obstacle has been removed and it is safe to continue racing, the Pace Car will complete one final circuit of the track, signified by the flashing of its orange roof lights. At the end of this lap, the race shall resume as before.'

And how.

The GDMCs re-start like game whippets on dope, and within two laps purple and white vehicles number 4 and 5 have established their predominance over the CZs, much to the great chagrin of the CZ pits.

'It's the occidental equivalent of the cargo cult,' Katy says four hours later as she stumbles out of the ebullient GDMC pitside hospitality zone beside Jack. 'It's like all these insignificant, stupid bloody little people gathered together to worship speed and power in the hope that some of it'll rub off on them and transform their grubby little lives.'

'My my, you are sharp aren't you?' he says, riffling efficiently through the quartermass papermass he's now accumulated in the puffajacket's pockets. 'There's a dinner somewhere tonight, isn't there?'

'Oh, I don't really particularly want to go,' she says. 'I don't think I could stand it. Those quails at lunch-time with their heads still on – it made me feel really queasy.'

'Yeah, you know it's gastroporn when the waiters start taking pictures of the food.'

Now they walk along the narrow concrete alley, down bare stone stairs behind the pits, past piles of tyres and spare bonnets, hoods and cowlings stacked up, waiting. And they move through the crowd, the trailers that hawk every kinda knick-knack and crass check-the-brand motor memorabilia – war-trophies for the speed voyeur – through the astringent smells of spiced meat and evil samosas, to the reserved white-zone car park where the Funky Hunk of Junk awaits.

'Do you want a lift back to Les Arcs?'

(The thrifty Madame Vauvatier annually turned over every spare room to paying journalistic guests.)

'Oh that'd be lovely. It's not putting you out, is it?'

'Really, it's no trouble. I've got to go back anyway at some stage and grab a couple of hours' shut-eye. I want to get up early, about three I think, to catch the rest of the race. And you know what they say – an hour before midnight is worth two after.'

He hears the cliché talk and baulks (They? Who are they? And what do they know about his sleep patterns anyway?) but excuses himself with a gliblet soupçon of rationale: clichés are clichés because they're true.

34 minutes later they're back at Les Arcs. Of their curious and eccentric hosts the Vauvatiers, no sign. All is still, except for the snores of a person they identify by the passes inside his neck as George Astbury, a motorsport trade hack who's passed out with his head on the giant leafed dining table, resting on the leather-patched arms of his brown tweedy chainstore jacket. He snoozes gently behind his spectacles and nicotine-stained moustache.

Nothing is said as Jack and Katy cruise past the stone fireplace with three arcane motifs carved above it. They see the picture of the crusty Vauvatier ancestor with the overbite on the wall above the fireplace, next to the regimented handcoloured military scenes.

Next frame? Past the wood that pops its sap in the fire. Move over rugs. Motor along wooden floors (next, next – keep moving!) up the frayed blue carpet on the stairs, past the rip in the last panel on the mural. And the baby fox still stares glass-eyed at the hunter with his gun.

Neither of them, for different reasons, comments on any of this.

Katy, because she has nothing to say. And believes that when one has nothing to say it is generally best to keep quiet – lest others take you for a gabbermouthed twerp.

Jack? He is older – he ought to know better. But all he knows is worse. Jacko feels like he's been shrunk to the size of that thin strip of plastic you sometimes find on pre-digital radios – and that something's pushing him beyond his frequency, out of his waveband, miles off the dial.

On the landing, they stop and look at each other for a moment.

HE: 'What's your frequency?'

SHE: 'What's your threshold?'

HE: 'What's your speed?'

SHE: 'You reckon you're fast enough for me?'

She goes to the bathroom and he sits on one of the tiny beds, his feet on the red Chinese rug, reflecting on the velocity his life has acquired. Some people get off on narcotics, some drink, others gamble, a few crave power. The world is full of neurotics; fat-sos; couch-potatoes; obsessive horticulturalists awaiting bizarre gardening accidents and anal-retensive corkscrew collectors. The psychopathic geography teacher who, on dismissal for his cruel and unusual punishments of his young charges, channels his destructive energies into constructing a mausoleum built from barbed wire. Jack – like many other mediaocrities – craves speed. He wants his life to move and move fast. This way, he reasons, there is less pain – the involvement is structured. The momentum of events limits one's exposure. Pace creates a hard, intimidating, protective cocoon that affords its apostrophated mechanic-owner-driver not merely the opportunity to observe, but frequently a means of adjusting details in the passing panorama as it fleets around him.

And the tempo is a rapid clip: too hip, gotta go – I personally do so sympathize with the terrible tragedy of your once happy family's devastation by this sadistic and sick psycho serial killer, but you can hear my bleeper screech calling me to another assignment – so if you'd just stand over there by the sweating flock wallpaper ('Positions please everybody') and tell me again ('Marker') just one more time ('Turn over and Action!') HOW DID IT FEEL? How did it feel when they told you your son had been found in an unmarked grave? How did it feel when you heard the tapes of his last moments, screaming and begging in sobs and pleas for mercy? Did you know an infotainment corporation is bidding for the rights so they can release the tapes as a boxed set? What's your reaction to that? What would you do to these people? Do you blame yourselves? Don't you ever feel that there's a reason why this happened to you? What is it like for you now? Can you reconstruct your lives again in the two minutes before our car arrives? HOW DOES IT FEEL?

And the filmed tape flies one place and Jack flies another to meet a different crew, who already are pre-planning how to tackle the grizzly Russian patriarch who'll break eggs to use their yokes for painting icons that'll hang on the walls of the Orthodox church, a church that lies on dry land within a city of water. And it's wild: here comes a fatly balding man with a cigarello, who refuses to let the camera hardware into the city on any of the cargo boats – on which he has a monopoly – unless he receives an immediate down-payment of 3,000 bucks per day for a minimum ten-day hire. Higher! Everything blurs.

Jack lives in a bubble in the blur. As do we all.

We are tourists lost in history, you and I, he and she. The edges blur and the gap grows soft in a space, the space where we live, a time between parentheses in human development.

Yet there are constants.

Katy has returned – she is even more beautiful than he could've guessed.

Her nipples are rosebuds.

'There are more crucifixes in this room than mirrors,' she says later, when she is happy again. She holds one in her hand – she's found it hidden in the shabbily painted green built-in cupboard by the bed.

As he watches her stand there something inside turns right round and his stomach catches the lift to his mouth. As she moves towards the beds he's pushed together in the heat of the moment, he sees in her a parallel life and it occurs to him that he could live it.

Live the dream.

A bigger life on a different canvas, splashier, a Gauguin in the commuter-club watercolour exhibition, worlds away from the Saturday-morning shopping and in-laws, the accelerating tension his secreted double-life and routine sexual warfare he'd known with Annie.

And he smells the foreignness of her, the other, as she lies on top of him and lets her soft tongue twist around his mouth, like some ancient Greek goddess placing her hand into a dark cave where there were snakes; inviolable, safe in her own vulnerability. And they roll over and fall on the floor.

'Owwwwww,' she howls.

He rubs the soft white milkiness of the skin on her thigh. He is patient, soothing her with noises that sound like a valentine card. He darts his tongue in her ear and slowly begins to rally, to sally and toss gamey foreplays this way and back. He turns her over and runs his lips down the entire length of her spine.

'Ohhhhhh,' she moans.

He doesn't stop and nor does she.

Her hands grip the cold red square tiles upon the sill, and he pushes her and she hangs right out of the window; and he has her there with her tits out in the night air, and she screeches over the dark gravel path, beyond the black water, into the grim hills where cows lie down under the struggling spread of tree boughs.

Love comes in spurts, short hard shots of hot jissim.

Travelling, moving.

And still.

They doze on the bed.

His mind whirs, turning over scenes and sensibilities like the movie projector that wanted to direct the apostrophated film, wild cutting random sprockets in the soft, warm celluloid; blowing through the barriers that separate each frame within the strip.

She drowses in flowing fantasies of childhood: burning cars and soldiers in green berets; petrol bombs and ritual stonings; disappearances and songs about dismembered stumps in vinegar; castles and louche boys called Johnny in silk smoking jackets, holding ivory and Bakelite cigarette holders as they drawled of playing a frightfully sportin' game of real tennis.

Tossing in her sleep, she screams, awakes and turns around.

'There, there.'

He hugs her.

'Look,' he says.

On the red tiled windowsill, Madame Vauvatier has left a bowl of fresh cherries.

EVERY TIME HE'D BEEN HERE, he realizes, something had unfolded, had revealed itself.

In the past it had been upbeat: socksiness, self-discovery, expansiveness – 'more of me' – pushing back the barriers, breaking through thresholds.

But now he's forced to face the fact that life is finite and there are two clear roads he can go down.

Down.

Or maintain – and then down suddenly.

This is it, he realizes.

Post-coital Triste?

Keep moving, Jack.

Back at the pits: smoke drifts through the hard-glare beams of the bright arc lights that cut through the night like knives. He pushes through the bodies huddled against the tape that cordons off the immediate work-area. Around the space before the raised dais arc the team manager and his purple and white pufforaked cohorts, grand marque groupies and sundry lesser bimbs with stopwatches, clipboards and endless streams of black coffee for the mechanics who, between changes, hang around like gangsters, picking their nails in nervous preen. Something wrong – Brocklebank skids GDMC number 5 inside. The team manager yanks open the door. The driver wrenches at his visor, and shouts at the crew. Blown a tyre. Co-ordinated frenzy as each mechanic moves to perform his appointed task. The go-faster squeegee wipedown to clear the insect bodies that inevitably splatter all over the windscreen at 260, 280, 300 mph. The double-ended gas fill, with the plastic funnel vacuum on the right, sucking out the surplus air. The rapido-rapido nuh nuhnuhnuh of the mechanical screw-driver as it removes and ejects the dead wheel. Mechanics put their hands up to show they're through.

But where's the replacement rubber?

'Move it,' the team manager bellows in exasperation.

'Use this one,' another mechanic in a dirty boiler suit shouts, as he rolls a tyre from number 6's pit towards the crew working on the Brocklebank car. The spark as Giles Brocklebank roars away in hot pursuit of shapes in the night. The whole operation has taken, Jack guesses, perhaps one minute. On the way in, Brocklebank still tenuously held the lead by the skim of his car's metallic sheath – CZ number 17 was right on top of it and closing.

60 seconds where perhaps there should've been 25.

Seconds.

Crucial micro-moments of too-late time.

Going, going, gone.

Going out, number 17 had nosed in front. By the time Jack reaches the press box, Klassen's CZ runs more than a lap ahead – and now car 16, piloted by one of the Salvatori brothers, is catching up.

'The rain is holding off and the CZ's nuclear-boost turbo-drive is now showing to advantage,' Jack hears one of the francophone commentators say into his microphone. He gazes intently at the heat-streak pictures that play on the battery of screens in the press room.

Jack treks along the towpath surrounding the circuit, imagining the two cops investigating city fraud in his projected treatment for a mini-series knocked up on Sunday afternoons with Kinkaid, his only remaining friend from Uni. He contemplates the history of Pam Tair, Annie's friend from the Realito Academy of Dramatic and Performing Arts who, in her role as corporate flack for the purple and toxic white Long Life Ciggie Co., has arranged this trip. Of Pam's unwise marriage to the RSM she'd met while she was a newsreader in the Middle East, and the way she'd fallen for that militaristic moron's bullshine faster than an Imam with a whip on a desert drinks party. He considers how easy it would be for a terrorist, or even that Joke-shop Killer, to assassinate the First Citizen in Venice by concealing a gun in a dummy TV camera.

He thinks of thresholds: the place where you run off the edge of the map; where there are no more signs, no cues, no clues.

He recollects the girl who'd sat next to Katy at that dinner in Maurey, the tone-deaf girl who'd avoided national service in Israel by becoming a troubadour folksinging to the troops all along the Wailing Wall, and he muses on the men who fought the needlematch around and behind him, and finds himself now walking over a mound of ground, where before him lies the Fair.

The Fair is a top-ranking attraction of the Torquemada 24-Hours. It pulls, as he knew from bitter experience, every pick-pocket within miles. Now he wanders nomadically among its garish neon.

Jack hands over 3.75 to see Utaz, 'the fattest woman in the world'. A portable red neon display announces she is 33 years old and weighs 421 kilos. She sits on two chairs as the curtains part. She sits glumly, silent, still, a mass of blubberation, veins pulsing out of flab, great wads of flesh rolling over one another in an obscene, splangle-lurex clad cacophony of obesity.

Jack makes his way to the back of the crowd. He catches her eye. And waves to her.

She smiles a wry grin. But she doesn't wave back.

Outside Other People mill around him. He sees small boys shooting on dodgy pre-shonked rifle ranges, the air-guns recoiling to bruise their shoulders, never to hit the mendacious targets which would travel with the prizes from town to town. He remembers once making a programme about fairgrounds for the regional TV station where he'd worked after leaving university – he'd then come to the conclusion that fairs were places where one discovered a new identity amidst the violent bustle, the loud noise (now overlaid by the screaming motor-whine that banshees through the night), the flashing lights, the tattoos, the giddy scream-machines, the burly competition, the sweet, tooth-rot candy-floss: the ephemerality of it – the frozen moments so large in a child's life, so formative, so 'this is bigger than both of us, daddy'. And no carnival could be more transient than this – for it exists for just eight hours during the long night of Torquemada as the headlights whir and whizz around the track.

Jack resists the urge to see the world's smallest ponies, somehow overcomes the lure of the naked lady in the pit with snakes, remains unamused by the prospect of 'Funny Girls from New York'.

But one booth draws him strangely.

It is set apart from the others somewhat. There is no blagger with a microphone hustling in the punters with chutzpah and tawdry challenge. Just a sad-looking woman, maybe 40 something, who sits outside drawn beige curtains. There are no signs which indicate what might lie behind. No one enters. No one leaves.

He asks the woman what's inside.

'Seven bucks, M'sieur,' she says wearily. She doesn't look at him. Her features are world-weary – but sharp. She has a pointy nose, feline eyes and a strong chin. On her fourth finger she wears one of the largest diamond rings he's ever seen.

'But what's inside?'

'Seven bucks, monsieur,' she repeats, as if talking to an extremely stupid child.

He pauses, baffled, victim of an indecision attack.

'Do you want to see the show or not?' she asks finally. 'If you do, give me your money and go in. If not, please move along so that others can see.'

In the distance car engines roar and he fancies he hears screams. But now, as if in a trance, he sees himself hand over the money. She operates a concealed lever beneath her desk and a door creaks open squeakily.

Inside, the show is screened off in such a way that one has to walk around to the back of the tent to view the exhibits.

What Jack initially finds is a series of glass jars set on narrow, upright wooden tables.

In the first, suspended in what he presumes is an alcohol/formaldehyde solution, is a monkey-faced foetus. It has grey gunk caught up in its brown hair, matted like an old-fashioned coconut gymnasium pad such as the one he had landed on many times at school.

He moves on, gripped, in spite of a gloss of grossed repulsion, to the next item.

Inside this jar is a tiny grey mermaid, half-torn as if it wants to split in two. It can't have been more than 24 inches high. It too floats in formaldehyde, perhaps suspended by some hidden string or wire. He is struck by its face, such a small face. Half human, half chimera, its features, pitifully contorted, seem to epitomize pain: all pain ever felt by human or animal everywhere throughout time. He tries to tell himself it's fake, but a part of him stares at the pleading grey eyes, dried out in the thin skin, as if they'd awoken one morning to see the Scapegoat waiting at the foot of the bed. It upsets him so much he wants to cry. His eyes water as he moves on to the adjacent exhibit and becomes aware of a voice talking to him. The voice is pitched falsetto. It belongs to a –

midget with a microphone.

The little man, dapper clad in a smart dinner jacket and dark trousers not dissimilar to those somewhere in that room at Les Arcs, where even now Katy probably slept and dreamt in the dolls' house bed.

He can scarcely believe it.

Long Memory: Micro-man pushing trolley sandwiched in a board that asked DO U JUJU?

The homunculus stands on a small rug, Red, Chinese.

Short Memory: Its pattern seems uncannily similar to –

No, no.

Must be tired. Fatigue. Media-lag. State of over-arousal. Stress.

The distinctive pattern on the rug swims before his eyes. He rubs his peepers, opens them, and looks around, forcing himself to notice things. The dwarf is surrounded by plants and speaks in some strange esoteric coastal pitter-patois-I-am-a-dialect with which he was infuriatingly unfamiliar. Jack moves along, his mind like an old leaf fallen in damp fog.

More bell-jars: he sees two babies that share one head, an enormously inflated domelike cranium; a pig embryo with two bodies joined to one hideously disfigured bonce.

The last jar contains a human foetus which had somehow sprouted two skulls. An embryonic person with two heads, in which sit cruel parodies of the human face that share the same flat, misshapen body between them.

Jack walks outside and makes his way back towards the white zone. On the way he passes a man wearing a baseball cap with a radio built in. The man checks the progress of the race through the white plastic wire that drops down from the cap into his ears.

'Gearbox, gearbox,' he mutters to himself as Jack passes.

They make tracks through the crowd in opposite directions.

Jack walks back to the track and stands by the Palladio straight, near the woods where, in years gone by, he'd habitually pitched camp. As the dawn breaks and sun comes up, he notices that, as always, fewer and fewer cars are lapping. Back at the press box he cogs on that the CZs have somehow regained the lead.

Short memory: somewhere during the night, he remembers watching GDMC number 5 come in far too fast on the Vaux chicane, hit the esses in the wrong gear and turn over in a spinning fireball. Death Fantasy Factor Five feeds the gasps and yells of the crowd. He re-visualizes the purple and white mess hurtle and turn. Remembers the confusion and alarums – foam spraying the crowd, ambulances seeming to join the race, the appearance of the Pace Car, and pilot Henri Enriques miraculously stepping from the burning shell, unscathed.

Auto-resurrection.

Heat. Sun. Noise.

The noise is now like the whine of the beast, the sound of an animal pushed to the very limit of its capabilities.

The sun beats down like thunder. It hovers, a yellow egg nestling in a powder-blue sky. And the heat, the heat is a recipe for misery: select high humidity and bake at 95 Fahrenheit for four days. Honey, the heat goes on. Time counts off. The sun is an egg and the egg cracks.

Here it comes again.

People hoon and gibber as the wildfire thrill of it all builds to climax EERROWW, spreads and burns incandescent, fagging out and draggin' down some well-knackered fatigue victims of spectator overheat; see them burn-out, slouched around the concrete blocks, prostrate on the green grass, aghast as they lumber into the cheap sideshows which surround the main event, prone to lurch in gearbox-gearbox attitudes of attrition and morose melancholy, weary and battered by fatigue and sleep-starvation, by drunkenness motorvated by the automatically febrile neuron postures of the engine-random-zealot-crazy.

And now the sun. And now the heat. And now the noise.

EERROWW.

He finds himself back at the GDMC pits. He watches mechanically now; each bend has a right line, every stretch of straight a blow-out point. He hears Pam Tair, stopwatch swingling perkily around her thin, fake-baked neck, squeaking in her tones of aspirational apricot that car number 6 has retired.

'But it was marvellous what they did with Umbonza in car 4. The cylinder casing cracked – so they glued it together with Superglue, isn't that marvellous, Jack, *Superglue*?'

She could just as easily have told him that the first horse to wear spectacles was fitted for a number seven lens or that 23,811 American tourists visited Fiji in 1982.

Two roads you can go down, he thinks.

'Are you OK, Jack?' Pam asks. 'You look a bit peaky. Let me get you a bacon sandwich.'

And now, some hours later (CZ have got this sewn up, no doubt about it), Katy Montcrieffe smiles at him beginily.

When she's sure no one's looking, she winks and dispels his exhaustion with her smile.

And the conflict surges within him again like some alien thing.

They don't stay to the end of the race. He drives her back to Les Arcs.

Roadrace!

In his mind, he leads the pack and the engine whines and he pushes it beyond its tolerance into some ultra-fast hero-burn to drown the roar of fantasy crowds. Somewhere out there in the dark of his unexplored interior is a crowd. Somewhere out there is fast-track fantasy, *a dream that might come true*.

When they arrive back at Les Arcs, he sees M. Vauvatier directly outside the front door of the main house.

The old man stands stock-still on the gravel, listening intently to his portable telephone, saying nothing as the sun beats down on his shiny, speckled head.

He is there when they come out, back to the diesel-fuelled micro-bus.

He stands, not seeing, not moving, listening intently to silent sounds from the other end of the radio-phone line. The party have to squeeze carefully past him, crocodile-style.

The fuel-considerate micro-bus travels through the ville.

And it's apparent that already the small town of Torquemada reverts to its natural state, a state of inertia, of stupefying provinciality and dull torpor. Once more the grey stone farm buildings cluster in suspicious, miserable huddles between barely cultivatable bleak hills; the monotonous patchwork of identically planted fields line the mean and grimy roads. The scattered tiny villages replete with cramped houses; derelict barns and the like with their ill-kept outyards littered by untidy piles of tractor parts, old bottles and plant debris; yes, afterwards they reassert their centuries-old predominance, their mastery of both the landscape and the minds of those who co-exist within it.

Until next year when again there will be 24 hours more in Torquemada.

And as the choppers whir and the small turbo-props clatter into action like metal midges, the afternoon sun bathes the airport in a singular light. It is an egg, it's a yoke, but the egg has cracked and ho ho ho inside the egg is a tiny baby crocodile with two snapping fang-filled heads.

Two paths you can go down.

Jack looks into Katy's eyes and sees a map of the Dreamtime – another city in another time. There are no specific directions.

Only clues, signs – common reference points along the trail.

But when they kiss, Jack tells himself that somewhere down the road he'll read a map, a hidden map of the interior where *x* marks the spot.

Then the plane's engine starts.

The gin toniques are all finito; the one-prop engine turns, the plane taxis its six passengers. It waits at the end of the runway, the aero-chauffeur pumps it up, the engine surges, the plane picks up the pace. It races down the runway and the tarmac's being eaten up and swallowed faster – Jack looks out of the tiny porthole in the protective fuselage, and watches as the world flies by, and tilts as the plane's wheels leave the ground and its nose climbs into the blue blue sky – and the blur begins all over again.

A Kiss to Die For

YOU'RE ON THE CITY'S outer edges, so far out on the periphery, down behind the Barrio, beyond the Shakespeare Zoom and Pardesi Parkway, edging down on the Deep Southside of Stewartstown. So far onto the edge that the citizenry there spend most of their hours keeping chilly stock-still for fear of cutting themselves.

And we glump around the abandoned tenement buildings, crashed out like an over-age drug-raddled showgirl, and pootering amongst the debris and scuzzy lowlife we see this run right down park, now called Meantime Community Gardens.

Get through the broken-down brick walls, over the piles of rubble, past the trashed up two-tone motor-car and splayed-out stacks of consumer disposables. The whole place is very quiet. No street-types taking the night air here.

They know this is an ungroovy locale to hang out in after dark. It's the fave dump-and-drop spot for the mob. There's a mudpile quagmire in the middle of the park, reputedly containing what's left of Joe 'Mad Dog' Kiaftovski and 16 of his henches and wenches after identities not unconnected with Carlos 'Mattress' Jacquenelli finished with them.

You're going in.

Among the ferns, straggy grass, rotting fronds and random cast-offs, lies a familiar form, half buried in the loamy reddish earth. It's – ulgh. It's – well, here it is. Here's a penis shape discarded in splodgy red goo – some kinda economy contract, they musta just stuffed the guy's balls in his mouth, a rush job.

There's a discarded off-pink beach towel covered with throw-up, splattered with stray sand from what? Ventura Beach, 70 klicks away? One of the construction projects around the corner? Who knows – and more significantly, who'll tell?

No one.

Look closely. There are traces of mayonnaise around and about and a blurred black and white polaroid print of some pimply John Lennon clone, severely illin'.

Zone in.

There's a vaginal-like aberration poking up through the soil can you dig it can you dig it?

Yeah, you can dig it.

It's the ice-picked apex of a skull. Skull of a black male, about 5′ 11″, 180 lbs, probably mid-30s, early 40s.

Think big, dig deep.

Through the blue-tinged earth its fetid features poke.

He wears some kind of shapeless gold lamé beret over long dreadlocks. His face looks inexplicably blissed out.

See the eyes.

The eyes are grey-blue, chilly gaze, filled with blank-it-out, mad eyes. Watch 'em stare, dead-set straight ahead. Dead? Dread eyes follow you around the lot, they're making everyone feel uncomfortable. The pupils burn bright in a humongous stare, like they're lit from inside. The rest of the eyes are filled with grains of multi-coloured sand and soil. The nose is broad, and vicious blood stuff has dribbled in trickling tributaries from the mouth's long, narrow slit.

Dig. Think about the money, honey.

He wears a black coat. The shoulders are narrow and stooped. The fists are clenched.

The hands are bloody, abraded.

The black coat's decorated with embroidered trick-on motifs of electro-voodoo, and hung with much gold and brass Hassidic and Masonic regalia, dangling with all manner of talismanic old fragments of bone,

six-pointed stars of purple neon,

sticks of rock crystal in various intriguing shapes,

shards of withered skin in small glass and metal, velvet-lined cases.

Now almost anyone with $\frac{1}{60}$th part of the cerebral cortex not actively dysfunctioning is gonna lam-bamb-outta this place ASAP. Contrary to popular reports of his demise, Jean Jean LePichon is alive, aliveo. It was like he'd just cocooned himself beneath the ground for a little nap but had been awakened in the middle of a bad dream.

And he gets up out of this filthy hole, wipes his eyes and hits the backs of fleeing feds with the big gab.

'Yowzer all such concerned pet owners and I ask ya – is your dog a vegetarian? Is he pure in mind and body? Are you all corruptin' an' condemnin' the pooches to Pit Bull karma in the canine afterlife? Are you stranding your leurved ones on the food chain? Alienatin' them from alla God's other little crits?'

Now you see some guy – local character by the name of Barking Ferddie, (so called because most of the streetpeople on Mattimoe Avenue reckon anyone who runs around with seven fat black hounds when he barely has enough to eat himself from the scraps he picks up out of the garbage cans they string up down that way to prevent theft of such a valuable item, has got to be singing off a different song-sheet) and Barkin' Ferddie and his pack are standing there looking at this apparition because Jean Jean Le P, camouflage pants and ersatz pearl necklace and combat sneaks two sizes too small and all, is striding towards them.

The dogs begin to bark. But as he comes closer, they sort of sit down on their puppies and just content themselves with a little whining and the odd snarl.

'I ask you, are your dogs vegetarian?'

You could knock Barking Ferddie, (who, despite the slightly irregular nature of his gourmet eat-up nutritional programme, is still a fair 16½ stones) down with a Barbie Doll's blowdryer.

'Hell no,' he says, so pianissimo.

'Well,' begins Jean Jean LePichon, but he gets no further because Barking Ferddie has reached inside the disgusting, dirty raggedy ass-wipes he calls his shorts to produce his only other known possession that ain't a dog lead, tawhit one Metropol standard-issue ultra-high frequency alarm whistle. And he blows on this silver tube with every bit of breath in his bulky bod.

The hounds go instant ape baskerville and Jean Jean LePichon's blah blah is curtailed by this ferocious pack, and the man takes off hot-foot down in the general direction of the city. And for someone who's spent the past 72 hours totally tranquillized beneath about a ton of squelshy red loam, he shows a turn of foot by no means slouchful, at that.

FAT TUESDAY.

Agggggggh. You won't believe that Fat Tuesday.

He arrives at Le Hot Club de Now, when that was still the bad money-making Richter scene-shaking liquid entertainment centre in gross^{n} floral polyester boxer short shorts. Their vehement orange and off-green colour-crash is enough to give Le Hot Club's resident sex therapist herpes complex and overnight celibacy. Even the turn-ups are size XXXXXXL.

'Babes!'

Eustace Vauvatier, clad in his Coke can coat could be heard to rattle 70 yards away on sighting the boy.

Fat? Tuesday is bloody humongous.

Tallboy, the black dude who runs an inner-city semi-automatic weapons franchise on behalf of the Evil Stone Lords, nudges Knocker, rarely to be seen without his ticky-tasky blue and yellow blazer at this time. Knock almost dies on the spot.

Here's some freckled 17-stone screaming faggot with a pudding-basin crop ligging around in his club with the Toy and Tranny Saul. Krocker can't resist it.

''ere,' he says to the Toy, poking same in ribs. 'I din know u were a ferkin chubby-chaser.'

Now the Toy is so sizzling hot at this time you could flash-fry a rump steak on his aura. Flavour of the month? Never mind the sanity, feel the myth. People out there were falling over each other in the stampede to pressure-sell the pirate videos,

floating franchises in yupster-niched Toy inconography,

Toy T-shirts with the edible comic-strip gum free in every pocket,

the personally endorsed bored-games,

the intimate fragrance range,

the porno-cartoon rights –

anything; 'cos the Toy's had four triple platinum hits that year and it was only July already. Hit the spot, get hot, take a shot at the top and bathe 'n' rave in that soak all over ya aura myth. Yeah, the Toy seems so hot he could melt any moment.

But this myth didn't match its public's expectation when its public wasn't around. Like now, the Toy don't like having a rib-cage shake from Knocker as he leans against the bar to warble noises-off from his next single (a sort of informal audition for same) into Tranny Saul's lug-hole.

So he ceases this activity momentarily.

'Tuesday,' says the Toy with that mein camper lurch in his voice, before resuming the coo-coo billet-doux in the earlobe of Tranny Saul.

And the Toy, decked out in the small silk cut-off pillar-box hat, the long white leather coat with the plastic dominoes sewn on next to the gypsy medallions – hey, he means business. And at Tuesday he looks. And the look on his face, Fat Tuesday notes, is imperiously high and says, 'Waste that creep.'

Tuesday moves in.

'Call that a coat, dear? Looks more like a condom to me. Full of slim prickings – shame they didn't have one in your size. Ooooooh 'scuse me it must be Christmas – look at all this snow falling on the floor at seventy quid a gram. Yeah go on, get down and grovel. It's only talc, but what'd you know? You don't know what time it is do you, babes?'

And Tuesday then overwhumps Knocker's digits in this fungal dorsal flab most disgustin' for the sensitive citizen to behold.

'Oooh, what strong hands.' Tuesday simpers and stares at him for a nano-seccie. If you listen, you can just catch the trace of the home-town Irish lilt in his voice.

'And what a cheap watch. I can spot a Rolex copy at two miles, babes, I used to sell 'em. You know? Oh, excuse me, you know naff all, dontcha?'

Now there's no almost in it. Knocker's, Standing Order, at that time some 15-year-old bimbette doing Page Three after eloping with a dodgy televangelist, looks at her man like he just say his tongue's dang dried up after filch-rimming a rhino.

What she wants to say is, 'Say something.' But no word leaves her lips. She wants to say, 'Defend yourself.' But she's scared Tuesday might step on her face next. And all the showbiz scions and faggot poseurs and scenesters and celebutantes die a little inside because they recognize here is one fresh blood.

But actually Tuesday just eases off lavwards with the Toy and Tranny Saul, who tonight looks v. fetching in its silver sequinned tutu, but is perhaps marginally miffed about all this attention Fat Tuesday and his outfit are copping and bopping to. Fat Tuesday dresses like this for a reason, that being stop the world – he wants to mouth off.

Like, he's the best DJ in the universe. Like, he won a drag competition when he was twelve. Like, he gonna model for *X* magazine. Like, he can recite pages 342–7 of the Freemans catalogue verbatim. Like, the Toy is his best, BEST FRIEND. So he repeats his lines:

'I was talking to that Diana Ross about you the other night.'

Mark: 'You weren't,' or maybe if they're lukewarm dumb, 'Oh, really?'

Fat Tuesday: 'Yeah. (Beat.) And she says WHOOOOO?'

That's why the Toy paid for him. Tranny saved him the trouble of looking pretty. And having Tuesday around meant he didn't have to tongue-thrash anyone any more. Leaving the Toy to wander high as a cloud, totally out of it, and no one, he guessed, would really notice overmuch – because between them, Tranny Saul and Fat Tuesday supplied the expected prerequisite dollops of global glamour to go, the nuclear bitch deterrent and hip-quipping tack it up and tear down the tracks, which is what his public expected. Or so he reckoned. At least in the increasingly rare moments when he wasn't one way or the other utterly oblivious to them, it and every other goddamn thing in the universe, except the cotton-wool around his spine or his Spectre-induced three minutes of total brain death.

So the duo would follow faithfully in their master's tootsteps. Yeah, they all went to the lavatory together.

'Our bladders aren't synchronized or something. That's why we spend so long in there,' Tuesday says when the troika shuffle their bustles outta the egregious ambi-sexual lavvies at Mr Cairo's or Rififi's.

But on the night in question, the Toy, Tranny Saul, Fat Tuesday and assorted liggerati are having a quiet, cosy dinner for 20 at Alchemy, this being the new chi-chi exclusive enclave of eaterie, the absolute *ne plus ultra* that's just débuted inside Mystic City Sign.

And on the night in question, the moon is full.

At the Toy's table Roberto Mad-Hat catches sight of same through the windowpane.

'Look at the moon,' he croon to Blond John, his first-date surfer hunk. 'He is like a beautiful young boy searching for his flaxen-haired, swainy concubine. He is like a lover preparing for the boudoir. He is pale and passive, anointing himself for sacrifice.'

'Yeah, uh, suppose so,' says Blond John, tuckering down to lip-pucker another gi-normous portion of broiled reindeer in aspic and raspberries. On the other side of the room – among the many booths whose inhabitants know past and see future to turn a buck for now, amongst the juggling fire-eaters and trick-cycling dwarf twins hawking duff sparklers and over-cultivated pearls – Morty 'Big' Kinsella, the 300-buck per hour black-collar legal eagle, looks out of the window and catches sight of this moon. The 310-pound repository of dark secrets, the man who knows where many bodies are buried (it's said, out of his hearing, that Big M. helped put a few of them away hisself with the back of a shovel – but Big. M. is an honourable man and giving many drop-dead dinners and also shows at most significant salons in elegant Belleville and St Cloud mansions; so the citizenry do not believe such contemptible trash, or if they do, tactfully refrain from the say so in his immediate vicinity) – and, having seen the moon, wishes he hadn't.

Big remembers hearing somewhere that catching sight of Mama Luna through glass will send the viewer mad as a meat-axe faster than J. Robinson; recalls hearing this half-formed thought someways back when he was a mere whippertysnappety barrack-room-lawyer brat. And in the hypercharged atmospherics of the Church of the Mystic City Sign, this bubbles right to the forefront of his mind to a point where he cannot resist confiding in his host.

'Hey – cantcha' gettem to put up some kinda curtain or sommink?' Big M. inquires of the dapper chap on his right. 'Full moons freak me right out, 'specially in this fuckin' spook trap.'

Petey Casales replaces his glass of Château Greedypig on the white damask tablecloth. He looks out of the window. He sees an opportunity to make a play.

'The moon looks like a widow waiting for her sons to return from war. She is a sad moon. She knows death,' he opines confidentially.

'Hey, kid, are you on drugs or what?' Kinsella says. 'I said kill the fuckin' moon, it's buggin' me, right?'

'Right, right,' Petey says and snappety fingers at non-existent staff.

Now up in the DJ booth Boosterfish is spinning the ultra-heavy defo funk down mix of B B Bax & the Chanel, Max Fax III, TFL Riotomatique Boys and Monsterpiece Meet Margot. It pound and drum and beat and thump like a solid sonic wall. For which there is a sound reason.

Tawit: in the centre of the room a hexagonal structure has been partitioned off from the rest of the Church, with a spiral white curtain that's wrapped around a tall tower which reaches, virtually, to the building's domed top. Sounds soniferate from this pit, the kinda caterwauling that White Jacqui and Barney Boosterfish quite correctly calculate will seriously upset the digestion of the diners, and the equilibrium of the boogie-down revellers entranced in dance.

Inside the tower and the caged-up pit beneath it lives Jean Jean LePichon. That night, it just so happens that some kooky troupe are doing a Martian Awareness Evening. Normally the Alchemy is illuminated solely, by the sacred candles – hundreds and thousands of sacred smoking candles – and a terrible fire hazard at that. But the pyrotechnics channelling the Martian Awareness's harmonic convergence energy (from seven continents in a global telethon link) cause this unprecedented power surge on the building's electricity system, which, in turn, Eisler minions have wired up on the fly, to offset the cost of their boss having to install the state-of-the-smart sprinklers, ultra-violet smoke detectors and all, to zip the lip of the fire marshall.

So it's most unexpectedly that Boosterfish is forced to shut down his wall-shattering, sensurround sound system.

And all around the floor this causes a distinct change of atmos as, high above in the rafters, various crews of techno-monkees summoned from hearth and home clamber around trying to figure out exactly what's stuffed up. Back down on the ground people can hear themselves think a bit, and the attention is focused increasingly intensely on the strange sideshows around and about them all. Now it just so happens that some of the Toy's party, and others of the Casales table, go walkabout and bump into one another in and around the Illustrated Man.

The Illustrated Man is this cabalistic booth with a life-size see-through perspex illuminated replica of the human body, anatomically absolutely accurate in each and every detail, illustrating the functions of lymphatic glands, nodes, sinews and the whole shebang of the hot-wired nervous system. Occasionally, by way of infotainment, the android replica will slowly turn its head, wave its arms, make with the in-and-out of regular human-type breathing wheeze, discharge its bladder into a small Grecian-style urn appropriately positioned below, or simulate whatever the body function of the day's been deemed to be.

Now really the Illustrated Man is just a blag for the booth inside, which consists of a number of most wondrous mirrors, again all life-size, empanelled in exquisite stone-cut ground-glass frames depicting mythical archetypes, a visual representation of the chemicals that form the human bod and much else, the whole hoopla set around myriad hyperdelic 4D mirrors. But you see none of that until you've forked over 10 bucks (negotiable donation).

But Blond John, Mad-Hat Roberto, Fat Tuesday, the Toy, Mini-ligger and one or two others have drifted in between courses. Among whom are Petey Casales and Ratso Roskoe. Roskoe –

alias Sloopy D. – is this scuzzy mulatto guy who actually does the dirty work on many mob hits. He stands at the booth's entrance, taking a pull on an ale, his bleached negroid features absorbing the mass of spells-for-sale,

instant karma incense sticks

and esoteric perfumes,

his stocky frame in its all-black threads and red patent lace-up shoes still as if in deep thought, perhaps creating some horrid new hierarchy of fresh bods to kill and fun ways to waste 'em. For some reason the prospect of deep mirrors supposedly revealing the myriad aspects and realities of his true soul does not make the strings of Ratso P.'s heart effervesce with that ol' up-beatin' rush of swing and zing.

But Blond John and Petey Casales literally bump into each other in their haste to check out the masked Mirror Mirror behind a velvet curtain at the far end of the kiosk. And these two strike up an instant rapport like they've known each other since the polar ice cap first froze over. But the Toy now behaves most agitato. The reason why is that since the music died he's getting Jean Jean LePichon's stream of abusage full in the face. And because of over-zealous dealings in that day's South American soft commodities market, the Toy gets The Fear.

'Fats! Fats! That awful man is slaggin' me off. Do something, Fats. Do something, you silly little queen!'

'Eh?' says Fat Tuesday, who's been somewhat preoccupied with a proposition being put to him by Blond John and Petey C. It seems that Petey C., in his capacity as entertainments secretary to the Teleciti-Sicilian social register, is most deeply desirous of seeing a full-on Fat Tuesday disc spin-that-disc show with fabby pyrotechnics, vitriolic verbal chat-attack, performing A-list celebutantes and all the whole rap for a very close, dear, personal friend of his brother Paul's daughter's birthday party.

But Fat Tuesday is refusing both adamantly and eloquently.

'Nah, I work only Tuesdays,' he says in his flat-pan drop-dead voice.

Petey C. offers him certain illicit substances which he assures the celebutantes are of premium, gold-standard quality.

'No dice, babes,' Tuesday negatives.

'Do something.'

The Toy is screeching in his face.

Fat Tuesday now finds himself in neo-traumatic mode.

'Listen to it!' the Toy shouts.

And everyone shuts up and cops the throaty rant unrabbling from somewhere within the tower.

'And this sodomite, he is dressed as a girlie and partake of that which no man should partake; and he is corruptin' the fibrous body of the city and lo he shall bring doom an' destruction on us all. Yet will ye cast him out from this holy place, O wimp-bod sons of Lachmaddadon and Kelly Marie? Nonceos like him yowsar hath no testiculars, and are poor sappy creatures accurséd of the great black son o'man whose stretchmobile yo'all aren't fit to lie down before. Oh accurséd harlot, whacked up wirehead scumbag son of the vile corporate hydra, get thy lame ass outta here. Come not near me thou pestilential pieca frog spitty, thou vultural turdy drop, thee blaspheming against all that is vital and good for small plants and other livin' stuff. Fou' they face right off stinky or be accurséd forever and ever and then some, twinky one two viper head.'

Fat Tuesday senses here is a mouth that could be some serious competition.

'I'll deal with it,' he tells his sugar-baby and shoots right off.

After more than the usual prerequisite tussle with security, he finally manages to wangle his way into the tower.

Inside, it's dark as death. After his eyes accustomize to this a bit, Tuesday makes out the shape of a table in the middle of a room and a beam running above it. In one corner is this huge old bronze cook-pot, decorated with many pentagrams and weird-out calligraphy. On the table itself are various cutlasses and other implements of destruction, plus miscellaneous tools of prophecy.

Tuesday's Irish eyes catch sight of one or two hypodermics, a welfare voucher-book made out to one Ms K. Velozquez, and various half-drawn astrological charts which show an unhealthy predominance of planets placed in the 12th house. Exploring gingerly, he finds there is an open floorboard at the back of the room. Tuesday stoops down to have a squiz. And he catches a glimpse of finery most splendiferous, various cloths which glint of gold and sparkling stuff of the sort that very much attracts Fat Tuesday and thus the Toy's credit-card collection wherever they come across them, be it up-town, down-town, cross-town, all over the world. He bends down to see if there's any way to jimmy up the other boards to get a better shufti – some secret lock or cryptic contraption. As he does so, something else kicks his ass so hard he falls over flat on his face. The foot belongs to the loinclothed figure of Jean Jean LePichon. He smirks, hyper-bad, his face illuminated by the camping gaz torch that burns in his hand.

'Thou flea-ridden catamite!' screams Jean Jean. 'Thou who consorts with public health risk number one now comes sleazin' around the Holy Pile, thievin' whatever it can get its grubby mits on for what blasphemy I wish to know not. Thou who hast slept thy way into the Babel palaces of this here today gone Gomorrah, thou who does the distinkin' and depraved acts with any scumbag slutboy to slake thy insatiable avaricious lust, get thee outta here afore I am applyin' the blowtorch to ya belly.'

'Actually,' says Tuesday, 'I just came down here to ask you

please try to be a little quieter and less vulgar.' He dusts down his Comme des Fillet suit and cops the reaction: mounting wrath in the chill grey-blue eyes. 'Your shouting is disturbing our dinner, I'm afraid, so I'd ask you, please, to stop it,' he says demurely.

'Yowser feastie on the craven bodies of innocent animals that will turn to ashes in your mouths. They shall rot ya souls, for he that eat the meat juice and do not lock their wifies in the coal bunker during menstruation are doomed to die in eternal char-grill flash-fry bothway agony.'

Jean Jean LePichon hits the flame-on button at the side of the burner. But Fat Tuesday just stares.

'Wow,' he says. 'You are really the most. Your skin is like the finest ebony in the G-plan catalogue, blacker than the coal mined from the deepest valleys of the industrial north, darker than midnight in a catacomb, smoother than the finest silks in the Droneboys Warehouse sale that I attended the preview of only yesterday.'

'Depart both thy faces from this place,' rages Jean Jean LePichon. 'Thou art of no account, the catamite that brings the plague upon this city, thou art a trollop toy of the evil one and oughta get thy grimy plates off sacred ground, unholy infidel.'

'Your hair's not bad either,' says Fat Tuesday, trying to run his fingers through the dreadlocks. 'It's like the finest calligraphed swirls on a hand-embossed Lauradonna invite, it's like walking in a field of highland heather, it's tressed as sensually as the silk wrap in which I stash my Bay City Rollers pube collection, and it's something that my hairdresser would die for.'

'Thou cyclops-eyed pieca pus! Thou rapscallion verminous toadie! Get away from the prophet, thou slimy pile of rubbish. Thou wilt cause all cash machines to jam. Lo all the drinks tix will be lost and the names struck off every guest list. All the DJ booths will be silent – listen!' His face is twitching uncontrollably

– as if some infernal Armageddon is exploding in the streets of his soul.

'But it's not your hair I desire,' says Fat Tuesday, who now forces his quavering quarry up against the wall, from which dangles the piece of material that swirls up to the ceiling and out of a hole therein to wrap itself around the tower. 'It's your mouth. Your mouth is the most beautiful thing that ever talked the earth. I have never seen anything so utterly drop-dead in my entire, babes. It smells of nectarine from sunlit valleys, it is styled up shapewise loads better than even the glitziest two-grand-a-day-model frame, it is the stuff which would persuade Dennis Hopper to star in *Red and Jeb*, the boys who won the hearts of the village by finding Lassie's lost pup. Did I tell you Denny's a close personal friend of mine? Ooooooo, I must have that mouth. Gimme a kiss, bigboy.'

And FT puckers up.

'Listen, sucker,' hisses Jean Jean LePichon. 'If your ass ain't outa here right now, I'm gonna blow your mother-fuckin' face off.'

LePichon reaches into the loincloth, produces his Magnum piece and whammies its cold steel snout straight in Fat Tuesday's facials to emphasize his point.

'Git git git git git git git out, white trash!'

Fat Tuesday scarpers in such triple quick-time that he's history before the scream's out of his mouth.

When he appears back at the table, looking as if it'll take six hours power-tannin' with the sunlamp kid to bring him back to anaemia, there's a major confabulation. Tranny Saul is dispatched to purchase a herbal suppository from an adjacent stall.

'You're giving him too much attention again,' hisses Tranny Saul in the Toy's ear as he and Tuesday disappear to the lavs for admin of same. 'I don't like it.'

Meanwhile Jean Jean blah blah onwards and roundwards

sometimes randomly repeating a word or a sound over and over for no discernible reason. 'Yo and there shall be a be-be-be-be-bee-beeeee beating of wings and it shall be in strict dread four-four time and the city will up-chuck its toxic substances and lo, just as I prophesied on Channel 62 many thousand times last night, y'all dumb dreck-heads, the stink of death shall assail the land.'

Up in the rafters there are occasional flashes and the crackling of short-circuitry noises. The duo return twenty minutes afterwards in a considerably calmer mind-set.

'OK, babes,' says Tuesday when Petey snakes back to their table with Blond John. 'I'll tell you what I'll do, as a special favour. If you do just one tiny thingette for me, I'll do the show for your friend's daughter's birthday party.'

'What is it?' says Petey. 'Name it. Anything.'

'Anything' says Fat Tuesday, turning to the entire liggerati who all listen right up.

'Anything,' says Petey. 'I'm a man of honour.'

'Then bring me the head of Jean Jean LePichon.'

'What?'

'C'mon, babes, don't mess about. That black man with the megaphone in the tower over there. I want his head,' Fats says. 'I want it delivered on a silver salver.'

'You can't be serious,' Petey snorts, his weasel features all shook up.

Fat Tuesday shrugs. 'No head, no show,' he pouts. 'Besides, you said I could ask for anything I wanted – and I know exactly who you are. So put up or fuck up, jerk-off.' And he turns on his heel and flounces off for more piggery.

Now Petey sits down at his table much troubled.

'Ya fix it for ma little princess?' grunts Big Mort between smackerings of sherry and almond trifle avec fruit de mer, this being the latest mix-up trend in the metroplex's groaning gourmet porn-stops.

'Sure, sure, it's all taken care of,' Petey replies. 'I'll get back to you with the dates.'

'Listen, Petey, it's gotta be the fourth, *não mexe*. My princess's birthday's on da fourth, and we already book the conjuror, see?'

'Si, si, the fourth,' says Petey, pushing his trifle aside untouched as he wipes the moisture off his upper lip with the napkin.

'Hey, Petey, I visited Alphonse the other day.'

Petey simulates enthusiasm. His retarded cousin was serving seven to ten in Tannertown for armed sodomy.

'He asked me to give you this.'

Petey glances at the envelope that has landed in his lap. Inside are piles of phials of pink powder and bundles of high C-notes.

IT TAKES BLOND JOHN three days and 2,000 bucks to buy the head from the owners of the Illustrated Man, and then another 48 hours for them to re-wire it.

'I don't know – don't you think it's rather *jejune*?' asks Fillet, the world's most perfectly formed fashion editor, as she tries on the rubber and broken-glass pillar-box hat in the fag-ash blond boy's basement workroom.

Roberto shifts. Fillet had never looked back since she'd made the cover of *Teleciti Times* Sunday colour sup six years ago, targeted as one of the Brightest and the Best of Happening Yewf.

'Oh no, Caroline,' – Roberto was one of the few human beings who could get away with using Fillet's first name and live – 'that hat's just you to a T, absolutely yeeeww, dear heart.'

At that moment Blond John bursts in through the front door. Carelessly, he has neglected to open it first. His demeanour hints that he is, perhaps, somewhat harassed and careworn. Underneath his left arm he carries a package wrapped in old newspaper. In his right is a manila envelope that is stuffed full of black and white polaroids. Sweat glistens on his forehead.

'Hey,' he says, grabbing Roberto by the scruff of the collar.

'Excuse me,' Roberto fumes, throwing his hands onto his hips. 'I'm in the middle of a consultation.'

'No time, dude, gotta move.'

Blond John uses his built-up physique to drag Roberto off his feet.

'Gwark, 'scuse I, Fillet, rush job,' the milliner sqwarks as the tall, guandom Iron Man of Montana County hauls him bodily into the claustrophobic back-bedroom.

He finishes the reconstruction exactly 24 hours later.

'I just want you to know how much I personally appreciate this,' Petey says, stuffing an envelope full of used notes into Roberto's dag-tired hand as he kisses him on each cheek.

'Whack him,' he told Blond John when they were back with their key cargo in the ancient black car. 'Maybe we could get some of the loot back. This whole shebang's running way overcost. Way way over.'

They picked up Muscles McKhan, a body-builder who made himself useful around Paul's limo business; Tallboy, keen to make a few career moves within Mr Casales's and Mr Culver's organization; plus Ratso Roskoe and Flaky Fake, a wispy boy of age indeterminate who looked even more morose and melancholy than usual. This strange crew met, as per script, at Pookie's Polka Bar and Grill.

When they hit the Church of the Mystic City Sign, Jean Jean LePichon made tons of noise and fought like an alligator at the dentist until Muscles and Blond John pinned him and finally kept him still long enough for Flaky to line up the spike and pump 500 mg of animal tranquillizer inside him.

Then they drove beyond the Barrio, past Pardesi Parkway, over to the edge of Stewartstown where it feeds into Mattimoe Avenue.

'Hey boss,' Ratso whispered. Ratso always whispered. Johnny Throat had stymied his vocal-chords in a bar-brawl some years ago. 'Boss, couldn't I just slap him around a bit?'

'No,' said Petey.

'Just a bit.'

'Oh,' Petey sighed irritably and rubbed the small purple sore on the back of his neck. 'Very well, then,' he conceded sulkily. 'But try and show a little finesse, dear. And do hurry up – I wanna go home.'

Petey didn't feel crash-hot. He had bad flu. Couldn't seem to shake it off.

And they did what they had to do, dig, while Ratso R. carefully indented his pièce de résistance, a fearsome, but largely cosmetic, gash at the apex of Jean Jean LePichon's noggin, with an ice-pick particularly selected for this very purpose.

And on the morning of the fourth, Fat Tuesday was awakened at his mama's 43rd-storey municipal apartment in nearby Stewartstown with a large package from Intrastate Express.

He looked inside and almost threw up.

Yet even today he still kisses the long mouth of Jean Jean LePichon on the low glass table by his bed before arising and dusting the cobwebs from his eyes each and every afternoon. He still refuses, at least in public, to believe it's a ring-in.

And Roberto? After his biz went bust, last thing anyone heard was that he was going back to Realito to study sculpture.

AGENCY

HERE COMES THE MAN.

Tracking . . .

. . . Locate.

On the other side of the Barrio, past the Shakespeare Flydrive Superzoomway, the constantly under-reconstruction 56-lane artery that bisects the city . . .

Frame location complete.

Connect frame.

Touch power to animate.

And it happens so.

. . . the man walks down the road. He is an Asian man. He wears a double-breasted grey suit. He carries a briefcase. The briefcase is red. It is handcuffed to his wrist.

Cutaway: Morrison's POV.

My number is one digit off a shrink called Dr Boris Kerenski. That evening I'd been at O² with Katy and Tiger. They were discussing the arrangements for Katy's wedding. Tiger was going to be the bridesmaid. Katy was telling her about a hen-night a friend of hers called Maxine had thrown, present lists, should I invite Great-aunt Bathchair or Miss Nazi, that sort of thing. I was bored and started talking to a director I know, a guy called Simon. I was trying to float Media-Cool, the thing I'd been working on with Terry Kinkaid, it's a metropol mini-series about a crime reporter who gets involved with the mob, routine prime-time fodder, very safe, Simon's girlfriend Fi came back from the lav in the middle of our conversation. She was out of it, boy she was really gone. She's this blonde bitch who dictates her novels in bed and dresses provocatively when out to understate it somewhat. I said, 'Yeah I remember you, we met once before – you took a slug at me in the Wah Wah Bar.' Then she comes on, it was so embarrassing, the whole I've-always-wanted-to-meet-you bit, she even remembers the Amcro mobile phone fraud thing which was one of the most goddamn pedestrian investigations I've ever done, and she starts wrapping her admittedly very long and not entirely unwatchable legs around mine, sticks her tongue in my ear, flirting out of her face the whole seven yards, awful. To be honest at one level I was really enjoying the attention but on another I was wincey with the cringe. Fi's got rep as a smackie, media-whore and motor-mouthing bitch. Her talent shades genius but she's so lazy that she prefers to make it to the top on her back. And you just don't behave like that in public. At least I don't and I don't expect the people I'm around to either. I don't know what you think or how you behave. But that's Fi's act – public sexual psychodrama. I can't remember what happened in any precise chronology but Simon made a move on me. Normally in a fight I just start flailing, completely freak out, but maybe it was the oxygen, I don't know, I was very calm, watched the guy make his move, grab me, let him hold the lapels, threw a kind of feint on the guy, twisted my foot around inside (a cruel parody of Fi's act) so I can throw him. And he ended up on the floor. For a moment I saw his face and the weakness there. Just for that moment I wanted to answer back that cravenness, I wanted to pummel him, totally stomp him into shit oblivion and, word, I could've done it because I was holding him there, very calm. But that shot through and I thought too hip, gotta go so I'm back at the apartment and I'm crashed out on the bedspread just in my socks. I always take all my clothes off except my socks when I wank and try and get off without touching myself. The socks are a personal thing, it's 'cos I lost my virginity with my socks on. It's a kinda paranoid view of masturbation, I don't wanna touch myself because I'm worried about catching something. Ha ha. All seriousness aside, it's sexier like that. I've fantasized about Fi because she's so sexual, whenever she's out she just wears this bra and very very few clothes. Her legs, oh God. Anyway. I'm crashed out on the bedspread in that rather interesting phase where you're asleep but you're awake. You know what I mean. But the fucking phone starts ringing. Which is a real bummer because in my head I've been composing this epic poem about a guy who writes commercials but who's trapped on this barge house and has to devise some mythopoetic way to end his exile. And there's this intrusive telephone ringing somewhere all over the second read-thru and now the only thing I can remember about the mythopoem in the dream is the Bumpers, which is like a Casino Society expression for the Ace King Queen Jack on the dice that spin on the clocks and my father's saying, 'Bumpers, Bumpers, you've got bumpers!' And I'm telling him, 'No, look at the face – it's just Ace Jack Ten Nine.' And I'm at this bit in the poem-sequence where there's some kinda stand-off between the writer and some old wrinklebat who's a tactical advisor to the Olympiad about liquorice and carpets. And in some way this is very central to the ad-writer's dilemma: he's got to out-manoeuvre this very old, very smart be-blazered carpet and confectionery maven to get the hell off the boat-house, which, in the context of the reverie, seems crucial, though surprise surprise I can't remember why now because the telephone call completely destroyed my concentration. So I reach out, pick up the receiver and this voice says, 'You gotta come, you gotta get here now, they've come for me, Doc, they're gonna kill me I know it I know it.' Oh shit, I start trying to explain it's 3.45 and they've a wrong number. But something makes me think, it's irrational, it's perhaps connected to heightened intuitive arousal during the dream-state but I ask, 'Where are you?' and they say, 'You know where I am, Doc, you've gotta come get over here now please,' and, OK I know I know I've been behaving strangely recently, but I suddenly get very angry with this old crone on the end of the phone and say, 'Whatdya think I am? A rotadex? Gimme your goddamn address. GIVE IT TO ME.' And they squeal me this address off hyper-fast and I scrawl it down in my dream-book on the table by the bed, and as I'm writing there's a sound in the background like a door being smashed down, and the party on the other end of the line is screaming, 'Help me, Doc, help me, they're gonna kill me, help me; and then there's a weird kind of noise like someone's driven into this quiet little suburban living-room with a tank and a terrorist unit has opened up, and then the party screams again most horribly and suddenly the line cuts dead. Now, oh reader, you ain't got this far without pickin' up a trick or two and me neither. You can guess what happens next and you can tell anybody you bloody like. Right, right I wake up the next morning, call into 95 and there's nothing much happening except Spyros says, 'Keep your eye on that Joke-shop thing, we hadda tip that they're gonna move this evening.' There's a Mongolian fuck cluster cross-town, biz slang for a totally newsless presser, you know press conference that's held for internal and/or political reasons when there's no fucking news. So Spyros says to chill and be ready to go this evening because our source, actually a money-grubbing little squit in Metropol whose got the green-eye about some adopted half-brother, a hyper-achieving Metropol wiseguy called Hutton, he says that tonight it's gonna happen and Mr Laughing Boy catches his. So I stagger back to bed, eat the Vitamin D shirt I'd been wearing the night before and get a flash on the Casino Society dream and then top-spin on some other weirdo fantasy that overflowed it where I think I'm talking to one of Boris's fucking crazies who's got The Fear in XXXXXXX giant economy size. So I'm trying to get back to the concept of what the hell was going on back on the barge-house, like am I frustrated ad tycoon or what, and open up the dream-book and shit, there's this address. Right, right you guessed I've gotta go down for the low-down, check it out, why not? Except Poodle phoned and I got side-lined into a drug-buy with her and then oh God actually fucking her because we're so out of it. We're nicely wound down, rapping along the usual lines of vulnerability as power, strengths qua weaknesses and all when off squeaks the bleep and Joe, who's Poodle's goddamn husband, is saying, 'It's on over at a fashion perpetrator party down on Riverside West. Pull ya finger out, pal.' Good job he didn't know from where. Such cruel ironies make life worth living, right? Anyway I have to ankle outta the brown room in the hotel on Roxburgh Drive like now and get over to WestZone rapido rapido, which is no furkin joke believe me because half of Shakespeare's clogged solid due to Sunday's hurricane or some burst bloody gas-pipe or both. So I ditch the car and short-lease it to a lay-by pool which is the kind of putty-head petty-fraud that gets people fired were certain other people at News-base to discover the transaction, because it's 95's car and there's at least an even bet that anyone renting cheap from a lay-by pool is gonna fuck it up pretty badly. Anyway I just abandon it, stash the cash and catch a purple bus over to Television Central Station where I meet this chick on the tube – it's an entire other story – and check in back to base and the word Joe gives me is hang-back hot-shot, stick ya feet in an icebox and cool ya heels. As always it's chaos at the centre. When it actually starts happening,

I'm in some club cross-town with this babe, and they're so wired at base that they bounce the bleep-signal straight onto my lobes. It's ultra-paranoid that. All news people, though, if they're any good at all, are always total paranoids. There's one old character up there, Charlie Yang, who's positively panphobic about faxbugs, protein-delivered cerebral false-positive transmitters and a whole lot of stuff nobody's even invented yet. But really, what the hell's bells buckets of blood do they think I'm doing – sitting in the goddamn press club pooling tips with BBC World Services? So I've got the message already, excuse me, move off with the chick to hit the binge where we hang out, blending, casing the action, trying to make some faces, work out the shots, check what kind of show this is gonna make but there are no names there, not in bulletin terms anyway, although some of the scenesters and celebutantes would probably make soft spots on First Reports. A bit of much needed colour for Bodycount – the Metropolitan Murder Programme – and would have the quaint midlifers who put Designer City together for all those middle-aged style-nostalgic numbers in the Western Slurbs positively pissing their pants for profiles and eye-witness stuff as a handle to fill up more and more of their ridiculously vacuous prime-time look-at-my-subtly-stitched-subliminally-corporate-branded-hemline-as-a- philosphical-agitprop-homoerotic-art-statement pop junk schlock slot. None of which is my problem, and, most assuredly, also not yours. The party itself just gets weirder and weirder – all those goddamn psychedelic drinks that I sloosh down to stay undercover scramble my motor-cortex more than somewhat which is frightmare drag 'cos I obviously have to keep certain bits of brain reasonably clear for when whoever the hell it is does the dastardly whatever they're going to do on yar boo hiss Mr Public Enemy Number One, he of Laughing Boy 44-Faced notoriety. And sure enough creepskate Hutton's right on the money to give him wha's due – not much probably 'cos 95 are big on front of house promise, mean on moulah bottomline unless it's part of a sixty-six 'continuing relationship' ninety-nine which is possible here I assume – because sure enough someone or, I suspect, *something* wipes out this pasty-facered-russet-thatched lawyer character called Nick Kingston Gore who splatters with a retching ignominious finality all over the bathroom. It's zoo-time: Maurey McClure, who's been doorstepping outside, has taken off in hot pursuit of a black GDMC Crusader and Maurey's in the Bloodhound so he ought to catch it without breaking second gear, right? Wrong – the killers lose him on Shakey Zoom which suggests that the Crusader's a Q-car and therefore this is an inside job. Simultaneously, the crew – who've spent the entire afternoon hiding inside a refrigerator delivery van parked in a side street – are all over the place trying to run up power-lines, rig babies, not trip over their coaxial cables and all the other mesmeric motions they ritually scuttle into to blap us on-air. Security's superheavy – I have a rather nasty tussle with a spook called Montcrieffe, yes, he's a relation, no, he doesn't want any filming at all. But the commissioner's office is there and of course, what with the Metropol contract coming up for tender in the fall, the commissioner's office is more than somewhat goddamn keen to get full-on splash-hot coverage and the situation deteriorates by the moment, because the commissioner's people are rowing with Montcrieffe (who I've got an inside line on which I'm trying to play to screw him for a lead on who this dead 44-Faced murder addict slash attorney is and why and how and the usual 8,000 questions), and his people are getting heavy with the crew who are in ape-frenzy mode because the switching system's crashed and Gallagher – the producer – is trying to do a deal to get some juice fed over from the porn-shop across the road, plus there are also these bogue ad agency people who are shooting a crash 30-second spot to go out tomorrow for the Commissioner and our crew are just having two-headed kittens because they're getting hassle from Montcrieffe's people who are very fucking heavy indeed, like lots of physical commitment, and they're catching flack from the Metropol bureaucrats who want things presented in shall we say a certain way and the crew's job (outside the disappearance of the extension lead that's got to be run over the road to the porn-shop, which is par for the course) is aggravated by the adge from the ad agency's very fucking freelance vid-paparazzi who have a whole set of problems of their own and I'm screaming at the sparks to get the fuck on with knitting a new fibre-optic or whatever because 21 or 7 or 92 or 62 are gonna be here any *second*, not to mention Frames, World News International, All Planet Coverage and the usual posse of sportsboys, goon-ghouls, hardware-toting opportunists, media-high-wired icon-hustlers and passing souvenir-seekers who this kind of situation invariably attracts. Miraculously, I get the story out, we have the footage of the bod in the bathroom, yer actual last look at the Joke-shop Killer, I mean exclusive fucking footage of the Man with 44 Faces blown away by some kind of extraterrestrial psychic predator – it's a bloody televisual dream, right, the stuff of which ratings orgasms are made, no? I finish the story, have the tape rushed back to base, ankle-scram the crew outta there and think if this doesn't get me that goddamn Golden Vidicon and a slot on the board bloody nothing short of resurrecting Howard Hughes and close-ups of his sex-life as Jack the Ripper will.

And then?

Silence.

They can it. The stuff we take to air – and 92, 62, 0/28, 21, 7, 4, 3 and 001 pump out is just – wallpaper. It's official wallpaper, it's shit-bland, hoary old chat-heads holding up a flim-flam re-edit

– I'm sure it's the stuff the commissioner's ad agency people shot, almost certain. Like, here's the top story of the day, maybe the top televisual event of the year already and somehow it's just been slung into electronic oblivion and replaced with wallpaper TV. Oh, God! I'm inna kinda frenzy at this point. I keep asking questions, busting into one stupid meeting after another, and it's knock-back knock-back. Right up the command chain, from Spyros and Charlie onwards, upwards and sideways right the way to Jimmy bloody Hennessy himself's office it's all shoulder-shrugs and raised palms and you-tell-me-buddy-you're-the-hotshot-go-figure and urbane quizzicality and 'no way can you have access to the tape until you've filled out this form' and 'he's-in-a-meeting-right-now' and 'Look don't worry about it, Jake, it's stable-door stuff now whatdya reckon on this airport scam is there a body there or what?'

Stop frame.

Cutback.

Location.

See the man get into a taxi. An Asian man? No. He is a white man. He wears a single-breasted black suit, cut long in the jacket and baggy on the legs. His ear-piece is connected by clear tubing to something inside his shirt. He carries a briefcase. The briefcase is red. It is handcuffed to his wrist.

Where is he taking the briefcase?

Why?

8,000 questions.

8,001: who wants to know?

Me – Morrison.

Stop frame.

Cutback.

Over to you and your Point Of View.

Haggard character mid-30s in sleazy bar down-town. The bar's called Two on One because it's at the intersect of Da Vinci Driveway and Second Avenue but someone liked the spaces between the buildings more than the structure itself and pulled down number one so even though the bar's the second building on the block, reality has it as the first.

What a dump. They're doing renovations that have continued here for approximately forever. The entire middle of the room is filled with building debris. Those messy Construction fairies have been here too! The clientele cluster round the L-shaped drink-serve area and –

Squeeze frame

There he sits in his nylon crime de fashion shirt, Jake Morrison, mid-30s, very weary and also wary about the eyes, hair greying, smoke-stained beard. He pulls out the paper-scrap on which he copied the address from his dream-book and thinks, 'OK – why not? Let's check it.'

And he pays Dolly Dagger, the peroxide pensioner who runs this place, and he moves.

Keep moving.

Morrison sees –

the car stop. The man gets out. Is he Asian? Hispanic? Black? Caucasian? He can't be sure. It all happens too fast. The purple taxi, with the doorside ad with the picture of St Jimmy Lee Lewis and the legend that asks DO U JUJU? ('You bet I do,' Morrison muses) drives away. The man is on the pavement outside a building. And he is moving.

Move in.

It is a big building, monolithic, behemoth, granite, flanked by two lions.

Stop dead outside the two lions, their ferocious expressions frozen in stone at the gates of the monolithic granite Lodge. They guard the heart of the city. They protect the architecture of appearances. They deter the faint-hearts, the dilettantes, the unwary and those not prepared from . . . meddling. From . . . interference. Who may touch the dream? They guard against intrusion, protect from predators, fend off Other People; Other People and Outside in the fantasy inside the city of your heart.

Only the man with the red briefcase walks up the steps, he strolls straight past the lions into the building's entrance hall. The briefcase is handcuffed to his wrist.

Jake checks the address from the dream-book – and follows him.

A guy walks towards the exit as Jake shoots through. A man deep in thought, his rectangular spectacle frames cast down to the chequerboard tiles on the floor. The sleeping partner in Eisler Realty has his hands clasped behind his frock-coat and a great deal on his mind.

Morrison follows the man's path past him. The man walks the briefcase to the back of the hall and disappears down into a dark corridor.

And Jake Morrison is hot in pursuit

At the end of the corridor a shaft of top-light illuminates a metal spiral staircase. His metal-tipped shoes echo on the stair. The briefcase-carrier is near the top.

Jack tracks.

He climbs the stair as quietly as he can in his shussh-proofed shoes. And at the top he sees . . .

. . . *something's moving.*

And his eyes are moving. And they see . . .

. . . that the second level is given over to plant. The space is totally undivided and open. Row after row of man-high grey-blue stacks stand in line after line after line after line.

Jack approaches – his quarry is already 100 yards away at the other end of the room. But there seems in this windowless place just one exit.

Just one last exit.

And the back of the man with the ear-piece and the red briefcase handcuffed to his wrist has just gone through it.

Jake listens.

Everything is very quiet.

Wait.

Not quite quiet. He can distinguish two noises: one is a soft air-conditioning sound. The other is almost subliminal. It is a whirrrr.

Jack runs his fingers along the cool, metallic sheen on the vertical surface of one box. He stops.

Each has a techno-designation written on metal plate. A sign.

This one says:

BUILDER.

This one says:

MOVE.

He moves.

He walks along the rows towards the exit door. He stops and looks around.

He mosies over to another row of machines. He examines the hieroglyphics writ thereon this too identical obelisk.

It says:

CREATE VALUES.

His eye is urbanely directional and it moves along between the spaces that separate the stacks. Overhead, concealed light fluoresces. Beneath his feet, soft floor caresses. He zig-zags, drawn to one stack, though why he knows not. He stops afront it and reads the legend there.

INTERCEPT.

He notices something.

Just below the eye-line.

On the top-most surface, right beneath his eye, is a recessed ridge set into the box at the front. He pauses and strokes the hairs at end of his beard between his right thumb and forefinger. Annie knows, Poodle knows this indicates he's pondering a dilemma. You know he's at the point where he's wondering which way to jump. He moves his hand away from his face, he's caught the point and realizes that he must make a move. He now runs his left index finger all the way along the smooth groove that's set into the top horizontal surface of the cool, grey-blue metallic surface of the casing.

Hear the air-con. Listen to the whirrrr. Overhead, the recessed lights diffuse their glow.

And now something's happening.

A new noise.

It's pitched higher; it's intense.

And the front of the casing . . .

. . . dissolves

to reveal:

a soft-tech console. No flashing lights, no techno-porn. Just a 14-inch screen that seems to be singing quietly to itself as it reflects a constantly cross-cutting vid-image of himself. Numbers and symbols periodically flash in fast tiny incandescent bursts. Jack stands there and examines the machine, the screen, the console.

At the bottom right-hand side of the screen, there is a tiny area glowing with a chimerically camouflaged legend

ON

He touches it.

Now the flat-screen abruptly sounds a lower pitched hum and almost instantaneously moves on an extending tumescent tube of rubber squeeze, like a cobra-head, from the stack-machine up towards him. Three inches from his face, it stops, it meets his eye.

The picture wipes.

White screen: empyrean.

He suddenly feels a curious image fill in his mind. He is a small boy and he sits in the branches of the huge oak in a boggy field and looks around.

'The tree,' a voice, unspoken, says, 'of knowledge.'

Before M.'s eyes appears on-screen some menu.

VALUE CREATE. SHAPE SCULPT. BUILDER. MOVE. FIND. FRAGMENT.

There's more but –

He hits: PROBE.

Up on the knowledge tree.

Negotiate – protocol.

'Ident?' asks the voice.

This time he doesn't respond. He listens. Spaces between the spoken word.

'It's the agency, Jack.'

Who said that? a voice inside him roars.

But the room is quiet. The silence of dead-air is broken only by the mix of the air-con's low-hum and the whirrrr.

No other humans are visible.

'Affirm identity please,' the voice cajoles. It is a soft voice, low, asexual, clear.

He taps onto the alpha-board, displayed lower left.

JAKE MORRISON.

'Sanctions lifted. The field is clear. You may now proceed safely, Jake Morrison. Have a nice day.'

He walks towards the last exit door.

Pushes.

And nothing happens.

He pulls.

Nothing happens.

'For crying out looooud,' he wails.

The door slides into the wall.

To reveal a chicane of narrow corridor, overlit by spots that lead through alternate phases of dark and light to a metal-grooved travelator, an ascending walkway.

At first it's bounded on both sides by white walls.

Then someone turns the light out.

But the travelator keeps moving.

He stumbles off it suddenly.

Dim lights return.

He stands on a ledge high. Very high, maybe a quarter mile above the rows of stack-boxes.

But he's not sure of distances, unconfident of his spatial perception any more.

Confused, he thinks to himself and it's his voice talking now. Maybe had too much in Two on One. But all this bloody weirdsome, onto something.

He's on the edge of the ledge.

He looks down at his feet. They perch on a mirror surface.

He looks up.

Indeed. Yes it too, the ceiling is a mirror.

They reflect, locking him into an eternal corridor of now.

No.

'No!' he screams out loud.

Spinaround.

There's the door and he moves towards it. It's a metal door, like a slaughterhouse or a safe – grey, low-sheen, he's closing.

Pushes on the bar that transverses it.

And he's inside this room.

The room is curved, almost spherical save the flatness of the floor that's grey-carpeted in luxury one-millimetre thin. The walls are decorated with symbols: hammers, pentagrams, dividers, globes, a sickle, the moon and the stars, the sun.

And names: painted into the gold-leafed scrolls that criss-cross the walls.

Abraham. Noah. Moses. Shem. Gebes. Alfarabi. Magnus. Aquinus. de Villeneuve. Bacon. Ripley. Agrippa. Borri. Morimus. Aluys. Van Helmont. Paracelsus. Boheme. Duval. Guzman. McCarthy.

Jake sees a man's arms open a red briefcase on the anonymous desk in front of the window back-centre in the room.

Stop frame.

Enhance.

Move in.

Inside the briefcase is a spool of two-inch broadcast tape. Magnetic memory track stripped and packaged in plastic, sealed in cellophane.

Release hold.

Animate.

The man behind the desk peels the cellophane away from the tape-casing.

Post-cellophane.

He rotates the casing.

'Yup,' he says. 'That's it, all right.'

He looks up and grins at the man with his back to Jake, the other man who, until just now, had the combination-code handcuffs attached to the red briefcase braceleted to his wrist.

'You get your crate of beer for this – as long as the tape matches.' And then he looks up at Jake.

'Morrison,'

he says.

'Welcome to the Dream Room.'

'That's it,' says Jake, moving towards the desk. 'That's my tape, isn't it?'

'Ah.'

He takes a handkerchief from his pocket and blows his nose.

'I think that's where we have a –' his voice is sing-song, unnatural. '. . . a difference of opinion, Mr Morrison.'

He glances at the man who's been carrying the briefcase. The briefcase, with the bracelets still attached, is on the table. It's closed. The guy's turned away, he's moving to go out the door but Jake just catches a fleeting glimpse of his features.

'Jeez!'

Almost burns his retina out.

He has no face – just a dimming white light where the shape of his face ought to be.

Only it isn't white.

It's phaeic. It's white. It's shade. Grey. Slopy. It's fading. It's moving.

'Channel 95 believe that they own the tape, Morrison,' H(ab-good) says. 'I suppose that strikes you as a curiously antiquated idea.'

'Tell me,' he says, 'what's going on.'

'Well, it's connected with the notion of real property. Things in action. We made an offer to your employers for this tape, and they accepted our offer. We gave them something of value – they gave us the tape.'

'But,' Jake begins. And suddenly his thorax feels like the Shakespeare Superhighway – all clogged up.

'Marvellously simple, really, isn't it, when you think about it.'

EERRROW.

The other, with the briefcase now, moves so fast he's disappeared.

Jake looks around, back at the door.

Didn't even see it open.

Habgood sits down in the nondescript chair.

He picks up a pencil and twiddles it around between his fingers. He sighs.

'You see', H (correct. H is always correct) begins.

Then sighs again.

'It's the agency, Jack.'

Twiddle twiddle.

'You were on a default assignment.'

Lock in.

Downstairs a hand –

Touch: reveal.

'The agency works on the principle that all of its agents function, Jack. They are performers – and that's all. If agents become too intelligent, they threaten the viability of the entire organism. So they have to be intercepted.'

'You mean censored.'

H makes a smacking noise with his lips. He spins slowly in his chair to gaze outside through the semi-circular glass.

'No,' he says. 'I mean intercepted.'

Out there are clouds. Out there are citizenry.

Their movie must go on.

Mirrors and masks.

30 hats, 44 faces.

And he spins back round to face him.

'Even on a default assignment – in fact, especially on a default assignment – you've got to know the rules. And Rule One? Remember Rule One?'

Jack's lips are stitched together grimbo-gribly.

Face the fucker out, he thinks. Face him out.

'Rule One is – You're Working for Us.'

H shifts in his seat.

'There are big pictures, Morrison, you're aware of that – visual shorthand, it's your stock in trade.'

He clicks his tongue against the roof of his mouth once.

Twiddle twiddle.

And then puts pencil down.

'Sometimes,' he says, seemingly suddenly fatigued, 'the factual implications of an incident, a series of incidents, could destabilize. Destabilize, yes – everything that we've all worked for. It's very complex, Jake, very very complex.' He leans forward and presses a button on the intercom on the desk. A voice says, 'Wanda from Dubrothonic on Line One,' but he ignores it and continues.

'Censorship? Well, if you like . . . yes. We prefer – responsibility. More, ah, civilized, isn't it, responsibility? Think of an animal, a dog or something that was totally orientated towards pure pleasure and the gratification of ah aha.'

Here H sneezes and blows his nose.

'Uh ahem totally pampered and experienced nothing but pure pleasure. The organism would rapidly break down. It wouldn't be able to compete when things turned round.'

He folds his upper lip down and says, 'And things are turning round Jake, they're turning round. Turn around.'

'What?'

'No, go on. Turn around.'

Very slowly Jake turns around.

And he sees, framed in the doorway, a blurred shape of a maybe-man cuffed to a red briefcase whose face is caught between channels.

Out of nowhere, it squeezes the remote once twice.

And there's an empyrean moment of total dazzle.

Outside the sun's up in the clear blue sky, beating remorselessly on the stream of cars locked bumper to bumper on the Shakey Zoom, the metal beneath their paint sweltering silently in its burning heat.

The city will be hot tonight, yeah.

SO WHERE ARE THEY NOW?

Rep married Rupies Gloss, the movie actor, in a high-profile showbiz ceremony at the Church of the Mystic City Sign.

Her father, Eddie Eisler, abandoned his idea of running for First Citizen on a soft-left ticket when they changed the gun laws: he's now a pillar of the local schul.

His wife has been having an affair with Nicolai Josh Rambuen, who joined the Future traders where Barney Boosterfish now works eight to six. Since he's started living with Katy, his betrothed, Barney doesn't go out much any more. Katy's pregnant. They've already decorated the nursery.

Closing the gun courts – and thereby effectively suspending all existing firearms legislation – affected others too: Morty 'Big' Kinsella, against all the pollsters' predictions, was returned to the city council on a low turn-out with a large majority.

Emma was killed in an armed hold-up at Gerrard Jewellers, where she'd recently started as the under-manager.

Lotti is back in China where she volunteered to be a missionary teaching English as a foreign language.

Zarah travelled too – she went to Iragua and fell in love with a revolutionary guard. No one's heard from her in a while.

Jenny is doing concurrent seven-year terms for fraud after Joe Poodle's security firm persuaded her to confess that she was blackmailing Eisler Realty after inducting a computer virus into their system.

Tallboy and his posse, headed up by Muscles McKhan, are on the payroll of one of Paulie's limosine companies. Mr Casales still eats at the best restaurants and is fêted by city councillors. This may or may not be unconnected with his silent-partnership in a low-profile – but extremely influential – political lobbying consultancy called Montcrieffe and Habgood.

Casales's associate, businessman Alex Culver, is awaiting the result of an appeal against charges of grand larceny and conspiring to file a fraudulent tax-return.

Petey Casales died from leukaemia following the collapse of his immune system.

Blond John joined the Brotherhood of St Francis and lives in their monastery up-country.

Papa Ivalliovitch had a coronary, successful triple by-pass surgery and is attempting to breed a super-pigeon.

Kelly R. Guervitz works part-time as a contract cartographer for NASA. Her shop is still listed in the city's yellow pages.

Blackjack lives with Daz, an unemployed guitarist, in a rented flat in the Barrio.

The Toy is working on his new album.

Fat Tuesday hosts an all-night gabfest on a syndicated TV show and is learning to play both golf and miniature croquet.

Tiger Lily and her stepfather Jerome still live in Belleville. Last year she opened an eponymously named nightclub on the site formerly occupied by Rififi's.

After his father died (the old man had a stroke while looking for his portable telephone which began ringing after he'd misplaced it earlier that afternoon in the hall of his large farm-house in Torquemada), Eustace Vauvatier moved to Geneva, where he'd been stashing the money he'd earned from his numerous clubs.

His maid, Tranny Saul, officiates at the soirées the couple throw periodically for visiting artists. Recently the couple fêted Robert, a former milliner, who stopped over en-route to open his show in Singapore.

The Torquemada 24-Hour Road Race was won last year by a GDMC Equipage XLX driven by Giles Brocklebank and Henri Enriques.

Vanda Jacquenelli played a cameo role in *Mother Teresa's Black Hole*, a B-movie which, although barely hitting break even at the box-office, won a minor prize at an esoteric genre festival. She was engaged to Bruce Dior for the 72 hours before his motorcycle crashed into a telephone box on Victory River Bridge. Following the coroner's direction that the jury return an open verdict on her fiancé's death, Miss Jacquenelli has begun to take photography classes part-time at City Uni.

Annie is on the dole following the break-up of her marriage to an alcoholic up-country farmer.

Fi died from a heroin overdose at the dinner-party thrown by Susie Splash to celebrate the signing of a contract with Bee Z. Melrose to volume-manufacture Splashwear.

Stinky Eddie married a celebutante called Mercedes. He sold his father's chain to a multi-national, and is currently involved in several projects of which the best known is the popularization of miniature croquet.

Richard Rayban was sued after he published a satirical profile of an ex-débutante called Miranda shortly after her marriage to the eligible young millionaire head of an internationally known furnishing company. The action, during which the editor broke down under cross-examination, bankrupted him and he now publishes a life-style magazine, *Winning Through Retirement* under Stinky Eddie's auspices.

White Jaqui was offered a slot in the all-girl pop trio, The

Sizzle Sisters, after one of the founder members dropped out to become a full-time mother. The group are currently on the Japanese leg of their latest S R O world tour, scheduled to end some time next year so the act can star in a feature film vehicle, tentatively entitled *Sizzling Hot*.

Knocker moved up-country last month to run a custom-car franchise north of the Mistral.

Cressida Crane was last seen, some time ago, in the Wah Wah Bar. She did not appear to be enjoying the best health and her voice was notably thick as she attempted to solicit a green spot from Terry Kinkaid in exchange for a blow-job.

Fillet amazed the world of couture when, after just 35 working days, she quit her coveted role as Fashion Director of the prestigious consultancy Media Decode to convert to the Baha'i faith and marry an internationally famous cricketer.

Snaps directs glamour films for one of Jimmy Hennessy's investment companies, Bimbo International, whose cable and satellite channels are beamed around the planet.

Snips still snips.

Gazza became a chintz-slinger. One of his first clients was Mrs Eleanor Burgoyne, who spent a small portion of her enormous divorce settlement in eradicating all traces of her previous husband from her house.

Christina Ivalliovitch was bound over after a charge of dog-napping against her was found not proved. She is writing her autobiography and researching a video-disc about poodle-breeding.

Jack Morrison – depending on who you believe – was either gunned down by security forces or has retired to live up-country and, under a pseudonym, adapt thrillers for Channel 0/28.

Jean Jean LePichon's facial tattoos are said to have developed stigmatic characteristics – the tear-shaped droplets reputedly wetten annually on 7 March. The veracity of this story is difficult to confirm – the day after a Metropol raid recently closed down the Church of the Mystic City Sign, Jean Jean LePichon returned to living on the streets.